Savage Apocalypse Book Two: The Howl Of The Dead

By Scott Dokey

This book is dedicated to my family, for their faith and belief in me always.

CHAPTER 1

Tommy Patterson always looked forward to Friday nights. It was a chance to finally spend some quality time alone with his dad. And he relished every moment of it. Sometimes it was watching their favorite movie together with a tub of popcorn between them on the couch. Other times, they played a board game or two. But this Friday night was the one he looked forward to the most; when they took their rods and reels to the small lake at the edge of the woods and fished for catfish. To a ten-year-old kid, this was like heaven.

At half-past seven, Tommy rushed out to the garage, where his dad, William, had just finished restringing the line on one of his reels. "Is it time, yet?" he asked anxiously.

William looked up at the evening sky for a second, scrutinizing the angle of the setting sun, and then down at his far-too-eager son with a soft smile, "Almost. It's still a little too light out right now. Give it a few more minutes and then we'll be ready to go."

Tommy nearly stepped on his bottom lip as he stood there, pouting.

"Hey," William said. "Don't go getting all upset like that.

The fish won't bite if you're upset."

"You're joking, right? I'm pretty sure my feelings have nothing to do with fishing."

William snickered. "Sure, they do. Remember, animals can sense emotion; even fish."

"Yeah, you've told me before. I just don't get how it works."

William ruffled Tommy's hair and chuckled, "Don't worry about it too much. What do I always tell you?"

Tommy replied, "Don't sweat the small stuff."

"And...?"

"It's all small stuff."

William smiled back at his son, suddenly realizing how much he had grown recently. "Just try to remember that," he said. "Life will be much easier. Now help me load the rest of the gear into the truck and we'll be ready to go."

Tommy grabbed his dad's tackle box and lifted it onto the open tailgate. When he turned around to get his own, smaller tackle box, he was annoyed to see his little sister, Kate, standing there holding her pink Barbie fishing pole in her hands. "What are you doing here?" he asked, his voice clearly irritated at her presence. This was supposed to be their special time alone, just him and his dad, and now his sniveling sister was trying to barge in.

Kate replied matter-of-factly, "I'm going fishing with you?"

Tommy turned around so he didn't have to look at her, knowing his temper would probably get the best of him, and then he'd do or say something that would probably get him in trouble and ruin the whole night, or worse. "Dad?" he implored.

William looked at Kate and smiled. *She's so determined to grow up,* he thought. "I'm sorry, Little Lady, but you're not quite old enough to be out so late."

Kate protested, "But I'm almost six years old!"

Tommy replied nastily, "So? I didn't get to go until I was eight."

"Well, that was you. Everybody knows girls are better than boys."

Tommy threw his tackle box into the truck and turned around, his face scrunched up as his eyes burned with anger, "I'll show you who's better than who."

William cut in between them, "Hey, that's enough of that."

Tommy argued, "But she started it?"

"And I'm finishing it," William stated firmly. He then turned to Kate, "Listen, next time we go fishing it'll be during the day so you can go too."

Kate's eyes grew misty for a second from disappointment until she finally gave in, "Promise?"

"I promise."

"Or maybe we can go sometime early in the morning when the frogs are still out?"

Tommy couldn't stop himself when the words quickly slipped off his tongue before he realized what he was doing, and said, "You look like a frog."

Kate stomped her foot and held her finger firmly jabbed in his face, "You take that back!"

When his dad looked at him sternly, he knew that an apology was the only thing that could still save their fishing trip. "Okay," he said. "I'm sorry."

William looked at Kate expectantly. After a moment, she finally said, "Fine. Pology accepted." Then, to show off to Tommy that she was dad's favorite, she went over and gave her dad a big hug in front of him, a wide smirk spread across her lips.

After a minute, William said to her, "Now go in and get

ready for bed."

Kate trudged off, still carrying her fishing pole. On her way out of the garage, she looked back at Tommy and stuck her tongue out at him when William wasn't looking, before turning and running into the house.

*****

Melinda was sitting on the small swing that ran along the back of the patio, slowly sipping a cup of tea, when William turned the corner. She didn't see him at first, so it gave him a minute to admire her as she sat there, her back against the soft pink glow of the setting sun.

She turned to him and smiled, "Are you spying on me, William Patterson?"

"Of course I am—any chance I get."

"I guess that means I better be on my best behavior, then?"

"You better. I'd hate to have to punish you for acting up."

"Oh, really?"

"Yes, really." Then he nuzzled up close to her and softly nibbled on her ear.

Melinda responded with a soft moan, before nudging him away and saying, "Don't you have a fishing trip to get to?"

William smiled, "I'd rather do some other kind of fishing."

"As tempting as that sounds, I think you better get ready to go. You already have a disappointed little girl on your hands. If you blow this off, you're going to have to deal with your son as well. And we both know he doesn't handle disappointment well."

William snickered, "You got that right."

She smiled back at him seductively, "Plus, when you get home, we can always pick up where we left off." After a passionate kiss, she pulled away from him, "You better get going before he starts getting antsy."

"One more," he said, and gave her a last, quick peck before he walked back into the house.

***

When William climbed into the driver's seat, he wasn't all that surprised to see King, their four-year-old Golden Retriever, sitting next to Tommy. "And what's this all about?" he asked.

Tommy said matter-of-factly, "King wanted to come too."

"Oh, he did, did he?"

"Yep, he sure did."

In reply, King let out a soft bark that made William chuckle as he scratched behind the dog's ears. "Okay, fine. You can come too. But you better not scare the fish." King barked eagerly in agreement.

William put the keys in the ignition, and a minute later they were pulling out of the driveway. Their neighbor Harvey Stratton, was sitting on his front porch drinking his evening beer. He was an older man in his sixties, who had lost his wife to cancer three years earlier. The alcohol was his attempt at erasing the pain of his suffering.

Harvey waved at them as they pulled away. Tommy gave a small wave back and then said to his dad, "He's a strange old man."

William chuckled, "He's not so bad."

"But he smells bad."

This time William laughed out loud, then said, "You should give the guy a break. He's been through a lot these last few years."

Tommy grew silent for a minute. At his age, he'd never really thought about how much Harvey had dealt with when his wife died. Instantly, he was embarrassed at the way he had acted. "I guess you're right. I'll be nicer to him from now on."

William added, "Plus, you have to admit that his jokes are pretty funny."

Tommy chuckled this time, "Yeah, he is kinda funny."

Then they were out of their neighborhood, heading toward Lake Cahuilla, and what he hoped would one of their best fishing trips ever.

Ten minutes later they reached Cahuilla Park Road, and followed that around the edge of the lake to W Access Road. William pulled the truck over and stopped at a little clearing about forty yards from the water's edge.

Tommy jumped out of the truck before it had had a chance to come to a complete stop. King bounded out after him.

When William joined them at the back of the truck, Tommy was struggling with the tailgate. William reminded him, "Remember, it sticks a little sometimes. You have to push it in while you lift the handle." He then demonstrated the trick and dropped the tailgate down.

It took a couple of trips for them to carry all of their gear down to the bank. Dusk was giving way to night, which prompted William to turn on the battery-operated lantern so they could see what they were doing. A soft yellow glow spread out over the small area.

For all of his eagerness to catch fish, he was still squeamish when it came to baiting his hook with chicken liver. "God, I hate this stuff," he exclaimed.

"I know, pretty gross, huh?" William replied. "But it's the best bait to catch catfish with."

"I just wish it didn't smell so bad."

"What's with that nose of yours? It seems like everything smells bad to you."

"Hey! I can't help it if my nose is sensitive."

"Fair enough. Let's get these lines out there and see if we can hook onto Big Bertha?"

Tommy asked, "That's just a story. She's not real, is she?"

William replied, "Oh, she's real, alright. I saw her once. Must have been nearly five feet long and a hundred pounds."

Tommy was shocked, "Wow! I bet it'd be awesome to hook onto something like that."

William agreed, "I'm sure it would. Maybe tonight's our lucky night?"

William got up from his camping chair after he finished baiting his hook and cast his line out toward the center of the lake. The bait plunked into the water about forty yards out. He let it sink to the bottom and then turned the crank a couple of times to remove any slack. When he was satisfied, he propped the rod up on a y-shaped stick he had pushed into the ground.

Tommy went after him. His effort wasn't as good as his dad's, but was still impressive for a boy his age, landing about ten yards in front of his dad's.

William said, "Nice cast, Tommy."

"But it didn't go out as far as yours."

"It doesn't matter how far it goes out, Tommy. The important thing is to find where the fish are."

King decided at that moment to knock over the bucket filled with bait, sending chicken guts spilling across the ground in a grotesque cascade. Though it seemed like an accident, the sight and scent of the raw meat triggered his instincts, and he immediately lunged for a mouthful.

"King, no!" William's shout pierced the air.

King froze, his ears drooping as he laid down, still chewing his prize. Seeing the look of hurt in his eyes filled William instantly with regret.

Tommy's face turned green at the mess. "Thanks, King," he muttered, barely suppressing his urge to vomit.

William sighed, regretting his outburst. "It was an accident," he said, shaking his head. "That tail of his is like a wrecking ball sometimes."

"I know, but it's still gross!" Tommy retorted, looking away from the mess.

"Yeah, but the fish won't mind." William bent down, using his pocket knife to scoop the guts back into the bucket. "Help me clean this up before it starts attracting bugs."

Tommy was about to protest when a faint light streaked across the sky. "Look, Dad, a shooting star."

William looked up, his eyes narrowing. "That's not a shooting star."

"How can you tell?" Tommy asked, puzzled.

"Because it's getting bigger. And it's heading this way."

They both watched as the fiery orb hurtled toward them. William's heart pounded as he realized its trajectory would take it right over the lake and into the surrounding woods.

"We need to get this gear into the truck now!" William said urgently. They began reeling in their lines as fast as they could.

As the meteor streaked over the lake, debris splashed into the water, causing it to hiss and steam. The air grew still, as if a vacuum had enveloped them. A tremendous boom followed as the meteor crashed into the woods, the ground shaking violently beneath their feet.

King barked incessantly at the commotion. William grabbed Tommy and shoved him into the truck, with King leaping in after him.

"We need to check it out," William said tensely. "There might be campers out there."

He backed the truck up and drove around the lake toward

the woods. Fortunately, because the heat of the desert summer creates a slow season for the park, they had closed the campsites for renovations.

They reached the entrance to the woods and took a narrow trail just wide enough for his truck to squeeze through. After a quarter mile, they reached the edge of a massive crater, about a hundred yards wide and three feet deep. The meteor had landed in a clearing, minimizing damage to the forest and its inhabitants, but still leaving a trail of destruction. Steam rose from the ground, creating an eerie fog.

William left the engine running and the headlights on, illuminating the area as he got out. "Get the flashlight from the glove box," he instructed Tommy.

The air was thick with smoke and the acrid stench of fire and ash. "Smells like burned hamburgers," Tommy said, covering his nose. King jumped down, immediately burying his nose in his paws.

A strong breeze blew through a moment later, making the odor bearable. William and Tommy pulled their shirts over their noses and walked the crater's perimeter. William's flashlight beam revealed a watermelon-shaped rock at the center, crackling like ice cubes thrown into a hot drink.

"That little rock did all this?" Tommy asked, incredulous.

"It was much bigger before it hit the atmosphere," William explained. "Most of it burned up on the way down."

They climbed down into the crater, moving closer to the rock. The crackling grew louder, followed by a hissing sound like the valve on a pressure cooker opening to release its pent-up steam.

"Don't get too close," William warned.

They were about twenty feet away when King growled, his hackles raised as if a threat were nearby.

"It's okay, Boy," Tommy said.

No sooner had he spoken those words, than the meteor exploded, sending a shower of rocky shrapnel mixed with a black, oily substance flying. The blast, though not lethal, was powerful enough to send stone fragments tearing at Tommy's face and arms. The flashlight flew from William's hand, and King yelped before he scampered away into the woods.

"King!" Tommy shouted urgently, but the dog had already vanished.

William retrieved the flashlight, checking Tommy for serious injuries. "Are you okay?"

Tommy nodded. "Just a few scratches."

William examined a cut on Tommy's cheek. "We need to get you home and cleaned up."

"But what about King? We can't leave him here."

"He'll be okay. He's probably just scared. He knows the way home."

"I hope you're right," Tommy said reluctantly.

They trudged back to the truck, brushing off clumps of grime and debris. Once inside, William maneuvered out of the woods. As he did so, Tommy peered into the darkness, hoping to catch a glimpse of his four-legged friend, fearing that he might never see him again.

CHAPTER 2

Justin's eyes were glued to the screen, his fingers flying over the keyboard as he tried to calculate the trajectory of the meteor that had just crashed. The tension in the control room was palpable; the other four meteors that had been clustered with this one had mercifully disintegrated upon entry into Earth's atmosphere. But this fifth one—larger and much more deadly—had broken through. His heart raced as he imagined the potential damage it could have caused on impact.

He was so engrossed in his work that he didn't notice the subtle shift in the room's atmosphere. Suddenly, the pungent odor of cigarettes and stale coffee assaulted his senses, snapping him out of his concentration. He stiffened, realizing too late that the NEOP director, Dr. Patrick Leonard, was now standing right behind him. The man's presence was oppressive, his breath hot on Justin's neck, as if the weight of his scrutiny alone could alter the course of events displayed on the screen. Justin swallowed hard, the taste of dread mingling with the acrid scent that clung to the air.

"What's the status, Justin?" the Director asked.

Justin replied, "Four of the five objects disintegrated upon entry, sir."

"What about the last one?"

"It looks like it came down somewhere in Southern California."

"Can you narrow down the point of impact?"

Justin slid his chair over a few inches and turned to another monitor, and began typing rapidly. "I'm pulling up satellite imagery right now."

After a few seconds, an image filled the screen. He zoomed in tight and peered closely at the screen. "It looks like it went down in a town called La Quinta. The crash happened in a wooded area surrounding Lake Cahuilla."

Dr. Leonard turned his stocky body around quickly and addressed the six other technicians manning stations of their own, "I want a field team mobilized within the hour."

The technicians began feverishly working at their keyboards, and within seconds, the room was filled with a myriad of voices. After a few minutes, Darcey, a young intern fresh out of Berkley, spoke up, "A team is gathering at Ames shortly."

Dr. Leonard said, "Good. Who's heading the team?"

Darcey replied, "Samuel Greenburg."

The Director nodded his approval. Greenburg was a good man in his book. A little intense but he certainly knew his stuff. They had even been roommates for a semester at Caltech. Then, after graduation, he had remained in California, getting a job as a research scientist at NASA's Ames research facility. Now, ten years later, he was head of the Space Biosciences Division.

Leonard was a little disappointed he hadn't stayed in contact with Samuel, especially after Samuel's wife had died in a car accident a few years ago.

"What's their ETA for arrival at the crash site?" he asked.

Darcey replied, "Their plane is currently on standby. It's a thirty-five-minute flight to Palm Springs International, and from there a forty-minute drive to the crash site."

"Good. Tell me when they're ready to be briefed."

"Will do," Darcey stated and then focused her attention back to her computer terminal.

Dr. Leonard turned back around to Justin, "Can you zoom in closer?"

Justin replied, "Sure," and hit a couple of keys so that the image zoomed tighter until they could make out a truck pulling up to the site. The picture was filled with smoke, but they could make out a man and a boy getting out of the truck and walk toward the center of the crash, with a dog trotting beside them.

The Director muttered, "Christ! I hope they don't do anything stupid."

The words had no sooner left his lips, when they watched the meteor explode on the screen, sending the man and boy reeling backward.

"Shit!" Leonard cried. "That can't be good"

He turned back to Darcey, "Call Samuel back. Tell him he needs to step on it."

He turned back to the screen just in time to see the truck pulling out of the area. "See if you can track that vehicle, Justin."

Justin replied, "I'm on it," and began feverishly typing at his keyboard.

For a quick second, as the Director looked closely at the satellite image of the crash scene, he thought he saw something in the woods. But then it was gone.

"I have a bad feeling about this," he mumbled to himself.

***

* * *

The fact that Samuel was a chronic insomniac was a blessing in disguise when the phone rang at eleven o'clock. The reason always hovered around thoughts of his wife. This night was no different, and he was silently grateful for the distraction.

At first, he thought about not answering it. When he was in this kind of mood the last thing, he wanted was human contact of any kind. Then the ringing stopped and he breathed a soft sigh of relief. That didn't last long, because a few seconds later, his phone started ringing again.

"Well, at least they're persistent," he muttered as he reached over and grabbed his cell phone off the night stand next to his bed. A quick look at the source of the call caused him to sit up quickly. He knew instantly that something big was going down.

He pressed the accept button on to connect the call and tentatively said, "Hello."

Darcey answered, "Dr. Greenburg?"

"Yes?"

"There is a serious situation that's come up. We need you to gather a team and assemble at the Ames main conference room in thirty minutes. You will be briefed upon arrival." Then the phone went dead.

An exasperated huff issued from Samuel, "You gotta love NASA's directness."

He scrolled through the contact list on his phone quickly, selecting three colleagues that would provide him with the broadest range of skills, given the fact that he didn't have a clue what their actual mission was.

***

The first name he thought of was Andrea Melborne, one of

the leading scientists in the Astro-biology Division. She was a spunky woman in her late thirties, whom he had had the pleasure of working with on a number of projects. Her vast knowledge would prove to be invaluable. Plus, there had been a little bit of a spark between them. His fear of intimacy with another woman after his wife's death had prevented him from acting on it, something he still regretted to this day.

Samuel's thumb hesitating over Andrea's number before he pressed it. The phone rang a few times, each ring amplifying his anxiety, until she answered in a groggy voice.

"Hello?"

"Andrea? It's Samuel," he said, his voice wavering slightly. "I'm sorry to call so late, but we have an urgent situation. I just got a call to get a group together and meet at the Ames main conference room in thirty minutes. Of course, the first person I thought of was you."

Andrea yawned. "You do realize it's eleven at night, right?"

"Yes, I'm aware. Believe me, I'm not happy about this either."

"What's going on? Is everything okay?"

Samuel took a deep breath, trying to steady his racing heart. It had been a long time since he'd talked to Andrea, yet his stomach was still filled with butterflies, as if he were a kid back in high school. "I don't have all the details yet, just that they said it's serious. We need your expertise, Andrea."

"And my expertise is all you need, Sam?"

Samuel was silent. The conversation had turned precisely the way he hadn't wanted it to go and now he was tongue-tied.

Andrea's tone shifted, as if she could sense Samuel's uneasiness on the other end. "Alright, give me ten minutes to get ready. I'll be there."

"Thanks, Andrea. I knew I could count on you."

"You realize you owe me big time for this, Samuel? You know that, right? I expect to be paid back for this in the very near future."

As he hung up, Samuel felt a slight sense of relief knowing Andrea was on board.

***

Samuel dialed Kelvin Knepler's number next, his hand shaking slightly. Even though Kelvin could be a hot-head there wasn't a better environmental scientist alive. The phone rang several times before a gruff voice answered.

"Who the hell is calling at this hour?"

"Kelvin, it's Samuel," he said, trying to keep his voice steady. "We have a situation. I need you at Ames main conference room in thirty minutes."

Kelvin groaned, his frustration evident through the phone. "Do you have any idea what time it is? This better be important."

"It is," Samuel insisted, his voice urgent. "NEOP called. It's something big, and I need your environmental expertise. Please, Kelvin."

Kelvin sighed heavily. "You know I hate being dragged out of bed for these things, Samuel."

"I know, but I wouldn't ask if it wasn't critical. You're the best at what you do, Kelvin," Samuel pleaded, his desperation evident in his voice.

There was a pause before Kelvin spoke again, a clearly agitated tone in his voice. "Fine, I'll be there. But this better be worth it."

"Thanks, Kelvin. We'll meet at the Ames main conference room in thirty minutes," Samuel said in relief.

"Yeah, yeah. See you soon," Kelvin replied, hanging up with a grumble.

***

Last on the list was Simon Wright. Formerly a brilliant neurobiologist, Simon had shifted his passion to the camera and had become quite an accomplished videographer. His camera skills would come in handy as they documented their findings, whatever they may be. Plus, he was also Samuel's best friend.

Simon picked up almost immediately, answering in his usual cheerful voice.

"Sam! What's up, buddy?"

"Hey, Simon," Samuel said, trying to mask the urgency in his voice. "I need your help. We have an urgent mission. Can you be at Ames main conference room in thirty minutes?"

"Wow, middle-of-the-night call, huh? Must be serious," Simon replied, his tone turning more serious.

"It is," Samuel confirmed, his voice wavering. "And we need to document whatever we find. Your camera skills are essential."

Simon chuckled, trying to lighten the mood. "You know I love a good adventure. I'm in. Anything else I need to know?"

"Not yet. I know as much as you do," Samuel replied. "We'll be briefed when we get there. Just bring your gear. I really need you on this one, Simon."

"Got it. See you in thirty, Sam," Simon said.

"Thanks, Simon. You're a lifesaver."

"Always here for you, buddy. See you soon."

***

* * *

As he hung up, Samuel took a deep breath, feeling a sense of calm amidst the chaos. His team had come together a little better than anticipated. He hoped it would stay that way.

Quickly, he jumped into the shower and got ready for what he knew was going to be a long night. After throwing on some clothes and grabbing a slice of cold pizza from the fridge, he was out the door and on his way.

The drive to the facility was almost exactly fifteen minutes, giving his mind a chance to make up all sorts of weird scenarios that he was about to walk into. An urgent call late at night usually signaled either an approaching disaster, or that one had already happened, and he certainly hoped that the latter wasn't the case.

Thirty minutes later he was walking down the hall, heading toward the Ames main conference room. When he entered the room, he saw that Kelvin and Simon were already there. Kelvin glared at him for a moment, while Simon merely nodded and went back to sipping his cup of coffee.

Samuel took a seat next to Simon at the table. "Thanks again, guys," he said.

Simon replied, "Any word yet on what's going on?"

Samuel shook his head. "Not yet."

Kelvin muttered, "Figures."

A minute later, Andrea entered the room, followed by the Deputy Director of the center, Ashton Brown, an older man in his fifties with white hair who looked like a cross between Albert Einstein and Colonel Sanders. Behind him walked a young man in his thirties, who was dressed more like a mafia hit man than a scientist. The stranger took a seat at the table opposite everyone else, and just sat there silently observing.

Ashton walked to the corner of the room and pressed a

button on the wall, which caused a panel to slide open, revealing a large screen. "Gentlemen... and lady," he said in a southern drawl that seemed totally out of place in California. "We have a serious situation that needs our immediate attention." He pointed a small remote at the screen and a second later the image of Dr. Leonard appeared.

The Doctor got right to the point, "Recently, a small cluster of meteors suddenly appeared out of nowhere perilously close to Earth's orbit. We were hoping they wouldn't pose a threat. We were wrong. Approximately forty-two minutes ago, they entered Earth's atmosphere. While most of the meteors disintegrated upon entry, one of them survived and crashed down in a wooded area near Lake Cahuilla, approximately thirty miles southeast of Palm Springs. Local authorities have already been contacted to secure the crash site until you arrive."

Kelvin spoke up, his grumpiness magnified even more, "So, this is nothing more than a simple bag-and-tag expedition?"

"Not quite," Leonard said. "Shortly after impact, the object exhibited some unusual behavior."

The group looked skeptical. "What kind of behavior?" Andrea asked.

Leonard simply said, "It exploded."

Samuel stated, "That's not uncommon, given the extreme temperature the meteor endured during its descent."

"This is true," the Director replied. "But this happened with civilians present, and they were exposed to some kind of substance when the explosion happened. We need to get there and analyze the site ASAP Once we've identified the civilians, we'll let you know so you can follow up with them."

The screen went blank, and then Ashton addressed them

once more, "NASA has placed this mission at the highest level of importance. Clause here has been hired as your driver and guide. He's familiar with the area and will be there to assist you in case there's any trouble."

Kelvin quipped, "What kind of trouble could there possibly be?"

"The biggest problem may come from the media, as they try to get a closer look at the crash site. But you may also run into some wildlife out there."

Andrea asked nervously, "What kind of wildlife are we talking about?"

Clause replied, "Mainly coyotes, but there could also be bobcats running around. Usually they stay away from humans, but something like this could cause them to behave erratically."

Ashton interrupted, "No need to worry everyone needlessly, Clause. I'm sure everything will go as smoothly as possible. Now, we need to get you on the road right away. Your plane is scheduled to depart in twenties minutes. A truck will be waiting for you in Palm Springs with all of your necessary equipment. We'll maintain constant communication during the entire mission."

With that, he turned and left the room. As the rest of them filed down the hallway toward the hangar, Samuel couldn't help but think that there was more to this 'simple' mission than what they were being told.

CHAPTER 3

After William navigated past the deserted camping area, he turned onto Jefferson Street, the tires of his truck crunching over gravel. With the meteor crash looming in his mind like a dark specter, the night turned thick and oppressive, the kind of darkness that seemed to swallow the truck's headlights whole.

As he rounded onto 58th Avenue, a sensation like searing fire ants erupted across his skin, burning and itching as if his flesh were being devoured alive. He looked over at Tommy and saw him squirming in his seat, clawing at his arms.

"What in the world is this stuff?" Tommy exclaimed in a panic. "It itches like crazy!"

William fought to keep his voice steady. "We'll be home in a few minutes, then we can get cleaned up," he said, though his mind was churning with unimaginable possibilities. Whatever it was, it wasn't from this world, and God only knew what that meant.

"It feels like I have bugs crawling all over me!"

"I know. Me too. Just try not to think about it."

Tommy fell silent, as he tried to ignore the immense worry hammering through his heart. After a minute, he said softly,

"I hope King's okay."

"I'm sure he's fine," William replied, though he wasn't entirely convinced. "Remember, this isn't the first time he's run off, only to come crawling back home a few hours later."

"I guess you're right," Tommy said.

The drive home seemed to take forever, but soon enough, they turned onto Salida Del Sol and pulled into their driveway. The truck had barely come to a stop when Tommy sprang from his seat and bolted out of the truck, sprinting into the house with a pained look plastered on his face. William followed behind, his body aching and his mind swirling as he tried to process the events that had just transpired.

Melinda met him on the porch with a worried look on her face. "My God, William!" she gasped. "What on earth happened to you?"

"It's a long story," William said wearily. "I'll tell you all about it after I get cleaned up."

"Where's Tommy? Is he okay?"

"He's fine. He ran in through the back door to get cleaned up too."

Melinda's eyes narrowed when she realized they were missing someone. "Where's King?"

"He ran off," William said. "That's why Tommy's upset."

"Again?"

"Yeah. Something happened at the lake tonight that spooked him."

With the mysterious substance clinging to his skin, William trudged up the steps, the weight of the night pressing down on him hard.

***

* * *

Tommy scrubbed feverishly at the tar-like substance smeared across his face and arms. Hand soap, body wash, even shampoo—all proved useless. The black goo clung to his skin, refusing to budge. He opened the medicine cabinet and spotted a bottle of rubbing alcohol. Desperately, he reached for it, just as Kate shuffled into the bathroom, rubbing her eyes.

"What are you doing up?" Tommy snapped.

Kate blinked sleepily. "You were making so much noise you woke me up."

She squinted at him, looking closely in the grime smeared over his skin. "Ewe, what happened to you? You look disgusting! And you smell bad too!"

"I don't know what this stuff is," Tommy replied. "It came from some rock that crashed down in the woods."

Kate's eyes widened. "Wow! You mean it crashed down from outer space?"

"Yep. I bet it came from Mars, or maybe even farther away, like Jupiter or something."

Kate's expression changed to doubt. "Nuh-uh."

"I bet it did," Tommy insisted, his voice rising.

Kate just rolled her eyes. "Whatever. Just finish cleaning up so I can go back to sleep."

Tommy shot her an irritated look and turned back to the sink. He was about to splash the rubbing alcohol on his arms when the black, oily stuff began to disappear, almost as if being absorbed into his skin. A few seconds later, he was clear of the mysterious substance.

"What in the world just happened?" Kate asked nervously.

Tommy shrugged, bewildered. "Beats me. At least it's gone. Now you can go back to bed and quit bugging me."

Kate stuck her tongue out at Tommy and flounced back toward her room. Tommy decided he was clean enough for now, turned off the bathroom light, and followed her into the hall. Suddenly, he cried out in agony as a crippling pain shot through his stomach, bringing him to his knees.

Kate rushed back, her eyes wide with worry. "Tommy, what's wrong?"

"It's my stomach," Tommy gasped through clenched teeth. "It hurts bad. Hurry and get Mom."

Kate dashed toward the living room, finding it empty. Panic rising, she sprinted to her parents' bedroom and burst through the door.

Melinda looked up, startled. "What are you doing out of bed, young lady?"

"It's Tommy! He's really sick," Kate blurted out.

Melinda jumped from the bed and followed Kate out of the room, leaving William alone in the shower. She reached the bathroom just as Tommy finished emptying the contents of his stomach into the toilet.

"My God, Tommy!" she exclaimed, rushing to his side. She grabbed a towel from the rack and began wiping up the black mucus that had splattered onto the floor.

Tommy looked up, his face pale. "I don't feel too well."

Melinda pressed a hand to his forehead, her worry deepening. "Oh, you poor thing. You look terrible."

Kate stood nearby, her eyes wide. "I bet it was the space rock."

"Space rock?" Melinda asked, confusion mixing with fear. "What in the world are you talking about?"

"Tommy said it crashed down into the woods and exploded. That's where all of that black junk came from. It was over his skin and then it just disappeared."

Melinda glanced at the towel in her hands and gasped. The black substance was moving. She quickly flushed the toilet and threw the towel into the bathtub, her heart pounding.

"Here, let's get you to bed," she said, her voice trembling as she helped Tommy to his feet. "A good night's sleep should get you feeling better by morning." But inside, she wasn't so sure. She had no idea what was going on, and was afraid to find out.

Tommy was asleep almost instantly when his head hit the pillow. Melinda bent down to kiss his forehead and recoiled in alarm. He was burning up.

She rushed back to the bathroom and returned with a cold, wet washcloth, placing it gently on Tommy's forehead. She tucked his blanket up to his chin, hoping to battle the chills wracking his small body.

Then she turned to Kate, "Okay, little lady, time for you to get back to bed."

Even though Kate usually acted like she hated her big brother, at this moment, seeing him in agony, she couldn't help but feel bad. "Is Tommy going to be okay?" she asked.

"He'll be fine, dear. He just caught a flu bug or something." But Melinda wasn't quite so convinced.

Quietly, Melinda ushered Kate out of the room, closing the door behind her with a soft click. A minute later, she was tucking Kate back into her own bed, smoothing the blankets over her daughter's small frame.

"Try to sleep, sweetheart," she whispered, brushing a stray lock of hair from Kate's forehead, before she kissed her goodnight.

As Melinda walked back toward her bedroom, a sense of unease gnawed at her. The uneasy feeling morphed into cold, hard fear when she heard a loud thud echo from the shower. Her heart leaped into her throat.

She rushed to the bathroom, her breath coming in shallow gasps. The sight that met her eyes was a waking nightmare: William lay sprawled on the shower floor, twitching uncontrollably. Water still beat down on him from the shower head, mingling with the wriggling, black mucus being sucked down the drain. Melinda's stomach churned when she saw the smear of blood on the wall where the back of William's head had struck the ceramic tile.

Panic threatened to overwhelm her, but she forced herself to act. She reached in and turned off the water, then grabbed a towel and gently placed it under William's head. His skin was clammy, his eyes vacant. She found another towel in the cabinet and draped it over his shivering body, her hands trembling nearly as much.

The shaking stopped after a minute, and Melinda kneeled beside him, her voice wavering. "Hold on, Hun. You're going to be okay. I'm just going to call an ambulance really quick, and I'll be right back."

She sprinted into the bedroom, her fingers fumbling as she dialed 911. The operator's voice was a lifeline. "911 emergency. How can I help you?"

Melinda cried into the phone, "It's my husband! He fell in the shower and hit his head!"

The calm, male voice responded, "Just try to stay calm, Ma'am. We're sending help right away. What's your location?"

"I'm at 1215 Salida Del Sol. Please hurry!"

"We'll be there as soon as we can. Don't attempt to move him until the paramedics arrive." The line went dead, leaving Melinda in a tense, agonizing silence.

She rushed back to the bathroom, relief flooding her as she saw William's eyes flutter open. His mouth moved slightly as he regained consciousness. A streak of black ran from the corner of his mouth and down the side of his cheek—the same vile substance Melinda had seen on the towel earlier. She watched in horror as the ooze dripped from his face and disappeared down the drain.

Suddenly, William's hand shot out, grabbing her arm with surprising strength. "A meteor," he stuttered. "Something's wrong—"

Melinda hushed him, her voice soothing. "Shhh. It'll be alright. I've already called for help. They should be here soon."

William's eyes closed, and he drifted back into unconsciousness. As Melinda looked down at him, a shiver ran down her spine. She had a strong feeling that the worst was yet to come.

CHAPTER 4

Normally, the block surrounding the La Quinta Police Station —tucked in the corner between City Hall and the La Quinta Community Services Building—was bustling with activity, as assorted charities, businessmen, and entrepreneurs filtered in and out in a consistent parade of bureaucracy. But at this late hour, after the establishments had closed for the day, only the police station buzzed with activity: officers answering phones, typing reports, and chatting over cups of coffee. The walls were adorned with community service awards and photographs of local events, giving the place a homey, albeit busy, atmosphere.

Captain Gerald Harrison, a tall, muscular black man in his fifties, was in his office reviewing reports, wishing he had listened to that little voice in his head earlier that had told him to go home for the day. Instead, he had glanced at the mountain of paperwork on his desk that had seemed to be mysteriously growing by the minute. With a deep sigh, he grabbed the file off the top of the stack and flipped it open.

As he finished signing off on the report a minute later, the phone on his desk rang. "Captain Harrison speaking," he answered.

Dr. Leonard's voice came through urgently, "Captain Harrison, this is Dr. Leonard from NASA. We have an emergency situation that requires immediate attention."

Captain Harrison sat up a little straighter. "NASA? What's going on?"

Dr. Leonard didn't waste any time. "A meteor cluster entered Earth's atmosphere about forty-five minutes ago. Most disintegrated, but one crashed down near Lake Cahuilla. It exploded upon impact, releasing an unknown substance. We need you to secure the area immediately while we mobilize a team of scientists to investigate the site."

Captain Harrison's eyes widened. "An unknown substance? Is it dangerous?"

"We're not sure yet, but we can't take any chances. We need you to keep everyone away from the site until our team arrives. This is critical."

Harrison nodded. "Understood, Doctor. I'll secure the area right away."

He hung up the phone and stood, his imposing figure commanding attention as he stepped out of his office. He spotted Officer Drew Hanson at his desk, sorting through a pile of paperwork.

"Hanson, get a couple of officers on the phone ASAP. We have an emergency situation at Lake Cahuilla. A meteor crashed and exploded. NASA needs us to secure the area immediately. Sanchez lives close by. Let her know she's on overtime effective immediately. And radio Rodriguez to join her."

Hanson's eyes widened. "Yes, Captain. I'll get on it right away."

***

* * *

Officer Maria Sanchez was enjoying a rare, quiet evening at home. After a long day at work, she had just settled onto her couch with a bowl of popcorn and a movie she'd been looking forward to for weeks. Then her phone buzzed. She groaned as she reached for it reluctantly.

"Officer Sanchez, this is Hanson."

A deep sigh issued from her lips. She knew before she even heard what was coming next that her rare night off was about to be shot to hell. "Hey, Hanson. What's up?"

"We need you to head to the Lake Cahuilla park entrance immediately. Secure it and ensure no one gets in, especially the media. It's urgent."

"Now?" she asked, her disappointment evident in her voice. "What's going on?"

The sergeant's voice came on, sharp and urgent. "No time for questions, Sanchez. Get moving. Now!"

She glanced longingly at the TV, the opening credits of the movie rolling along in a mocking rhythm. "Copy that," she said, her tone resigned, as she pressed the button on the remote to turn the TV off.

"God, this job fucking sucks sometimes," she said as she grabbed a large handful of popcorn from the bowl before she sat it on the coffee table.

Luckily, she'd been too tired to change out of her uniform when she got home, so she was ready in a matter of minutes. As she grabbed her keys and headed out the door, she couldn't shake the feeling that something was wrong, and the unknown was far worse than any movie could portray. She jumped into her squad car and sped down the quiet streets, her mind filled with all sorts of horrifying scenarios.

***

* * *

Officer Juan Rodriguez sat in his patrol car, parked under a flickering streetlight at the edge of town. He was halfway through his nightly routine of filling out paperwork and sipping on a lukewarm coffee when his radio crackled to life.

"Unit 54, this is Dispatch. Over."

Juan set his coffee aside and grabbed the radio. "Unit 54, go ahead, Dispatch."

"We need you to secure the entrance to Lake Cahuilla park immediately. Officer Sanchez is en route to meet you there shortly. No one is to be allowed in, especially the media. It's urgent."

Juan sighed, glancing at the half-finished report on his clipboard. "Copy that, Dispatch. What's going on?"

There was a brief pause, followed by the sergeant's gruff voice. "Just get there, Rodriguez. Now!"

Juan felt a pang of frustration. He hated being kept in the dark, but orders were orders. He quickly gathered his things, tossing the paperwork onto the passenger's seat. *At least it gives me an excuse not to finish this stupid report,* he thought before he started the car, the engine rumbling to life as he peeled away from the curb.

He couldn't shake the feeling that something big had happened. The sergeant's tone had been unusually serious, and Juan's mind raced with possibilities. Maybe it had something to do with the strange tremor he had felt earlier.

The sky was blacker than normal as he navigated his patrol car down Jefferson Street, the oppressive darkness swallowing the road ahead, which was eerily deserted at this hour.

Glancing in his rear-view mirror, he saw a second squad car trailing close behind. He hoped it was Sanchez, the petite, brunette officer whose desk was in the opposite corner from his. He had never mustered the courage to ask her out, but tonight he wished he had.

Just as he refocused on the road, a large dog darted in front of him. "Holy shit!" he cried, swerving to avoid the animal. His headlights illuminated the beast, revealing a grotesque sight. Half of its face had been torn away, leaving raw flesh and bone exposed. The remaining fur was matted with blood, and it snarled at him through a fleshless mouth.

His heart was pounding rapidly as he continued to the park entrance, pulling over just inside and stepping out of his car. Officer Sanchez joined him a minute later, and despite the dread pooling in his stomach, he couldn't help but smile as he watched her approach.

"Nice move back there, Rodriguez," she said sarcastically.

"Hey, a dog ran out in front of me," Rodriguez replied defensively.

"Sure, it did."

"You should have seen it. Its face was all mangled and ripped apart."

"That sounds really disgusting! Let's just hope we don't run into whatever attacked it."

"I couldn't agree more."

Juan's nerves were already on edge, so when he heard a low growl behind him, he whipped his gun from its holster and spun around.

"What the hell was that?" Sanchez asked nervously.

"I don't know. Just stay close," Juan replied.

Sanchez pulled out her flashlight, the beam cutting through the darkness as she drew her own gun. The light stopped on a gruesome scene, making her stomach lurch. A large Bighorn Sheep lay on its side about twenty yards away. The enormous animal snarled angrily as it tried to paw its way toward them, its body gruesomely severed in half. A pair of coyotes chomped hungrily on the sheep's stomach, their eyes reflecting the flashlight's beam with an eerie glow.

The two officers backed away slowly until they were right next to Juan's car. He was about to go around to the driver's side when a third coyote emerged from the shadows, blocking his path. This one had a dark, empty socket where one of its eyes should have been, and its right front leg was chewed off up to the joint, causing it to lurch awkwardly. Thick, black blood dripped from its mouth as it growled.

Juan squeezed his gun tighter, preparing himself. The beast lunged, and he jumped sideways, barely avoiding its gnashing fangs. He spun around and pumped a round directly into the coyote's stomach, sending it crashing to the ground.

He was about to turn to Sanchez when, to his horror, the wounded animal got up and started coming for him again. He shot it directly in the chest this time, and it dropped with a thud.

At that moment, he heard Sanchez fire two shots of her own. He spun around to find that the other two coyotes had turned on her. Both were down, one with a bullet in the head and the other through the chest. The one with its brains splattered on the ground stayed down, but the other one got back up and came at her again. Quickly, she shot it between the eyes, and this time it stayed dead.

Juan was so distracted by Sanchez that he failed to notice the coyote that he thought was dead had gotten halfway up and was shuffling toward him. He cried out in agony as the creature's jaws clamped down on his left leg, tearing his calf muscle in half. His gun slid under the squad car as he fell to the ground.

The mangled canine released its grip and lunged for his throat. Its jaws were inches from his flesh when another shot rang out, hitting it in the side of the head.

Sanchez rushed over to Juan, her face a mask of fear. She set her gun on the ground and quickly ripped off his pant leg to inspect the wound. Even though the sight sickened her, she still had the presence of mind to remove her belt and secure it around Juan's leg as a tourniquet. A sharp cry flew from his mouth as she tightened the belt as much as she could. Then, his body started to shake as the first stages of shock set in. He looked at her in terror for a second before his eyes started rolling back in his head.

"Stay with me, Rodriguez!" she commanded.

As blood poured profusely from the wound and created a large pool around him, the sound of her voice snapped him back to the present. "I don't think—"

"Don't start talking crazy now, okay? I'm gonna get you into the squad car and we're getting the hell out of here," she said as she opened the rear door to the squad car and fought to lift Juan's blood-soaked body into the back seat.

Suddenly, a low, guttural growl filled the air. She looked up to see a big, black mangled German Shepherd bearing down on her. She reached for her gun but it was out of reach.

Juan looked at her and smiled weakly. It was an easy choice, deciding in that moment to sacrifice his life for her. He just prayed that his last act would give her the chance she needed to survive. As the dog drew closer, he picked up a rock and hurled it with the last of his strength, hitting the animal hard enough to divert its attention. The beast turned and lunged at Juan. "Run!" he cried.

He fended the beast off for a few desperate moments, but his injury had sapped his strength. Finally, the dog's jaws clamped down on his neck, ripping his windpipe out in a spray of blood.

Everything had happened so fast that Sanchez was paralyzed with terror as she watched the gruesome scene unfold. She didn't notice the blood-soaked bobcat creeping up behind her until its claws raked down her back, sending her falling forward under the weight of the maddened feline. A brief scream erupted from her mouth before its sharp teeth sank deep into her skull, silencing her forever.

CHAPTER 5

The plane shuddered as it sliced through a patch of turbulence, sending a jolt through Samuel's seat. He gripped the armrest, his knuckles whitening with tension. The hum of the engines was a constant reminder of how high they were above the ground. As an astronomer who had devoted his life to studying the vastness of space, Samuel found it ironic that flying unnerved him. Every bump in the air sent his mind racing with possibilities of what could go wrong.

The cabin was dimly lit, with only the occasional flicker of lights indicating their progress through the night sky. The crew moved silently, their faces calm and composed, adding an eerie calmness to the atmosphere. Across the aisle, Andrea and Kelvin were deep in conversation, their voices low, but Samuel could tell they were discussing the mission. He tried to focus on the conversation, anything to distract from his nerves, but his thoughts kept drifting back to the mysterious nature of their task.

Clause, sitting a few rows ahead, was the picture of calm. He had been on his phone for most of the flight, speaking in hushed tones that Samuel strained to catch. Clause's presence on this mission seemed out of place, and Samuel's instincts told him to remain wary.

When the plane finally touched down at three minutes past twelve, Samuel exhaled a long breath of relief. The wheels screeched against the tarmac, jolting everyone back to the reality of their mission. As the plane taxied into the private hangar, Clause rose immediately, speaking urgently into his phone. His expression remained impassive, but Samuel could sense an underlying tension.

The stewardess released the latch on the exit door with a metallic clunk, and passengers began to gather their belongings. Samuel watched the pilot emerge from the cockpit, murmuring to the stewardess before handing her a small envelope. She nodded solemnly and passed it to Clause as he walked by, a gesture that set Samuel's mind racing. It felt clandestine, like a scene from a spy thriller.

Inside the hangar, the air was cool and smelled faintly of jet fuel. The dim lighting cast long shadows across the concrete floor, adding to the sense of secrecy surrounding their arrival. A black panel van idled in the corner, its engine rumbling softly. Clause strode over to the van, pulling the envelope from his pocket and extracting a piece of paper and what appeared to be a photograph. He studied them briefly before slipping them back into his jacket.

"Time to move, people," Clause called out. "We're pulling out in two minutes."

Samuel took the front passenger seat, his eyes fixed on Clause. He needed to keep him in sight, to gauge every nuance and gesture. As the others filed into the back of the van, Simon turned on his camcorder, hoping to document the journey.

"So, Kelvin, what do you think about this little scavenger hunt we're on?" Simon asked, pointing the camera at him.

"Bullshit, is what I think it is," Kelvin replied tersely.

"Now turn that fucking thing off and let me try to sleep for a few minutes."

Andrea grunted in agreement, leaning her head against the side of the van and closing her eyes. Simon thought briefly about turning it toward Clause, but a stern look from him in the rear-view mirror suggested it might not be a wise decision. With a sigh, he switched off the camera and rested his head back to join the others in a brief nap.

As the van pulled away, Samuel observed Clause texting on his phone, fingers moving rapidly over the keys. He felt a knot tighten in his stomach, suspecting that there was more going on than they were being told. Clause's quick glance over at him was enough to make Samuel shut his eyes quickly to avoid suspicion.

The van sped through the deserted streets, heading toward an uncertain destination. Samuel's thoughts swirled with anxiety, wondering if they were stepping into a government conspiracy. His mind replayed the details of the flight and the clandestine hand-off in the hangar. He hoped his fears were unfounded and merely a product of an overactive imagination.

But as the vehicle hurtled into the night, Samuel couldn't shake the feeling that they were on a collision course with something far more dangerous than they had anticipated. He nestled his head against the cool glass, trying to calm his racing thoughts. Eventually, despite the tension that hung in the air, he drifted into a restless sleep, haunted by the unknown that awaited them.

CHAPTER 6

Dr. Leonard sat at his cluttered desk with his eyes fixed on the computer screen displaying a map of the La Quinta area. The flashing red dot marked the location of the officers sent to secure the crash site. A heavy weight had settled in his gut as he picked up the phone to call Captain Harrison back.

The phone rang twice before a gruff voice answered. "Captain Harrison speaking."

"Captain Harrison, this is Dr. Leonard," Leonard said, trying to keep his voice steady. "I'm calling about the officers you sent to the Lake Cahuilla crash site. What's the current status?"

Captain Harrison's voice hardened. "We lost communication with them about an hour ago. It's not like either of them to go silent. I've tried reaching them multiple times with no luck."

Leonard leaned back in his chair, a sense of dread creeping over him. "Is there a chance it could just be a technical issue?"

"I'd like to think so, but something feels off," Harrison admitted. "The area near the crash site is isolated, but they should still have signal. We're dispatching another team to check things out, but I have a bad feeling about this."

Leonard tapped his fingers nervously on the desk, considering the implications. "We believe the meteor might have released something... unusual. I advise extreme caution, Captain."

"You think it's dangerous?" Harrison asked.

"We're not sure what we're dealing with yet," Leonard replied, choosing his words carefully. "But it's crucial we contain the area. I'll coordinate with your team to provide any assistance you need."

"I appreciate that, Doctor. I'll keep you updated on any developments," Harrison said. "And I'll make sure my officers know to proceed with caution."

"Thank you, Captain. We'll do the same on our end," Leonard said before he ended the call.

Leonard rubbed his eyes, fatigue setting in as he picked up the phone again and dialed Ashton's number, the tension rising in him with every second. The call connected, and Ashton's voice came through, calm but with an edge of concern.

"Ashton here."

"Ashton, it's Leonard. We have a situation," Leonard began, trying to keep his voice level. "We've lost communication with the officers sent to secure the crash site. It's been over an hour now."

Ashton was silent for a moment. "What do you think happened?"

"I'm not sure yet. Captain Harrison is sending another team to investigate, but there's a possibility that the meteor released some kind of substance when it exploded. We need to be prepared for anything."

Ashton exhaled sharply. "We'll double-check our equipment and make sure the team is ready for anything.

Keep me posted on what Captain Harrison's team finds."

"I will," Leonard assured him. "And we're ramping up our analysis here to try to figure out what we're dealing with. I'll have more information for you soon."

"Good. We can't afford any surprises," Ashton said. "Make sure everyone on your end stays alert."

"Absolutely," Leonard replied. "I'll keep you updated on any developments."

Without another word, Ashton abruptly ended the call.

Leonard set the phone down and turned back to the computer, watching the red dot blink on his screen that represented the silent officers. He considered for a moment about having Justin pull up the satellite imagery again, but then thought better of it. *No need to throw everyone into a panic,* he thought bitterly. The reality was that he was afraid of what he might see. He knew, deep down inside that something very bad had happened. And he was responsible.

***

Ashton was more than a little frustrated when he got off the phone with Leonard and learned that the La Quinta police had lost contact with the officers that had been sent to secure the crash site. While it was certainly possible that it was merely a communication issue, he didn't think so. Something big was happening and his team needed to be prepared for anything.

He immediately called the plane and talked to the pilot, giving him a rundown of the situation and instructions to pass on to Clause. He didn't tell him everything, of course—just what he needed to know. Clause would be able to figure out the rest.

The more the deputy director thought about the

possibilities, the more he got excited. He needed to call Patrick back and alert him of the update, but he knew the good doctor wouldn't share in his enthusiasm. He decided that he would simply advise him of their current status, without giving him any details, and leave it at that.

He dialed Dr. Leonard again, and was relieved this time when a young man answered. Instead of having to speak with the director a second time, he was able to leave a brief message to pass on. He simply stated that the group had touched down and were currently in route to their target. Then he hung up.

As the details of the event replayed themselves in his mind, he could hardly contain himself. First, the prospect of finding an alien life-form was the stuff that every scientist dreamed of; and second, this discovery would finally put him where he deserved to be. He was far more qualified to lead the research facility than Dr. Rhodes, the current director, would ever be. Rhodes had gained his position through simple politics and business acumen. Ashton, on the other hand, had PHD's in biology and astrophysics, along with a Master's in Astro-biology, and had even dabbled in pre-med for a while. In his mind, Rhodes was an idiot and a fool.

When he presented his discovery to the board, they would have no choice but to declare him the new director. Either Rhodes would step down voluntarily, or Ashton would find a way to make sure the doctor was no longer able to fulfill his duties.

A little buzz escaped from Ashton's phone and he glanced down to see that he had received a text message from Clause. "Right on time," he muttered softly.

The message simply read: *Got your note. On alert. Leaving airport now. Will update soon.*

Ashton shot him a quick text back: execute ADAR

initiative. Then he slid the phone back into his pocket.

His pace quickened as he headed down the hallway toward the restricted elevator that would take him down to the sub-basement. This was his sanctuary—his private lab that he had built, away from prying eyes, where he could delve even further into the darkest mysteries of the universe. And now that opportunity had finally arrived.

Only a few of his closest and most trusted colleagues were even aware of its existence, and even fewer knew of his personal agenda.

He chuckled as he descended the elevator, for he knew that the discoveries made this night—his discoveries—would alter the fabric of humanity forever. And he would be the one to lead the world into a new age.

CHAPTER 7

The drive back home from the crash site had been tense, filled with fear and a strange, nagging anxiety that William couldn't quite shake. From a very young age, the stars and the celestial heavens above had fascinated him, and now the heavens had decided to drop something terrifying into his life. By the time the paramedics arrived at the Patterson house, William had fully regained consciousness, though he wished he hadn't. His head throbbed with a dull ache, and the world seemed to tilt slightly whenever he moved.

Against Melinda's better judgment, William had dragged himself out of the shower, each movement a struggle against the pain and confusion, and stumbled to the bed like a man emerging from a nightmare. She helped him into a pair of sweatpants, her hands trembling slightly as she propped him up against the headboard with a couple of pillows. She could see the fear lurking in his eyes, an emotion she rarely associated with her husband.

Before she could press him for answers, the blare of sirens cut through the night, their wails like mournful ghosts. The room flickered with the red and blue lights of the approaching ambulance. Melinda stood up from the edge of the bed, casting a worried glance over her shoulder.

"I'll be right back," she said, forcing a calm she didn't feel. "No going to sleep. Got it?"

William managed a weak smile, though it didn't reach his eyes. "Got it," he replied, his voice barely a whisper.

As Melinda left the room, William shifted uncomfortably, trying to find a position that didn't make his head spin. His mind reeled back to the shower, to the moment when he had stepped under the water and everything had gone wrong. The black substance had been waiting for him. As soon as the water touched him, it had slithered across his skin, cold and alive, before it disappeared, absorbed into his body.

Then the pain had come, a searing agony that dropped him to his knees. He had slipped, his feet skidding on the slick tiles, and then there was a blinding flash of light as his head met the wall. After that, darkness—until he woke to find Melinda's tear-streaked face hovering above him.

His thoughts drifted to the meteor, the fiery rock from the sky that had seemed so innocuous at first. But now, it seemed like a harbinger of something far darker. Before he could ponder the incident further, Melinda returned, leading the paramedics into the room.

The paramedics set to work examining William thoroughly. One of them, a burly man with a reassuringly calm demeanor, began asking William questions, his voice a steady anchor in the storm of confusion. As the second paramedic wrapped a bandage around his head, William's thoughts turned abruptly to Tommy.

"How's Tommy?" he asked worriedly.

Melinda replied, "He's fine now. He got sick earlier, but he should be okay by morning."

The one paramedic finished wrapping William's head and stood back, assessing him critically. "No signs of a concussion," he announced, his voice carrying a note of relief. "The cut isn't deep enough for stitches. You're lucky. Falls in the shower often end much worse."

Melinda offered a grateful smile, though it didn't quite reach her eyes. "Thank you for everything."

The paramedic nodded, turning his attention back to William. "If you start feeling sick or dizzy, get to the emergency room right away."

William nodded, absorbing the words through the fog of his thoughts.

A minute later, as the ambulance pulled away, the night air settled back into uneasy quiet. Melinda curled up next to him, her warmth a welcome contrast to the chill creeping through his bones. "Are you sure you're okay?" she asked, her voice barely a whisper.

"Yeah," William replied, though the lie tasted bitter on his tongue. "I think I just need some rest."

Melinda held him tighter, the fear in her eyes mirrored in his own. "What happened out there? First Tommy gets sick, then I find you unconscious in the shower. I was scared to death!"

William closed his eyes, gathering his thoughts. "What happened with Tommy?" he asked.

"Right after you got home, I found him in the bathroom, vomiting. That same black stuff was everywhere—the same stuff I saw in the shower with you."

"Are you sure Tommy's okay now?"

"Yeah, he'll be fine by morning," she assured him, though the worry etched into her brow said otherwise. "What's going on, William?"

He opened his eyes, meeting her gaze with a grim certainty. "I wish I knew. But I think it has something to do with the meteor we found tonight that crashed down near the lake."

Melinda was about to press further when Kate, their daughter, padded into the room, her small face creased with concern. "Is everything okay, Mommy? I saw the ambulance and got scared."

Melinda made room for Kate, pulling her close. "Everything's fine, sweetie. Daddy just had a little fall in the shower, but he's okay now."

Kate peered at her father, relief softening her features. "I'm glad you're okay, Daddy."

William managed a smile, though it felt like a hollow thing. "Me too, Munchkin. Me too."

Melinda sighed, brushing a hand through Kate's hair. "Why don't we get you back to bed so we can all get some sleep?"

But Kate wasn't having it. She gave Melinda her infamous pouting routine, accentuating it with her puppy dog eyes. "Can I sleep with you guys tonight? Please?"

Melinda hesitated, knowing that letting Kate stay meant a night of restless tossing and turning. But the fear in her daughter's eyes made the decision for her. "All right," she relented, "but try to stay still, okay?"

Kate nodded solemnly, already nestling between them, her small body a warm comfort. Within minutes, she was asleep, her breathing soft and steady.

But sleep eluded William and Melinda. They lay awake, the darkness pressing in around them, each lost in their own swirling thoughts. The meteor , the black substance, Tommy's illness—it all felt like pieces of a puzzle they couldn't quite fit together. And in the quiet of the night, as Kate slept soundly between them, William couldn't shake the feeling that something was very, very wrong.

CHAPTER 8

Nancy Beckham lay staring at the ceiling, counting the tiny cracks in the plaster. It was a ritual she had perfected over two years as a field reporter for KESQ, a late-night habit to soothe her restless mind. But tonight, her heart beat a little faster, her thoughts chasing an elusive dream: the anchor desk. That shining symbol of success was always just out of reach, glinting like a prize at the end of a long and winding road. But earlier today, she had learned that one of the long-time fixtures at the studio was retiring, paving the way for someone to get promoted. That person needed to be her.

Her dreams of glory were abruptly interrupted by the sharp crackle of her police scanner, a device that had become her lifeline to the chaos of the world outside. Tonight, it buzzed with an urgency that set her teeth on edge, hundreds of voices rising in a cacophony of alarm. Each call brought the same strange message: a light overhead, not like anything anyone had ever seen before, followed by a short but intense earthquake. She had felt the tremor, but thought nothing of it given their proximity to the fault line and the frequency of minor quakes on almost a daily basis. Now she knew this was something completely different.

Nancy quickly sat up in bed as the ground beneath her seemed to shift and rumble with a low, menacing growl once again. She leaped to her feet and grabbed her phone from the nightstand. Her hand trembled as she dialed Josh Bryant, her cameraman. Each unanswered ring brought a level of tension rising inside her.

"Come on, Josh," she muttered, her frustration mounting as the call went to voice-mail. She took a deep breath and left a message, trying to keep the desperation out of her voice. "Josh, it's me. Call me back right away! I think something big's going on."

Nancy tossed the phone onto the bed and hurried to her closet, rifling through her clothes with the speed and precision of a seasoned veteran. Then, her phone buzzed with Josh's name flashing on the screen.

She answered with a rush of relief. "Josh, thanks for getting back to me."

"Sorry," he replied. "I was a little preoccupied when you called a minute ago."

Nancy rolled her eyes, knowing exactly what "preoccupied" meant in Josh's world. It meant he'd been entangled in yet another night of naked Twister with some chick from the bar who would be forgotten by morning. She wished he'd take as much interest in her as he did in his endless parade of one-night stands. *Someday...*, she thought wistfully, before pushing the idea aside.

"Preoccupied, huh? What was it this time? Naked Twister with some bar bimbo?"

Josh chuckled. "Something like that."

She sighed. "Anyway, I need you to get your ass over here, right away."

"Why? What's up?" Josh asked tersely.

"I don't know, but the police scanner is going crazy,"

Nancy replied with a distinct edge in her voice.

Josh hesitated, his silence stretching just a little too long. "And you want to be the first on the scene so you can catch your big break?"

The words stung, though she knew he didn't mean them that way. Was she really that transparent? She paused, letting the silence speak for her.

"Look, I'm sorry. I didn't mean it like that," Josh said, his voice softening, with a hint of regret pouring through.

Nancy opened her mouth to reply, but a woman's voice drifted through the phone, laughing and snorting at something funny, and she felt her mood souring. "Just get over here as soon as you can," she snapped. Then she hung up before he could respond, tossing the phone onto the bed with a sigh.

***

Josh Bryant reclined lazily on his worn leather couch, with his eyes fixed on the flickering glow of his television. The dim light cast long shadows around his cluttered living room, which was a testament to his chaotic lifestyle. The remnants of last night's takeout sat on the coffee table surrounded by empty beer bottles.

The movie playing on the screen was one he had seen countless times, a comfort in its familiarity. Josh let his mind drift, allowing the dialog and music to wash over him after a long day at work, which was also coupled with some intense family drama. Just as he was finally starting to feel a sense of calm wash over him, his phone rang.

Josh groaned as he fumbled for his phone, which lay half-buried under a pile of crumpled clothes. When he saw Nancy's name on the caller ID, he hesitated. He knew she only called at odd hours when something was up—usually something big. Or at least something she thought was big. He couldn't help but smile at her ambition; it was one of the things he liked most about her.

But tonight, he was tired and didn't have the energy for one of Nancy's wild goose chases. He let the call go to voice-mail, hoping she'd get the hint. He settled back into the couch, closing his eyes for a moment as he listened to the familiar hum of the TV.

His brief moment of peace was shattered by a loud crash from the apartment next door, followed by a string of muffled curses. Josh winced. His neighbor, a disgruntled old man named Mr. Fredericks, had a knack for breaking things at the most inconvenient times.

"Great," Josh muttered, shaking his head as he reached for his phone. He dialed Mr. Fredericks' number even though it probably would've been better to go over there in person. He just didn't have the energy to venture next door, knowing that not only would he get roped into helping his neighbor clean up whatever mess had occurred, but that would be followed by a long, rambling conversation that sometimes droned on for hours.

The line rang twice before his Mr. Fredericks picked up. "What do you want, Braylon?"

"Hey, Mr. Fredericks," Josh said, trying to sound casual. "Everything all right over there? Sounded like something fell."

The man grumbled something unintelligible, but Josh caught the words "damn cat" and "bookcase." He stifled a laugh, picturing the scene in his head. "You need a hand?"

"No, no," Mr. Fredericks replied. "Just a bit of a mess, is all."

"Alright, then. Just let me know if you change your mind."

Josh hung up, shaking his head as he placed the phone back on the table. He had no sooner done that when his phone buzzed with an incoming voice-mail notification. He knew it was Nancy before he even checked.

Sighing, he listened to the message, Nancy's voice crackling with urgency. "Josh, it's me. Call me back right away! I think something big is going on."

He leaned back on the couch, staring at the ceiling as he considered his options. He could ignore it, let her find someone else to help with her story, or he could do what he always did—call her back and get swept up in whatever adventure she had concocted this time.

Josh ran a hand through his hair and did what he always did. He dialed Nancy's number. The phone rang twice before she picked up.

"Nancy," he said, keeping his tone light. "Sorry. I was a little preoccupied when you called a minute ago."

He could almost hear her roll her eyes. "Preoccupied, huh? What was it this time? Naked Twister with some bar bimbo?"

Josh chuckled. "Something like that."

She sighed, and he knew she was biting back whatever sarcastic comment had come to mind. "I need you to get your ass over here, right away."

"Why? What's up?"

"The police scanner is going crazy. I think it's something big."

Josh hesitated. "And you want to be the first on the scene so you can catch your big break?"

The silence that followed was telling, and Josh felt a pang of guilt for teasing her. He softened his tone. "Look, I'm sorry. I didn't mean it."

A woman's laugh erupted from the TV in the background. As innocent as it was, he knew it wouldn't help Nancy's mood. "Just get over here as soon as you can," she snapped before hanging up.

Josh let out a long sigh before he stood up and pulled on a jacket as he grabbed his camera bag and headed toward the door. Then he stepped out into the cool night air, wondering what kind of chaos he was walking into.

***

Nancy knew she didn't have any right to be upset, but the tight coil of frustration in her gut told her otherwise. The real problem was that she was mostly upset with herself. Josh had asked her out a long time ago, shortly after they had started working together. She had turned him down, claiming she wanted to keep their relationship professional. That was the worst mistake of her life! He never asked her out again, and now, she was stuck with the image of him wrapped around a body that wasn't hers.

She sighed heavily, trying to dispel the ghosts of what could have been, and forced herself out of her sour mood by completing her rummage through her closet until she settled on a blouse she was sure would look good on camera against the night backdrop—a white and yellow chiffon with a ruffled collar, professional yet trendy, the kind that said she meant business even when the world was falling apart.

Nancy slipped on the blouse and raced to the bathroom. She quickly revived her hair, smoothing down errant curls, and dabbed on some fresh makeup. Within ten minutes, she was done with her lightning-quick makeover.

As she gathered her things, an undercurrent of something electric pulsed through the air, setting her on edge. It was a feeling she couldn't quite shake, a sense that this night was different. The police scanner continued its relentless chatter, a symphony of fear and chaos that fueled the excitement growing inside her.

She rushed down the steps from her apartment toward the white studio van parked at the curb. It stood in stark contrast to the blackness of the night sky surrounding it. Nancy carried her shoes in her hand as she shuffled to the passenger door, her heart racing with anticipation. This was it—the story she'd been waiting for, the one that would change everything. She just hoped she was ready for whatever waited for her out there in the dark.

Josh barely acknowledged her when she opened the door and climbed into the passenger seat. She knew he was irritated from having to leave his little rendezvous and rush over, but it was his job to be able to drop everything on a dime and react to breaking news. She considered reminding him of that fact but thought better of it, deciding it would only make matters worse.

A minute later, they pulled out of the apartment complex and turned onto Monterey. "So, where are we going?" Josh asked.

"Lake Cahuilla Park," she replied.

As Nancy reached down to put her shoes on, Josh glanced over, raising an eyebrow. "Are you wearing heels?" he asked.

"Of course I am," Nancy replied.

Josh grunted. "Are you sure that's a good idea?"

"Why wouldn't it be?" she shot back, more defensive than she intended.

"I don't know? Maybe because it'll be dark outside, and who knows, you just might not be able to see where you're going? High heels probably aren't the safest things to wear."

Nancy had just about had enough of his sarcasm and was just about to respond when his voice softened, almost apologetic. "Look, I'm sorry. It's just been a crappy day, and

I'm taking it out on you, plus, believe it or not, I actually don't want you to get hurt."

Immediately, Nancy felt guilty for getting upset. "Is there anything you want to talk about?" she asked gently.

"Nah, it's just some stupid shit with my brother."

Ah, Nancy thought, understanding dawning on her immediately. Jared was Josh's loser brother, a man who was nothing more than a pimple on the ass of humanity. If he wasn't locked up for dealing, then he was out at the local bar picking fights—the kind of guy who liked to kick puppies for fun.

"What'd Jared do now?" she asked.

Josh shook his head, indicating he didn't want to talk about it. She let it drop, figuring he'd tell her when he felt like it.

A few minutes later, they were turning left onto HWY 111, heading toward La Quinta. Nancy flicked on the police scanner mounted in a cradle under the dash to see if there was any update on what was going on.

A myriad of calls crackled through the speakers, officers going on about wild and rabid animals. Then she heard the dispatch calling repeatedly for two officers at the park location. When they didn't answer, she heard the dispatch call for assistance.

"That doesn't sound good," Josh said, a note of concern creeping into his voice. "If there's a pack of rabid dogs running around, there's no telling what they might do."

They were just about to turn left onto 54th Ave. when something big splattered against the windshield of the van. "Holy shit!" Josh exclaimed. "What the fuck was that?"

Nancy cried out, her heart leaping into her throat, and looked at him in shock. He pulled the van over, breathing hard, and sat there for a moment, trying to collect himself.

Two more large objects thudded against the windshield, each leaving a bloody trail as they slid down the hood and onto the pavement.

Even though Nancy was scared, she knew they had to figure out what was going on. "Get the camera," she said to Josh as she slowly opened her door, her voice steady despite the fear clawing at her insides.

He hesitated. "Are you crazy? I'm not going out there!"

"We have to figure out what's going on here, Josh. So, find your balls somewhere inside those pants of yours and grab your camera!"

Josh gave her an angry glare, but reached down between the seats and grabbed his camera. If it had been anyone other than Nancy, they'd have had a mouthful of his fist by now.

Luckily, traffic was light, so he had no problem getting out of the van and walking around to the front. What he saw made his skin crawl. A pair of large blackbirds lay on the pavement, flopping around like fish out of water. Their wings were clearly broken, but what was so bizarre was the way they kept gnashing out at Josh's feet. "How are these things still alive?" he asked in disbelief.

"I have no idea," Nancy replied, staring in horror. "I've never seen anything like it. With injuries like this, they should have died on impact. Make sure you get it on camera."

Josh was already focusing in on the bloody birds when Nancy cried out. He brought the camera up quickly, the light catching a fleeting glimpse of another bird as it tried to nip at Nancy's feet. Apparently, it was the first bird that had hit the windshield and had somehow managed to crawl itself toward them. "What the hell?" he said in a shaky voice.

Nancy stomped down hard with the heel of her shoe, impaling the thing through the head. Just then, they heard a chorus of squawks coming toward them. "Shit!" they both exclaimed before they scrambled back into the van. They slammed the doors shut just as a barrage of winged missiles slammed into the van, a flurry of feathers and fury.

Nancy cried out, hysteria bubbling up as the birds battered the van, some hitting hard enough to send spidery cracks through the windshield glass. Josh waited for the attack to stop and then stomped on the gas. The truck bounced as it drove over the bird carcasses, continuing down the road with a lurch.

Josh's hands gripped the steering wheel with white-knuckled intensity, panic filling his voice as he exclaimed, "What the hell was that?"

Nancy had no answer.

"That was some end-of-days, apocalypse-type shit right there!" he continued, his voice rising in pitch.

Nancy finally gathered her wits about her and replied, "Let's just keep going. Maybe if we get to the park, we can see what's really going on?"

The problem was, Nancy wasn't sure she wanted to know. The darkness felt increasingly thicker with each mile they covered, bringing them closer to whatever awaited in the shadows.

CHAPTER 9

Harrison slammed the phone down in frustration. The lines had been ringing off the hook for the last hour, each of them going on about crazy lights and wild animals. Add that to the fact that they still could not reach Sanchez and Rodriguez at all, and then had lost contact with the other team he had sent to find them. His blood was about to boil!

Finally, he stormed out of his office and yelled at the nearest officer, "Get me that son-of-a-bitch from NASA back on the phone so he can tell me what the hell's going on here!"

The officer, a young man in his twenties and probably fresh from the Academy, was the unfortunate soul who bore the brunt of Harrison's frustration. Quickly he picked up his phone and said, "Yes, Sir!" while dialing the number.

"Put it on speaker," Harrison said. The officer pressed a button and Darcey's voice filled the room as she picked up the line at the other end and answered with a polite, "NASA's Deep Space Department. How may I help you?"

Harrison replied gruffly, "This is Captain Harrison of the La Quinta Police Department. I need to speak to Dr. Leonard right now so he can explain to me what the hell is going on here!"

"Of course, sir," she answered. "I'll get him immediately."

Her voice was replaced with boring elevator music as Darcey put them on hold to call the director.

***

As soon as Darcey had heard the captain's voice on the other end, she paged Dr. Leonard to the control room. He came strolling in a minute later.

"What is it, Darcey?" he asked.

"Sir, Captain Harrison from the La Quinta Police is on the phone. He sounds rather frantic and is asking for details about the incident. What do I tell him?"

"Shit! I was afraid of that," he said. Then he turned to Justin, "Any updates?"

Justin replied, "I've been tracking the team since they touched down. They should be at the sight within the next twenty minutes. And we were able to locate the residence of the civilians who were at the scene when the 'incident' happened."

"Good. What about ground zero? Have you been able to see anything else?"

Justin replied, "It was quiet as of ten minutes ago. Let me pull the satellite back up." He swung back over to the other terminal and pressed a couple of keys. The sight itself looked secure, but Justin saw something just at the corner of the screen for a brief second. He panned the image to the left so that it showed more of the entrance to the park and gasped.

Leonard heard his gasp and looked at the screen. He was alarmed when he saw the pack of crazed animals attack the two officers. When one animal kept advancing after it had mortally wounded, he feared for the worse. Then he saw the dismembered Bighorn laying yards away, and watched as it clawed and struggled to move when it clearly should have been dead.

The Doctor was at a loss as to how to explain what he was witnessing. Sure, he had seen all the horror movies, the ones where the dead come back to life with a hunger for flesh, but he never thought anything like that could happen for real. Until now.

Justin's voice brought him back to the present, "How is that even possible?"

Leonard replied, "It's not. At least not on this planet." And his own voice confirmed what he had suspected—that an alien organism may have been living inside the meteor, and was now loose upon this world.

Darcey spoke up, "Sir, the Captain is on the other line. What do you want me to tell him?"

Leonard replied, "Put him on speaker. I'll talk to him."

"Captain Harrison," he said. "What can I do for you?"

Harrison responded in a harsh voice, "First you can start by telling me what the fuck is going on here. And I want the truth."

"Of course, Captain. What I can tell you, is that not long ago a meteor crashed down near Lake Cahuilla. Because of the unknown origin of the subject, we have dispatched a field team to examine it and determine if there's any threat to the public."

Harrison's bullshit meter went off, "Tell me the whole story, Doctor. You're hiding something. I can smell it."

Leonard heard the desperation in the man's voice, and something stirred inside him. At one time, he had been a passionate man, concerned with the wellbeing of his fellow man above all else. Then career and politics hardened him. His reputation and achievements replaced the real important things in life, and suddenly he felt guilty and ashamed of the man he had become. So, he came clean to the captain and told him everything he knew. "What we have just learned, only moments ago, is that some kind of substance was released from the object. Two civilians were exposed, William Patterson and his son Tommy. We have confirmed their address as—"

"I know Patterson's address," Harrison interrupted. "He's a good friend of mine. What happened to him?"

"We don't know," Leonard replied. "They left the scene within minutes of the crash and went home. What we do know, is that an ambulance was called to his home shortly after."

***

Harrison turned to one of his officers, "Get someone over to Patterson's house right away. See if he's okay.'

"What else aren't you telling me?" Harrison asked.

Leonard replied, "Don't get excited, Captain. Panic right now will only make matters worse."

Harrison shot back, "Who said anything about panic? Shit, I'm just trying to get this situation under control. I've got calls coming in by the dozens about wild, crazy animals terrorizing the area. And I can't seem to get ahold of the officers I sent, per your request, to secure the park entrance."

Leonard was silent for a moment, trying to find the words to describe the grizzly images he had seen on the screen.

"Doctor? Are you still with me?" Harrison asked.

***

Leonard spoke up, softly this time, "We saw your officers on the satellite images. I'm afraid there's been a terrible incident..."

While the Director was talking to the police, Darcey pulled out her cell phone and typed a few quick lines of text and then hit the send button. Then she discreetly pushed the phone back into her pocket.

CHAPTER 10

William had just fallen asleep when the doorbell rang. The sound was sharp, almost violent in the stillness of the night. Melinda stirred next to him, her brow furrowing as she blinked awake. The bell rang again, persistent and insistent.

"I'll go see who it is," Melinda mumbled, slipping out of bed carefully to avoid waking Kate, who lay nestled between them snoring softly. She wrapped herself in her bathrobe and shuffled quietly from the room.

The hallway was dark, shadows clinging to the corners like cobwebs. She hesitated at the door for a moment, listening to the faint hum of the refrigerator and the creaks of the old house settling around her, before opening it cautiously. She found herself face-to-face with her neighbor, Harvey Stratton.

Harvey stood on the porch, the faint glow of the porch light casting eerie shadows across his weathered face. He was dressed in a blue plaid bathrobe, the kind that had seen better days, and there was a concerned look in his eyes.

"Harvey," Melinda said, surprised to see her neighbor at this late hour. "What can I do for you?"

Harvey stuttered as he spoke, his voice trembling slightly. "I'm sorry for bothering you so late, Ma'am. I was just concerned when I saw the ambulance and wanted to make sure everything was okay?"

Melinda forced a reassuring smile. "It's okay, Harvey. Everything's fine. William just had a little accident, is all."

Harvey's brow wrinkled. "Are you sure he's okay?"

"Yeah," Melinda replied, nodding to emphasize her words. "The paramedics said he was fine. He just needs some rest."

"What happened?" Harvey pressed.

"He slipped and fell in the shower."

"Oh, no! That's terrible. He's lucky he didn't get seriously hurt."

"Yeah, I know."

Melinda tried her best to be polite, but she knew this conversation could stretch into hours if she didn't find a way to end it. Harvey was the type who could talk a subject to death and then resurrect it for one last round.

Harvey continued, undeterred by her subtle hints, "I had a niece once, Norma, who died like that. Well, not exactly. She wasn't in the shower, but she fell in the bathroom and hit her head on the tub. Died almost instantly."

"I'm sorry," Melinda said, her voice softening. "That sounds terrible."

"Yeah, it was. My wife, Sherri, was a mess for months afterward. It was her sister's kid." Harvey's eyes began to tear up slightly as he thought of his wife and the tragedy that had shadowed their lives for so long.

Melinda saw his mood shifting as a current of sorrow started seeping in, and was just about to suggest he go home when a squad car pulled up in front of the house. The vehicle's lights cut through the darkness, casting flickering patterns on the pavement.

Harvey took this as a sign to leave, mumbling a quick excuse before shuffling back across the street, his slippers whispering against the concrete.

Officer Jerry Durant stepped out of his car as he watched Harvey shuffle back to his house across the street.

"Jerry!" Melinda called out, a genuine smile breaking through the weariness. "What brings you here?"

Jerry approached the house with a quick stride, giving Melinda a tight hug and a light kiss on the cheek. "Sorry to bother you so late, but the captain heard that William was hurt, and he sent me to check on him."

Though Melinda had just gone through this whole scene with Harvey, she was glad to see Jerry. He was a good man, and a good officer. He had also been William's partner a while back, before a knee injury had forced William into early retirement. "William's fine," Melinda said, her voice warm with gratitude. "He just fell and hit his head."

"That's good," Jerry said in relief. "I mean, not about falling, but that he's okay."

Melinda chuckled softly, appreciating Jerry's awkward sincerity. He always got a little tongue-tied around her, and she suspected that maybe he harbored a secret crush. "I know what you mean," she said.

Then Jerry's tone changed, becoming stern and serious. "You need to make sure you stay inside and lock the door. There's some crazy stuff going on out there, and you'll be safer inside."

Melinda looked at him in confusion. "What in the world are you talking about?"

"It happened at the park," Jerry said, lowering his voice as if the shadows might be listening. "Some kind of meteor crashed down, and now all the animals are acting crazy."

"I'm sure they were just spooked. William told me about the meteor. King was with them and took off after it crashed."

"Just be careful if you see him," Jerry warned. "There's no telling how he'll act. Two other officers have already gone down at the jaws of a pack of rabid coyotes."

Melinda was shocked, her hand flying to her mouth. "My god, Jerry. I'm so sorry."

Jerry nodded solemnly. "Like I said, just stay inside and be careful." Then he added, almost as an afterthought, "And tell William I stopped by."

"Will do," Melinda said solemnly.

Jerry offered a weary smile before turning back toward his car. A minute later, he pulled away from the curb, his headlights carving a path through the darkness as he headed back toward the station.

Melinda watched him go, her mind spinning with the unsettling news. She closed the door and locked it securely behind her. She took a deep breath, trying to shake off the unease as she returned to her bedroom, where she found a sliver of comfort in the rhythm of William's steady breathing, coupled with Kate's soft snores. Then she heard a distant howl, almost imperceptible, but it was enough to send a cold chill down her spine. Suddenly, life seemed very fragile.

***

Harvey shuffled slowly across the street, his feet dragging as if each step carried the weight of the world. The night air was cool and crisp, but it did little to clear the fog of regret clouding his mind. He was upset with himself for bringing up his wife, Sherri, for letting the memory of her slip past his lips so easily. With the mention of her name, the sadness was back, as sharp and relentless as it had ever been. It was why he had started drinking so much in the first place. After a few beers, the emptiness didn't hurt as much, the edges blurred just enough to get by.

As he trudged up the steps to his porch, the fact that his front door stood ajar by a couple of inches didn't entirely register. It was just another detail lost in the haze of his grief and self-pity. Absently, he walked through the door and closed it behind him with a soft click, shutting out the world and everything in it.

His first stop once inside was the refrigerator, the hum of the appliance a familiar comfort in the silence of the house. He grabbed a Bud Light, the can cold and reassuring in his hand, and popped it open with a satisfying hiss. A good, long swig helped a little, the alcohol burning a path down his throat, numbing the ache inside. He took another, and the stupor he had come to welcome began to settle in, a warm fog wrapping around his senses. He quickly finished the can, the empty husk of aluminum clattering to the counter, and reached in for another, seeking the oblivion he craved.

That's when he heard the growl behind him, a low, menacing rumble that sent a shiver crawling up his spine. His hand trembled as he slowly set the can back down on the shelf and turned around.

He was relieved when he saw King standing there. Even in his compromised state, he recognized the red collar around the dog's neck, the same one he had seen him wearing countless times before when Tommy walked him around the neighborhood. But this wasn't the same King. There was an aura of death surrounding him, something poisonous and unnatural that sent a jolt of fear racing through Harvey's alcohol-addled mind.

King's eyes, once bright and playful, were now clouded with a wild, feral madness, rather, one of them was. The other one dangled grotesquely from its socket, swaying with each subtle movement, while half of his ribcage protruded from his flesh, exposing the tissue and organs beneath.

The sight was enough to cut through Harvey's haze and bring a surge of panic clawing quickly to the surface. He tried to run from the nightmare standing in his kitchen, but King was on him in an instant. The dog lunged, teeth bared and snapping with a feverish intensity, and Harvey felt a blinding pain as they sank into his flesh, tearing and ripping with a savage ferocity.

The room spun around him, the walls closing in as he staggered back, a scream lodged in his throat, too late and too futile. The world faded into darkness as the life was torn from him, piece by bloody piece, until there was nothing left but the echoes of his pain and the quiet, relentless march toward oblivion.

In those last moments, as his vision blurred and his body went numb, Harvey thought of Sherri, of her smile and her laughter, the way she would hum softly to herself as she moved through their home. He hoped, with what little remained of him, that he would find her again, that they would be together on the other side of life. And then, mercifully, the darkness swallowed him whole.

CHAPTER 11

When Ashton got the text from Darcey, he felt a surge of excitement ripple through him. The message on his phone was the confirmation he'd been waiting for, the catalyst that would set everything in motion. His plan, long in the making, was now at the cusp of realization. Clause had to come through on his end; that much was crucial. The real challenge was to orchestrate the involvement of the rest of the bumbling crew without raising any suspicions, to manipulate them into helping him acquire what he needed without them ever realizing the full scope of what they were part of.

He felt a little more spring in his step as he walked into the main room of the restricted lab. The space was vast, a sprawling complex divided into various workstations, each a hub of activity and innovation. The far wall was lined with three massive containment units, five-by-five structures that stretched from floor to ceiling, their surfaces fortified with three inches of bulletproof glass. To his immediate left, a long bank of computer terminals served as the command station, a nerve center for the lab's myriad operations.

Ashton made his way to the center of the command station and began typing on a keyboard. The screen flickered to life, and the ADAR program began to initialize. The acronym stood for Advanced Deployment of Alien Recovery, a sophisticated system that Ashton had painstakingly designed. He anxiously watched an array of windows and data streams popped up on the screen as the program booted up.

Two other scientists were working in the lab, the only ones Ashton had trusted with his secret; the only ones who knew the lab even existed. Dr. Frank Vogel, a long-time friend and fellow MIT graduate, sat at another terminal, his fingers flying across the keyboard as he busily typed. Dr. Victoria Kafka, meanwhile, was at the containment units, putting the final touches together to ensure they were ready for what was to come.

Ashton had only known Dr. Kafka for a short time—she had transferred to the AMES facility approximately eighteen months ago—but he was immediately drawn to her. It wasn't necessarily her looks, though she was quite attractive, with long, dark hair and mesmerizing eyes. It was the way she carried herself that attracted him, her drive and passion for her work that few others possessed. She was a kindred soul, a fellow seeker of knowledge and power. Because of that, Ashton had approached her, and she had eagerly accepted his invitation into his inner circle.

The facility had taken approximately eight months to complete, with Dr. Vogel and Dr. Kafka playing crucial roles in its creation. It was a marvel of engineering and subterfuge, brought to life with a healthy amount of NASA's funding, which Ashton had redirected with a touch of creative accounting. The trio had planned meticulously, developing hundreds of scenarios and protocols to follow when the time came. Now, that moment was upon them.

As soon as word had come down about the meteor and its possible extraterrestrial inhabitants, Ashton had sprung into action. It was a best-case scenario, the kind he had only dreamed of. When he learned from Dr. Leonard that there was indeed unknown activity surrounding the meteor and its effect on local wildlife, he knew it was time to bring Clause into the fold. Clause would help ensure any potential specimens were secured, their secrets captured for Ashton's purposes.

Now, Clause was an interesting man, a cousin of Dr. Kafka. Though he lacked scientific skills, he possessed other valuable traits. Simply put, he was a hired gun. His military background made him a formidable adversary, and his unwavering loyalty to his cousin made him a useful ally. When Ashton's coup unfolded, Clause's skills would prove indispensable.

Ashton called his two trusted assistants over. "If all goes according to plan, our first specimens will arrive at this facility within the next six hours. Are all the systems in check?"

Dr. Vogel replied, "I just ran a series of complete diagnostics. Everything checks out."

Dr. Kafka answered, "The containment units have been pressurized, and everything is ready to go."

"Good. Just double-check everything. We can't afford to have anything go wrong."

Satisfied with their responses, Ashton excused himself and exited the room, heading back toward the elevator. But instead of ascending back upstairs, he walked to a sconce on the opposite wall and pressed a key into a hidden keyhole behind it. When he turned the key, a panel in the wall slid open, revealing a long, dark corridor with a pair of doors on each side and one at the far end. Ashton withdrew the key and stepped into the sloping corridor, feeling the familiar thrill of secrecy. The panel closed behind him, sealing the entrance from view.

This hidden wing of the lab was Ashton's pride and joy, a part of the facility only he knew about. The construction workers had known about it once, of course. That was when Ashton first learned of Clause's prowess. One by one, each of the men who had built the secret wing had met with untimely deaths.

Well, not all of them, Ashton thought as he reached the end of the hallway and entered the door there. The room was a cavernous expanse, approximately twenty-five thousand square feet with a twenty-foot-high ceiling. It was lined with an assortment of computer terminals and control centers, but the main attraction was the array of eight-foot-high glass cylinders that dotted the main floor.

Thick metal ducts rose from the tops of the tubes, converging in a large array suspended by beams from the ceiling. Each cylinder was equipped with metal tubing that jutted from the sides about a foot from the bottom, curving down to disappear into the floor.

All the cylinders were empty except for one. The cylinder closest to the entrance housed a man who had once played a vital role in the creation of this masterpiece. Ashton had deeply admired Juan Castro, the foreman of the construction project. Juan had demonstrated creativity and ingenuity, even completing the project on time and under budget.

Ashton stood before the cylinder, admiring the man suspended within, floating amidst a synthetic liquid developed by NASA to keep embryos in stasis. He tapped on the glass a couple of times, watching as Juan's lips quivered slightly in response. Ashton smiled, a sense of satisfaction washing over him.

This was just the beginning, the first step in a grand design that would change everything. With Darcey's text and Clause's support, Ashton felt invincible. The world had no idea what was coming, and he would make sure it stayed that way, at least until it was too late for anyone to stop him.

CHAPTER 12

As Josh turned onto 58th Street, the memory of the unnatural bird attack just moments ago lingered like a dark cloud over him. The police scanner in the van crackled to life again, delivering an urgent alert from the captain. The message warned all officers to be cautious of any wild animals in the area exhibiting extreme behavior. The warning did little to ease the fear hanging in the air between him and Nancy.

Nancy broke the tense silence first. "What the hell is going on here, Josh?" she asked, her eyes wide and her voice shaky.

He glanced at her, trying to mask his own nerves with an impression of calm. "I wish I knew. Just be careful tonight, okay?"

Nancy nodded, her lips trembling, while her eyes began to mist over as the reality of their situation sank in.

Josh continued, attempting to inject some confidence into his words, even though that was in short supply right now. "Like you said, maybe when we get to the park, we can get some answers?"

As they neared Jefferson Street, a sense of dread settled over them like a thick fog. After that, it was just a short trip to Cahuilla Park Road. Nancy's eyes darted around, catching dark shadows that seemed to scramble through the bushes and around the trees at every turn. Her imagination was running rampant, painting the night with terrifying shapes and sounds that waited to attack with savage abandon.

"Maybe this wasn't such a good idea," Nancy said fearfully, her voice barely above a whisper.

Josh replied, "Look, I know we're both scared. Hell, I'm freaking the fuck out over here. But we're almost there. And we need to see what's going on. If it's something dangerous, we have an obligation to tell the public so they can protect themselves." His words were meant to sound brave, but inside, he was trembling, and every instinct screamed that bad things lay ahead.

When he turned onto Cahuilla Park Road, the night seemed darker than he had ever seen it before.

"Slow down," Nancy urged in a tight voice. This time, the dark shadow she saw darting through the bushes was terrifyingly real. As the large dog passed by them, she saw its red eyes peering back at her from a mangled skull. The dog had clearly been in a horrendous fight, yet the extent of its injuries should have killed it. Nancy let out a small squeal as a shiver ran down her spine.

Josh asked, "What is it?"

Nancy was visibly shaken. "This dog just ran past us with half its head all chewed up. How does an animal live through an attack like that?"

Josh wished he had an answer, but the thought of undead animals roaming in his own backyard sent his mind into a tailspin. It was like something out of a nightmare. The black birds that had slammed into the van minutes ago should have died on impact, yet there they were, clawing and scraping toward them on broken wings, driven by an insatiable hunger. "What if it didn't?" he mumbled.

"What are you talking about?" Nancy asked nervously, her lips trembling again to signal that the same thoughts had entered her mind.

"I know this sounds crazy, but what if we're in the middle of some terrible nightmare? What if these animals aren't normal animals anymore?"

Nancy turned to look at him, her eyes filled with fear.

"It makes sense," he continued. "Something's affected the wildlife in this area. That's why they're going crazy."

"So, what do we do?" Nancy asked desperately.

"I don't know," Josh admitted. "But we'll figure it out."

As they neared the entrance to the park, Josh brought the van to a crawl, peering intently ahead. The headlights caught glimpses of movement, but the figures always slipped back into the shadows just out of view, as if intentionally hiding from the light.

They reached the entrance and immediately spotted the police car standing idle. Josh brought the van to a stop about twenty feet behind the cruiser and put the vehicle in park.

"Stay here," he instructed, reaching down to grab his camera.

Nancy's voice was full of worry. "Be careful," she said softly.

Josh nodded, slowly opening the door and stepping out. He closed the door softly and set the camera on his shoulder, then began walking cautiously toward the abandoned squad car.

At first, the only sounds were the soft hum of the van's engine and his own footsteps shuffling along the pavement. Then he thought he heard a soft growl from somewhere nearby, and instinctively slowed his pace.

After a few more steps, he reached the back of the squad car and noticed a second squad car parked off to the side.

Distracted momentarily, he nearly tripped over the ravaged body of a police officer. "Holy shit!" he cried out, bringing the camera down to capture the gruesome scene.

He had to stifle the urge to vomit at the sight of the officer's intestines trailing away from his stomach, half his face and skull eaten away, and one arm missing entirely.

Just then, a low growl sounded again, this time much closer. He swung his camera toward the sound, the light catching the face of a bobcat snarling at him, its mouth clamped around the officer's severed arm.

Josh backed away slowly, careful not to provoke the animal. The bobcat watched him with wary eyes. After a couple of cautious steps, the bobcat dropped the arm and let out a throaty roar. The sound was immediately answered by a chilling chorus of howls that filled the air, a symphony of nightmare creatures converging from every angle.

Inside the van, Nancy watched Josh carefully. As he backed toward the van, she saw the bobcat step into the light of the van's headlights. She couldn't help but cry out, which caused the cat to jump.

Josh's only hope was to turn and run for the van. He got within a few feet when he suddenly felt a searing pain in his left leg and stumbled to the ground. The momentum of the bobcat's charge carried it past Josh as he fell, but he knew he only had a second before it whirled around to finish him.

As Nancy watched the bobcat attack, she frantically managed to reach into the glove box and pulled out the handgun hidden there.

When Josh went down from the attack, she quickly moved to the driver's side and threw the door open. As the bobcat lunged past Josh, she fired a flurry of shots in its direction. The darkness made it difficult to aim, but she heard at least one bullet thud into the animal's flesh, hoping it would buy them enough time to get Josh into the van.

Quickly, she jumped out and rushed to Josh's side. The headlights provided just enough illumination for her to see his outline. She threw one of his arms over her neck and helped him stagger to his feet. He tried to walk, but his left leg dragged uselessly beside him. As they neared the van, she could hear the bobcat's low growl close by, praying they had enough time to make it.

Nancy struggled to push Josh into the driver's seat, silently wishing the van had been parked differently to allow easier access to the side door. Still, somehow Josh managed to slide over to the other seat, giving Nancy room to climb in.

She was halfway into the van when she screamed in agony as the crazed feline's jaws clamped down hard on the back of her right foot, and with a savage jerk, ripped out her Achilles tendon, sending a fountain of blood spraying out.

The bobcat fell back, momentarily off balance from the sudden release of tension, giving Nancy a brief second to close the door on her attacker. She looked at Josh feebly, her voice barely a whisper. "Maybe this wasn't such a good idea after all," she mumbled before losing consciousness.

Josh followed her into darkness a moment later.

CHAPTER 13

About twenty minutes later, the research van had passed through Palm Desert and was approaching the Indian Wells Tennis Garden. Clause, gripping the steering wheel tightly, gradually slowed down. The van's flashers pierced the darkness, and finally, he pulled over to the side of the road. The sudden stop of movement stirred the rest of the group from their fitful naps.

"Why have we stopped?" Andrea asked groggily, blinking at the unfamiliar surroundings. "Are we there already?"

Clause shook his head, his eyes focused on the road ahead. "No, there's just something I need to check out."

He stepped out of the van, pulling on his driving gloves with a deliberate snap, and walked into the beam of the headlights. Ahead of him lay a cluster of birds plastered across the pavement, their dark forms glistening under the artificial light. He crouched down to examine the nearest one. It lay dead, its head grotesquely caved in. What puzzled him, though, was the question of impact. From the spatter of blood —or the lack thereof—it seemed unlikely that it had met its end against the pavement. A vehicle had undoubtedly been involved.

A flicker of movement caught Clause's eye. He turned his head sharply to see a second bird just a few feet away. This one bore the grim evidence of a tire mark through its midsection, its innards a gruesome puddle of jelly. Yet, shockingly, its head continued to move, beak opening and closing feverishly, emitting a high, unnerving screech.

By now, the rest of the group had joined Clause, each reacting first with repulsion and then with intense curiosity. Simon had his camera out, documenting every unsettling detail. "How in the hell is that thing still moving?" he muttered, unable to tear his gaze away.

"You're the neurobiologist. You tell us," Kelvin replied.

Simon shrugged helplessly. "Beats the hell out of me. This thing should be deader than a doornail."

Andrea chimed in with a smirk, "That's a real scientific observation."

Samuel interjected, "Obviously, we won't know what's going on until we examine it."

Clause stood up and walked purposefully to the back of the van. Moments later, he returned with a large, metallic box. After setting it down beside the avian anomaly, he pressed a series of codes into the panel atop the box. With a soft click, the lid sprang open, releasing a thick vapor that spiraled into the night air.

Without hesitation, Clause lifted the dead bird and placed it into the box. Then he carefully retrieved the still-moving one and deposited it into the chamber beside its lifeless companion. Instantly, the creature's movements ceased.

After securing the specimens inside the unit, Clause returned to the back of the van with the box. "Time to go," he announced, jumping back into the driver's seat.

Samuel shook his head, processing the eerie discovery as he made his way back to the van.

A minute later, the van was once again hurtling down Highway 111 toward La Quinta, where, they hoped, answers awaited.

As they turned off Jefferson Street onto Cahuilla Park Road and approached the park's entrance, Samuel's apprehension grew when he spotted the red taillights of a studio van parked ahead. Clause maneuvered their vehicle alongside it, illuminating the police car parked in front.

"Wait here," Clause instructed, always a man of few words, before stepping out of the van and closing the door softly behind him.

With a small flashlight in one hand and a gun in the other, he moved cautiously toward the studio van. As he approached, the soft hum of its idling engine filled the air. He shone the light over the vehicle, spotting an ominous trickle of blood seeping from beneath the passenger door.

Holding his breath, Clause wedged the flashlight between his teeth and reached for the door handle. As it swung open, Josh's limp form nearly toppled onto him. He caught the man and eased him back into the seat, checking for a pulse. Josh was still alive, but barely. Then he noticed the second injured occupant and urgently signaled for help.

A low growl rumbled from the shadows at the van's front. Clause spun around to find a bobcat, dragging itself toward him on three legs, the fourth reduced to a bloody stump. Without flinching, Clause fired a single, precise shot, dropping the beast with a resounding thud. Immediately, a chilling chorus of howls and growls echoed in the night. Clause knew their time was running out.

When the others joined him, Clause barked orders, his voice sharp with urgency. "Simon and Andrea, help the people in the van. Get blood samples and stabilize their wounds if you can. Samuel and Kelvin, we need samples from this bobcat and anything else in the area. You have five minutes."

As everyone scrambled for their gear, Clause advanced past the fallen bobcat, skirting its lifeless form without a second glance. His role was not to analyze, but to ensure no more surprises lay in wait. Rounding the police car, he was greeted by the horrific sight of two officers, their bodies savagely mutilated. It was clear now that this situation was more dire than anticipated.

Clause approached Officer Sanchez, who lay face down in a pool of her own blood, and pried the gun from her lifeless hand. As he did, his eyes fell on the remains of several coyotes. To the untrained eye, it might have appeared as though the animals had been scavenged. But Clause sensed something far more sinister at play. Just then, the howls erupted once more, closer and more menacing.

He turned and swiftly made his way back to the van. "Time to wrap this up," he declared urgently.

Kelvin began to protest, insisting on more time, but the renewed chorus of howls—accompanied now by guttural growls—silenced him.

Meanwhile, Samuel was sealing a blood sample from the bobcat in a small test tube, which he stowed safely in his coat.

Inside the studio van, Andrea and Simon worked frantically to aid the injured. Although not medical doctors, their extensive knowledge of biology and first aid was put to use. They maneuvered Josh from the front seat to the back, where he could lie flat. They did the same with Nancy, stretching her out on the floor. Andrea swiftly applied a tourniquet to her calf, securing it with gauze. Kelvin, meanwhile, cut away the remnants of Josh's pant leg with a pocket knife, revealing deep, jagged claw marks that ran down his thigh. Andrea met Kelvin's grave look with a nod.

They both understood the grim reality: without urgent medical attention, these people wouldn't survive.

Clause appeared at the van's side, his expression inscrutable. "Will they live?" he asked.

Andrea responded, "We've stabilized them for now, but they've lost a lot of blood. They need a hospital, or I'm afraid they won't make it."

Clause sent a rapid text on his phone. "Help is on the way. We need to move now or we'll have company."

"We can't just leave them here," Andrea protested.

Clause's face remained set in stone. "We don't have a choice. Our primary objective is the crash site. They'll hold on until help arrives."

As if on cue, another round of howls pierced the air, this time much closer. Without further prompting, Andrea and Kelvin exited the studio van and dashed back to their own. Clause secured the studio van's door and raced to the driver's side, barely making it inside as a pack of coyotes emerged from the darkness.

In less than a minute, a formidable wall of beasts had formed, blocking their path. Most were dogs, but coyotes and bobcats stood among them, along with an array of felines. Each creature, though, bore the chilling mark of death's grip, defying the natural order in a gruesome display of undead terror.

CHAPTER 14

Each beast that stood before them was a grotesque vision of Hell's own spawn. Blood dripped and congealed on their mutilated forms; limbs had been severed or chewed off, leaving ragged stumps and raw, exposed muscle. Organs and intestines dangled grotesquely, dragging through the dirt like nightmarish appendages. The guttural noises that emanated from their throats were like echoes from the abyss, deep and throaty, resonating with a primal terror that defied comprehension. The worst part, however, was the eyes—if they still had them. Those that did were filled with a sickly red hue surrounded by impenetrable darkness, dead eyes that seemed to harbor an insatiable hunger.

Andrea's voice trembled as she cried out, "What the hell is going on here?"

Samuel turned to her. "Calm down, Andrea. Panicking now will only make things worse."

Simon replied in a shaky voice, "My best guess is it's related to the meteor. Maybe it released a chemical that's messing with their behavior?"

Clause interjected, "All the more reason to reach the crash site immediately."

"But how are we supposed to get through that?" Kelvin asked nervously as he pointed to the growing horde, which now numbered at least fifty.

Suddenly, the van jolted violently as something enormous and powerful slammed into it from behind.

Clause immediately slammed the van into drive and floored the gas pedal. He maneuvered the vehicle around the studio van and between the two police cars, a loud screech resounding through the vehicle as metal scraped against metal. The horde surged forward with a ravenous fury, clawing and gnashing at the advancing vehicle, the madness inside each one obliterating any instinct for self-preservation.

The van shuddered and rocked violently as it crashed through the wall of twisted creatures. It wobbled side to side as it mowed over several of them, like a macabre game of bowling where the pins were mangled, undead horrors.

Then came the inevitable disaster: a tire blew with a deafening bang. The van swerved sharply to the right before Clause wrestled it back under control. It lurched forward unsteadily, struggling like a wounded bird trying to maintain flight.

In the chaos, Clause managed to retrieve his cell phone from his coat pocket and activate the GPS. He glanced briefly at the screen to orient himself toward the crash site. That momentary lapse nearly cost them their lives. As he looked up, a crazed Bighorn sheep, its throat savagely ripped apart and gaping, was charging toward them. Although a Bighorn near the lake was not unheard of because of the proximity of the Santa Rosa Mountains, encountering an undead one was a different kind of terror.

Clause swerved sharply to avoid a head-on collision with the beast, but the blown tire exaggerated the swerve, nearly tipping the van onto its side. The phone slipped from his grasp as he fought to regain control. A swift turn to the left brought the wheels back to the ground, but they clipped the Bighorn with the front left fender. The impact sent the creature rolling violently away, giving Clause a fleeting window to avoid crashing into a nearby tree. He pressed the gas, accelerating forward as quickly as he dared.

Andrea screamed repeatedly, her voice sharp and piercing. Simon clutched the armrest, his knuckles whitening under the strain, while Kelvin sat beside him, his face drained of all color. Samuel muttered a silent prayer for their survival, his gaze fixed on the horrors outside. Only Clause remained seemingly unaffected, his focus unwavering.

Clause maneuvered the van until he located a small path and followed the GPS directions. He cursed silently for dropping his phone and prayed it wouldn't fall into anyone else's hands. Right now, though, bigger threats loomed.

After what felt like an eternity, Clause stopped the van in front of the crater. The headlights cast an eerie glow, revealing an unsettling silence in the area. The stillness was almost as unnerving as the chaos they had just escaped.

Clause began to open his door, but Andrea's voice stopped him. "You're not going out there, are you?"

Simon added, "Are you crazy? Look at what we just went through!"

Clause's expression remained firm. "We still have a job to do." He reached under the driver's seat and pulled out a compact automatic rifle, the metal gleaming ominously in the dim light.

Samuel's eyes widened at the sight of the weapon, fueling his growing suspicions about Clause. Knowing that trying to stop him would be futile, Samuel didn't protest, desperately hoping that Clause wouldn't lead them all to doom before this nightmare ended.

As Clause closed the van door behind him, Samuel's foot accidentally kicked something. With a covert smile, he reached down and retrieved Clause's cell phone, slipping it subtly into his pocket for later inspection.

Clause took a moment to shine his flashlight around the area. Remarkably, the vicinity was devoid of wildlife, both living and dead. He yanked open the side door of the van. "We need to be quick," he said sharply. "Samuel, Andrea—collect any samples you can from the crash site. Kelvin and Simon, you're in charge of changing the tire. The spare's under the rear of the van."

Simon asked, "And what about you?"

Clause looked at him sternly. "I'm planning on keeping your asses alive, if that's alright with you?"

Kelvin, looking around nervously, "But where are all the animals?"

"My guess is they're heading toward the city, toward human population," Simon answered.

Andrea's voice trembled, "What's happening here? Most of those animals had wounds that should have killed them, yet they kept coming."

Simon said what the others were thinking, "What if they were actually dead? What if some alien organism is controlling them?"

"That's ridiculous!" Kelvin retorted, but his eyes betrayed his own fear that what Simon had just suggested was now their reality.

"Is it?" Simon countered. "We've all seen zombie movies before. Maybe this is the same thing."

Clause cut in with an edge of urgency, "We don't have time for this now. Let's finish what we need to do, and we can speculate later."

The team slowly exited the van and gathered their gear,

each one looking around cautiously, ready to run at the first sign of the beasts. As Samuel walked back around, he caught Clause searching through the van, no doubt looking for his phone. Samuel put on his best poker face as he walked past. As soon as Clause saw him, he gave up his search and started a slow, sweeping cover of the area.

The group grew even more nervous as their self-proclaimed protector wandered away, but each moment that passed without incident helped ease their fear, if only a little.

As Samuel and Andrea made their way slowly toward the center of the site, each one carrying a small bag in one hand and a flashlight in the other, Samuel whispered to her, "I need you to cover me for a minute when Clause isn't looking."

Andrea gave him a questioning look. "Why? What's going on?" she whispered back.

"I don't trust him. I think he's up to something. He dropped his phone at one point and I found it. I want to check it out and see what's going on."

Andrea replied, "Okay, but make it quick. We still need to get what we came for and then get the hell out of here."

Samuel nodded.

Along the way to the center of the crater, Andrea stepped on something that went crunch under her foot. She stopped to shine the flashlight down and saw that she had stepped on a rock fragment. When she bent down to get a closer look at it, she noticed a black, oily puddle on the ground next to it.

"What is that?" Samuel asked.

"I think it's a meteor fragment, but there's some kind of black substance here as well."

Samuel bent down to look at her findings. As he did so, he pulled Clause's phone out. "This is the perfect opportunity. While you gather these samples, I'll check out his phone."

Andrea gave him an irritated look, but didn't object. Instead, she opened her bag and pulled out the supplies necessary to contain the samples.

Meanwhile, Samuel turned the phone on and immediately checked the messages. Most of them were short and cryptic in nature, and all of them involved Dr. Ashton Brown. And there was one message in particular that worried him. It mentioned ADAR, a project NASA had discontinued a few years ago because it called for extreme measures that, often times, seemed barbaric. Recovered specimens were to be tortured and dissected, experimented on, and then discarded when they expired. Of course, the government would always maintain plausible deniability.

Then he saw Clause's flashlight coming close and quickly slipped the phone back into his pocket. "We have a problem," he said to Andrea. "I'll explain later."

Samuel breathed a sigh of relief when Clause turned and continued to walk the perimeter of the area. Quickly, he helped Andrea finish gathering the samples, then they continued toward the center.

***

"This is bullshit!" Kelvin said as he crawled on his back under the van. "How did I get stuck with this job?"

Simon smiled and replied, "It's simple: you're younger than me."

Kelvin shot back, "Just remember that, old man, when we're running from those things out there and you need my help."

That statement instantly brought them both back to a somber moment. Then they heard a flurry of low, guttural howls. Luckily, they were farther away than before.

Simon handed a crescent wrench to Kelvin and he began to loosen the spare tire and jack with a renewed urgency. After a minute, Kelvin scooted out from underneath the van pulling the tire and jack with him.

Quickly, they worked their way to the front passenger's side tire. This time, Kelvin held the flashlight while Simon loosened the lug nuts on the tire. After he had loosened them all sufficiently, Kelvin slid the jack under the frame and began cranking. Together, they had the tire changed within a couple of minutes.

***

A rancid and decaying smell had begun to fill the air as Samuel and Andrea approached ground zero. They were twenty yards away when they stopped short and just stared in astonishment. A large pool of the black, oily substance had gathered there. But that wasn't the worst part of it. The worst part was that it was moving.

CHAPTER 15

Jerry took one last look at the Patterson house and sighed before he drove away. Since the first time Melinda had come into the station a few years ago, he had always felt like a love-struck schoolboy when she was around. He knew it was foolish, but he couldn't help it. And it wasn't like he was going to do anything about it, but a little fantasy never hurt anyone, right?

Instead of heading directly back to the station, he decided a trip through the Taco Bell drive-through might satisfy him. After placing his order, he was happy to see Isabel at the window. She was a young, petite Hispanic girl with a smile that always made the world around her brighter.

"Good evening, Isabel," he said as he handed her a twenty for his order.

She took the bill and flashed that smile of hers. "Good evening, Officer. How are you tonight?"

He shook his head, "Can't lie. It's been a rough night."

Isabel frowned, "I'm sorry." Then she handed his change back to him and turned to grab his order. She didn't notice the black shadow that flew through the opened window while her back was turned, and Jerry was occupied with the

A/C knob in the squad car.

A minute later, she turned back to him with his bag. "Well, I hope your night gets better," she said.

Jerry replied, "It just did," and drove off to park in one of the spaces nearby.

***

Inside the brightly lit restaurant, the atmosphere quickly shifted from the hectic pace of late-night service with customers in various states of agitation—a number of them clearly under the influence of some sort of illegal substance—to something far more sinister. Isabel had just turned away from the window, humming softly to herself, when a frantic scream tore through the air from the kitchen. Her heart leaped into her throat as she whirled around, just in time to see her coworker, Mario, flailing wildly, trying to swat away a black bird that had somehow gotten inside. The creature's wings flapped furiously, its beak snapping inches from his face.

"What the hell is that?" Isabel gasped, taking a step back as the bird darted through the air, its eyes glowing with an unnatural red light.

Before she could react further, the front door opened and three young men stepped inside, laughing and joking. Their laughter instantly died in their throats when they saw the black bird, now perched on the counter, with its head cocked in an eerie, unnatural way.

"Is that thing... dead?" one of the guys muttered, his voice shaky.

As if in answer, the bird let out a bone-chilling screech and launched itself at the group. They scattered, knocking over a number of other customers in their panic. The bird's claws raked across one man's face, drawing a stream of blood as he screamed in terror.

And then the windows shattered.

More of the undead birds, their wings tattered and bodies mutilated, swarmed into the restaurant, drawn by some dark, unholy instinct. They descended upon the terrified customers and employees, their guttural screeches filling the air as they attacked with a ferocity that defied nature.

Isabel found herself cornered behind the counter, tuck into the little drive-thru cubby with her back pressed against the wall. Mario was on the floor, trying to fend off two of the creatures with a mop, but their relentless assault was overwhelming him. One of the customers had managed to grab a red, plastic tray and was swinging it wildly, but for every bird he knocked away, two more seemed to take its place.

The air was thick with the stench of blood and the screams of terrified customers. Each of the birds' eyes glowed with that same eerie red light, as if they were driven by some sinister, unstoppable force. Isabel's heart pounded in her chest as she frantically searched for a weapon, anything to defend herself. Her hand landed on a large metal spatula caked with food residue that had clattered to the floor in the chaos. She gripped the handle tightly as one of the undead birds swooped toward her.

Isabel swung the utensil back and forth frantically, panic causing her to react in a desperate and futile attempt at defending herself. The creature avoided the weapon easily and dove toward her with savage fury. It impaled her arm with its beak, and together with its talons, maddeningly ripped through her flesh. Pain seared through her like fire. She screamed, her vision blurring as she fought to fend it off. The spatula clattered to the floor as the bird latched on, its talons digging deeper into her flesh.

"Help! Somebody, please!" she cried out, but her voice was drowned in the cacophony of screeches and cries around her.

The restaurant was a scene of bloody carnage, the walls spattered with blood, bodies littering the floor, and the screams of those patrons still alive filling the air with desperate pleas for salvation. The undead birds, with their rotting bodies and soulless eyes, were relentless in their assault, tearing into flesh and ripping apart anything in their paths.

And as the lights flickered and dimmed, casting long, ominous shadows across the chaos, it seemed as if the very darkness itself had come alive to claim them all.

***

The atmosphere inside the police station was a powder keg of tension waiting to explode. Phones rang incessantly, overlapping in a cacophony that gnawed at everyone's nerves. Officers shouted over one another, trying to make sense of the sudden wave of animal attacks sweeping across the valley. And each report was so much more bizarre than the last that no one could keep up.

Captain Harrison stood at the center of it all, barking orders, trying to bring some semblance of order to the madness. "What the hell is going on out there?" he demanded, his face flushed with frustration. "Get someone on the line with animal control—no, fuck that, get the damn National Guard! And I want every available unit out there—if it's got four legs and it's attacking, I want it put down!"

The front doors of the station suddenly flew open and officer Frank Fender stumbled in, blood streaming from a deep gash on his forehead, his uniform shredded. "They're everywhere!" he gasped, his eyes wide with terror. "They—they don't die, Cap! I shot one in the chest point blank, and it just kept coming!"

The room fell into a stunned silence.

"What do you mean, they don't die?" Harrison finally asked, his voice trembling ever so slightly.

Before Fender could answer, the station's power flickered, plunging the room into brief darkness. The lights came back on a moment later, but only at minimal power, casting eerie shadows along the walls. Then the phones stopped ringing all at once, leaving a deafening silence in their wake.

"What the hell..." Harrison started, but his words were cut off by the sound of shattering glass.

The front windows exploded inward as a mass of bodies hurled themselves through. Coyotes, dogs, cats—each one a grotesque mockery of life, their fur matted with blood, their eyes glowing with an unnatural crimson light. They moved like things possessed, driven by a hunger that defied reason.

"Holy shit!" someone screamed, as the animals surged forward. A number of officers drew their guns, firing wildly into the oncoming tide, but the bullets barely slowed the creatures down as they charged into the room.

Harrison barely had time to react before a giant Pit Bull with half its face torn off lunged at him. He raised his arm just in time to block the beast's jaws, but the force of the attack sent him crashing to the ground. The dog's teeth sank into his forearm, tearing through muscle and sinew. He let out a howl of pain, wrestling desperately with the beast as it thrashed wildly, trying to rip him apart.

Nearby, Fender was dragged down by a pack of feral cats, their claws raking across his flesh, tearing him apart piece by piece. His dying screams echoed through the station.

The precinct quickly turned into a slaughterhouse. Blood

splattered the walls and pooled on the floor as the animals tore through everything in their path. Officers were pulled from their chairs, their screams cut short as teeth and claws savagely found their throats. Others fired until their guns were empty, but the creatures were relentless, an unstoppable wave of death.

During the chaos, Captain Harrison managed to get his free hand on his sidearm. With a loud cry, he pressed the barrel against the Pit Bull's skull and pulled the trigger. The dog's head jerked to the side, and it went limp, sliding off him in a heap. Almost immediately, another animal was already lunging at him.

As he raised his gun to fire again, the power went out completely, plunging the station into pitch blackness. All that remained were the sounds—the wet tearing of flesh, the guttural growls of the undead animals, and the dying screams of the officers as the station was overrun.

CHAPTER 16

Jerry was unwrapping his third chicken soft taco when he heard a loud click through his police radio. With his free hand, he reached up to his shoulder and pressed the button to respond. He was answered with static and then silence.

He gobbled down the last bite quickly and pulled out of the parking lot, heading back to the station. If he had taken a last look toward the restaurant, he would've seen the people inside feverishly fighting off an attack by a murder of black-winged devils. And he would've heard Isabel's desperate cry for help.

Instead, he turned onto HWY 111, oblivious to their deadly crisis. Ten minutes later, he pulled in front of the police station, a shiver of terror creeping up his spine as he took in the scene before him. The place looked like it had been hit by a bomb. The glass in the front doors had been shattered, fragments glittering like cruel diamonds across the steps. A handful of patrol cars were parked haphazardly, their windows smashed in and their hoods dented, as if something heavy had repeatedly jumped on them.

But it was the bodies that made his skin crawl. The first one he saw was Hank Rogers, a veteran officer who had served nearly twenty years. Frank was slumped over in the driver's seat of his cruiser, his face turned toward Jerry—but only half of it was there. The other half had been torn away, a gruesome mess of blood and muscle.

Jerry held his breath as he forced himself to get out of the car. His feet felt like lead as he approached the station, every nerve on edge, his senses straining for any sign of movement. He could hear the crunch of glass underfoot, but it seemed distant, as though the sound originated from someone else far away.

Then he saw the second body—Jon Durman, the rookie. Jon had been young and eager, always trying to prove himself. Now he lay crumpled at the foot of the steps, his uniform soaked in blood. From the look of it, Jon had tried to make a run for his car, but hadn't even made it to the first step. Whatever had attacked him had been fast, brutal, and relentless. It had torn into his back, then dragged him down the steps like a rag doll before finishing him off on the pavement.

Jerry swallowed hard, forcing down the bile that rose in his throat. His hand gripped the gun at his side as he approached the entrance, his every step cautious and deliberate. The exterior parking lot lights flickered, casting an eerie glow on the streaks of blood that smeared the steps like some grotesque artist's canvas.

He stepped through the shattered doorway of the station's lobby, right into something from a nightmare. His eyes landed on the first of many horrors—a dead coyote lying in a pool of black blood, a bullet hole in its head. Not far from it was another dog, smaller, also downed by a bullet to the skull. But there was something off about them. Their bodies were broken, torn in ways that didn't make sense, as if they had been dead long before the bullets found them.

Jerry stepped gingerly around the carcasses, his breath shallow, his pulse pounding in his ears. As he moved deeper into the station, a low growl stopped him in his tracks. He crouched down, his heart racing, and looked toward the sound.

What he saw made his blood run cold.

In the middle of the main area lay Juanita Alvarez, the station's dispatcher. She had been with the force for five years, always reliable, always a steady presence in the chaos of the job. Now she was nothing more than a bloody heap on the floor, her body torn open, her insides spilling out. A coyote, its fur matted with blood, was feasting on her remains, the sickening sounds of its jaws ripping her flesh apart echoing throughout the building.

Jerry watched in horror as a large Siberian Husky, padded into view, its eyes glassy and dead, yet somehow alive with a ruthless hunger. It joined the coyote, tearing into Juanita's body with savage abandon.

Then Jerry saw more of them—undead abominations, twisted and grotesque, their forms shuffling in and out of the shadows, each one more horrifying than the last.

Fear gripped Jerry's chest like a vise as he struggled to contain the terror rising inside him. Moving as silently as he could, he began to retreat, his breath coming in short, shallow bursts. He was almost to the lobby when a low, throaty growl made him freeze.

He turned slowly, his blood turning to ice.

A large, white house cat stood there with its back arched and its fangs bared. Its fur was matted with blood, and its tail was only a gnarled stump. Deep claw marks crisscrossed its back, exposing raw, red flesh. The cat's eyes locked onto his, filled with a hatred that seemed almost human.

Then, with a hiss that cut through the silence like a knife, the cat lunged at him, its mouth open wide, aiming for his throat.

The sound of a gunshot rang out, and the cat dropped to the floor, its body twitching as blood pooled around it.

Jerry spun around to see Captain Harrison standing in the doorway of the records office, his gun still smoking.

"Get in here, quick!" Harrison shouted.

Jerry scrambled into the room, and the captain slammed the door shut just as a mutilated Mastiff crashed into it from the other side. The impact shook the entire room, and the two men braced themselves as the door shuddered under the force of the blow.

"What the hell's going on, Captain?" Jerry asked, his voice barely above a whisper as he huddled beside a desk, his heart racing.

Harrison slunk down next to him, wiping the sweat from his brow. He looked like a man who had seen hell and lived to tell the tale—barely. The deep gash on his right arm oozed blood, and his face was a mask of anguish and fear.

"I wish I knew," Harrison muttered. "It all started when Fender left his damn radio in the car. He stumbled back into the precinct, his clothes all torn to shreds. He started going on about crazed animals and then the lights went out. A minute later, a horde of these creatures charged through the front windows. Before we knew what was happening, the whole place was swarming with these... things."

He shook his head. "They wouldn't die, Jerry. We shot them, over and over, but they just kept coming. It was like nothing could stop them. It wasn't until we started shooting them in the head that they finally went down—just like in those goddamn zombie movies."

Jerry felt a chill run down his spine as he pictured Fender's body, torn apart like some kind of sick, twisted puzzle.

"What about the others?" he asked, dreading the answer.

Harrison's face darkened. "I don't know. It all happened so fast. The first dog got Rodriguez by the throat, and in one quick jerk, it ripped his windpipe out. After that... after that, it was chaos. Everyone just scattered. I don't know if they made it or if they're..." He trailed off, unable to finish the thought.

Jerry's mind raced, images of his colleagues—his friends—lying in bloody heaps flashing before his eyes. The station, once a place of safety and order, had become a tomb filled with the undead.

A sudden, bone-chilling howl echoed through the halls, followed by the sound of claws scraping against the door. The Mastiff was still out there, along with who knew how many others, all of them waiting, hungry, and relentless.

Jerry looked at Harrison, his heart pounding in his chest. "What do we do now?"

Harrison met his gaze, his face set in grim determination. "We survive, Jerry. We survive, and we find a way to put these things down for good. Because if we don't... we're all as good as dead."

CHAPTER 17

The pool of inky black ooze spread out before them like a living shadow, its surface roiling and churning with a sinister energy. It was roughly eight feet in diameter, but it felt as if it could swallow the world whole. The dark liquid bubbled and hissed, spitting up little globules that popped with a sickening squelch, like something out of a witch's cauldron in the darkest of fairy tales. At first, Samuel thought it might have been some kind of residual effect from the intense heat of reentry, a byproduct of their descent through the planet's atmosphere. But as he inched closer, he could see that the substance had a life of its own. It pulsed and writhed like a living organism, a nightmarish blob that defied logic.

The stench hit them before they even got close—an acrid, choking smell that made Samuel's eyes water and his stomach lurch. Andrea gagged, covering her nose with her hand as she approached the pool, her steps hesitant. "Oh my God, that smells horrible!" she managed to choke out, her voice muffled by her hand. "What the hell is it?"

Samuel didn't have an answer, not one he was comfortable voicing. His instincts screamed at him to keep his distance, but the scientist in him pushed forward, compelled to understand the unknown. "I don't know," he said, his voice tight with unease. "But we need to get a sample. Just... be careful not to touch it."

Andrea's eyes widened in mock horror. "Oh, I'm not the one who's getting the sample, you are," she shot back with a feeble attempt at humor.

Samuel tried to muster a smile, but it felt strained. "And what gives you that idea?" he asked, even as his hand moved to his bag, knowing full well she wouldn't volunteer.

Andrea's lips curled into an anxious smirk. "Just a hunch," she replied.

Samuel considered arguing, but the futility of it washed over him like an icy wave. He sighed, pulling out a pair of vials from his bag, their glass surfaces gleaming under the dim light of the moonlit sky. The thought of dipping them into that vile substance made his skin crawl, but he knew they had no choice. He crouched down, the ground beneath him feeling oddly soft, almost spongy. He froze, his breath catching in his throat as a deep, ominous rumble vibrated through the earth, reverberating up his legs. It was gone as quickly as it had come, leaving him wondering if he had imagined it.

As if on cue, Clause appeared, his presence as unwelcome as ever. He loomed over Samuel impatiently. "We need to wrap this up," he growled. "The threat could return at any moment, and we need to be ready to move out if it does."

Samuel didn't look up, his eyes fixed on the bubbling pool before him. "We're going as fast as we can," he said. "But if we don't follow proper protocol, the samples will be contaminated. And if they're contaminated, they're useless."

Clause grumbled something under his breath as he turned and stalked away, leaving Samuel to his work.

Once Clause was out of earshot, Samuel turned to Andrea.

"Can you finish the samples? I need to make a quick phone call."

Andrea's eyes narrowed. "Don't think you're getting out of this that easy," she warned, her tone sharper than usual.

"Look, Andrea," Samuel said, his voice dropping to a hushed whisper. "I'm not playing around. Something's going on here, something bigger than we know. I need to talk to Leonard about this directly."

Andrea hesitated, the disappointment clear on her face, but after a moment, she snatched the vials from his hand with a huff. "Fine," she muttered, begrudgingly kneeling beside the pool. As she carefully gathered the viscous fluid and soil samples, her face twisted in disgust, Samuel stepped back, pulling out his cell phone. His fingers trembled as he scrolled through his contacts until he found Leonard's name.

He hit the call button, pressing the phone to his ear as his heart pounded in his chest, the distant rumble beneath the earth echoing his growing dread. The phone rang, the sound unnervingly loud in the oppressive silence.

****

Leonard nearly jumped out of his seat when he felt his phone vibrate in his pocket. He had been busy dissecting the satellite footage, trying to determine the amount of damage already done, and any repercussions yet to come.

As soon as he saw who the caller was, he answered it, "Samuel, what's the status?"

Samuel replied, "Patrick, I only have a minute, so listen closely. There's something crazy going on here, and Ashton Brown is at the center of it. I got hold of a cell phone and found out he's implementing the ADAR program."

Leonard was shocked, "ADAR? But that program was shut

down years ago."

"I know. But there's a guy here by the name of Clause that Ashton hired as our driver. He acts more like a mercenary. And I think you better alert the military. By the looks of it, there was some sort of chemical reaction to the environment which has caused the local wildlife to become hostile."

"Hostile? How so?"

"There's already two dead police officers by the park entrance that were ripped to shreds, and we found a studio van parked by the entrance with a couple of people inside that were severely wounded. Then, on the way to the site we were attacked by a large pack of wild animals."

Leonard was deeply worried, "Is everyone okay? What happened?"

"Everyone's fine. But it was the scariest shit I've ever seen. The pack was a mixture of domestic and wild animals, dogs and coyotes, even a bobcat, and they all had the same hungry look in their eyes. But the worst part was that they wouldn't die. Clause shot a couple of them square in the chest and they got right back up. It was only when he shot them in the head that they stayed down."

"What exactly are you trying to tell me, Samuel? And don't give me any bullshit."

"I know it sounds crazy, but I saw it. These creatures were dead, yet they still kept on moving. And some of them had wounds that should've killed them long before Clause's started shooting at them. I hate to use the word zombie, but that's the only word I can come to grips with."

Leonard had started putting a theory together in his head, and didn't really like the direction it was going. "Okay. I'll contact the Marine base at Twentynine Palms and the March Air Reserve Base in Riverside, and have them on standby. I just need to know exactly what to tell them."

"Until I can get to the lab and get these samples analyzed I won't know exactly what we're dealing with. The problem, though, is Ashton. Somehow, we need to make sure he doesn't get hold of the samples. If he does, there's no telling what he'll do."

"In order to do that you'll have to get by this Clause fellow. Maybe I can talk to the local police and run some interference for you?"

"Let me try to figure something out first. This guy's wound pretty tight. I don't want to spook him."

"Got'cha. Just keep me updated."

"Will do."

***

Samuel ended the call, his mind racing with the possibilities of what was really going on. But there was no time to dwell on it—Clause was already rounding the corner, his expression as grim as ever. Samuel bent down to help Andrea finish, but the moment his eyes locked onto the puddle of ooze, he froze in shock. The once sluggish pool was now a seething mass of darkness, bubbling and gurgling with an intensity that seemed almost alive. It wasn't just the surface popping anymore; the entire mass was heaving, as though something within was fighting to break free.

The ground beneath them began to tremble, a subtle vibration that quickly grew into a bone-rattling quake. Samuel and Andrea scrambled backward, their hearts pounding in their chests as they tried to make sense of the madness unfolding in front of them. The air around them felt charged, like the moment before a lightning strike, and the stench from the ooze grew stronger, more suffocating.

Clause reached them just as the tremors intensified, his

eyes widening at the sight of the churning pool. "What the hell is going on here?" he asked, his voice edged with a hint of fear, a rare crack in his usually impenetrable demeanor.

Samuel shook his head. "My first thought was an earthquake, but this... this is something else."

Andrea, her face pale and drawn, pointed a trembling finger toward the now-roiling mass. "I think we need to get out of here, now," she whispered, her voice barely audible over the growing roar.

All three of them turned to look, just in time to see the center of the pool begin to twist and contort, forming a vortex of dark, malevolent energy. The ooze was no longer just a puddle; it was rising, stretching upward like a creature awakening from a long slumber. The vortex spun faster and faster, growing taller by the second until it resembled a primordial cyclone, a whirling column of darkness that defied the laws of nature.

"Run!" Samuel shouted, the word tearing from his throat as the three of them bolted for the van.

Kelvin and Simon, who had just finished changing the tire, looked up in confusion as the rest of the group barreled toward them. For a brief, disorienting moment, they just stood there, paralyzed.

"Move!" Clause bellowed, snapping them out of their stupor with a sharp tug. The urgency in his voice was enough to propel them into action. They abandoned the jack and the blown tire where they lay, rushing to the van and scrambling inside, their hands fumbling with the door handles in their haste.

Clause jumped into the driver's seat, slamming the key into the ignition. The engine roared to life, and the headlights flared on, slicing through the darkness to illuminate the horror before them. The ooze had grown to nearly ten feet in height, a towering column of spinning blackness that seemed to reach for the sky. It spun faster and faster, the roar of its motion filling the air with a deafening sound that made their ears ring.

And then, without warning, the column dropped, collapsing in on itself with a sickening squelch. The brief silence that followed was almost worse than the noise, a moment of trepidation where everything seemed to hang in the balance. But the respite was fleeting. With a violent shudder, the ooze erupted upward like a geyser, a monstrous spout of black liquid shooting thirty feet into the air. The ground shook violently beneath them as the spray rained down in thick, inky droplets, each one hissing and sizzling where it landed.

"Go, go, go!" Samuel yelled.

Clause slammed the van into gear, but the trembling ground beneath them made it hard to get any kind of traction. Not wanting to risk immobilizing them yet again, he let up on the gas and put the vehicle into park, hoping the unholy storm would soon pass and that something even more horrifying wasn't waiting for them when it did.

CHAPTER 18

The Director had just hung up from Samuel, tension still coiling in his chest, when a sharp knock rattled his office door. "Come in," he said, his voice steady despite the unease creeping into his thoughts.

The door creaked open, and Darcey poked her head in. "Sir, there's something you need to see."

He studied her for a brief second. "What is it?"

"There's been more activity at the site," she replied, her tone almost too measured, too calm.

Leonard's gut twisted, but he nodded and strode past her without another word. He didn't notice the way her eyes flicked over his computer screen as he moved, nor how her fingers twitched as if by habit. She caught sight of the Twentynine Palms Marine base page still open on his monitor. A shadow of a smile crossed her lips before she quickly pulled out her phone. Her fingers danced over the keys, sending a swift, coded message to Ashton: *Activity escalating. Director on edge. Watch the base.* The text disappeared as fast as it had been sent, and she slipped the phone back into her pocket just as Leonard glanced over his shoulder.

"Darcey?" he prompted.

"Right behind you, sir," she replied, her tone even, as if nothing had just transpired.

Leonard didn't question it and just kept moving. They reached the operations center where Justin stood hunched over his console, his face pale in the dim light of the monitors.

"What's happening?" Leonard asked in a tight voice, betraying the urgency clawing at him.

Justin didn't look up, his fingers flying over the keyboard. "I don't know, sir. But I've never seen anything like this. These images came in just a couple minutes ago."

Leonard leaned in, his breath catching as he watched the screen. The footage showed a twister of inky blackness ripping itself from the earth, spiraling upwards before exploding violently into the air. "Dear God," he whispered, eyes widening. "What the fuck just happened?"

Justin swallowed hard, finally turning to meet Leonard's gaze. "It appears the same substance that erupted from the rock earlier has somehow multiplied. It's causing a severe reaction in the surrounding environment. We're seeing... well, it's almost like a chain reaction."

Leonard's eyes darted to another monitor, freezing when he saw the van parked precariously close to the edge of the chaos. "Were they exposed?" he asked nervously.

"No," Justin replied quickly, shaking his head. "They retreated to the vehicle just before the activity began."

Leonard exhaled, a small but intense relief washing over him. "Thank God."

Justin hesitated, then asked, "What do we do now, sir?"

Leonard's mind raced, but he kept his voice calm. "Monitor the situation closely. I want to be alerted immediately if there's any change, any at all."

Justin nodded. "Yes, sir."

As Leonard turned to leave, his thoughts already racing ahead, he didn't notice Darcey lingering near the doorway. She watched him carefully, her eyes calculating, as if weighing the implications of what she had just witnessed.

Back in his office, Leonard didn't waste a second. He picked up the phone, his hand steady as he dialed the number for the marine base, his mind replaying the images he had just seen. But as he waited for the call to connect, he couldn't shake the feeling that something was off—something more than just the chaos erupting at the site.

Meanwhile, Darcey slipped away, her mission clear. Ashton would need to know everything, and soon. The stakes were higher than she'd ever anticipated, and the game was far from over.

***

The shrill ring of the phone sliced through the quiet of the night, jarring Major Thomas O'Malley from a deep, peaceful sleep. He bolted upright, his Irish-Catholic upbringing doing little to temper the surge of irritation that flooded his veins. Whoever was on the other end better have a damn good reason for disturbing him at this hour. He snatched up the receiver, his voice a low growl. "This better be good."

The voice on the other end was steady, but urgent. "Major O'Malley, this is Dr. Leonard, Director of NASA's Near Earth Object Program. I apologize for waking you, but a situation has arisen that requires your immediate attention."

O'Malley's brows knitted together as he tried to shake off the remnants of sleep. "What situation?" His tone was clipped, the words coming out with the force of a command.

Leonard replied, "Earlier this evening, an object crashed

down near Lake Cahuilla in La Quinta. It's caused some... adverse reactions in the local wildlife."

O'Malley's grip on the phone tightened as he sat up straighter, his mind starting to clear. "And what exactly does this have to do with the Marines, Doctor?" His voice was laced with venom, still not entirely convinced that this warranted the interruption.

Leonard's voice took on a grave edge. "The adverse reaction I'm referring to, Major, is that the wildlife in the area have been somehow contaminated. They've begun attacking the local population. If this isn't contained—and soon—whatever's affecting them could spread. We may be looking at a rapidly escalating crisis."

O'Malley's lips thinned into a hard line. "So, you're telling me you want my Marines to play animal control for you in the middle of the night?"

Leonard took a deep breath, fighting to keep his frustration in check. "It's far more serious than that, Major. We believe there's a virus spreading through the area, affecting both domestic and wild animals. It's already infected close to a hundred creatures, and we have confirmation of at least two fatalities."

The mention of deaths snapped O'Malley into full operational mode. "Is this virus only affecting animals?"

Leonard hesitated for the briefest of moments. "As far as we know, no humans have been infected—yet. But we do have two subjects we're monitoring closely. And Major... we have a team on-site collecting samples, if they manage to get out alive."

"What the hell does that mean?" O'Malley's voice dropped an octave.

"They were attacked minutes ago by a pack of these crazed animals. Fortunately, they've got a hired gun with them—he managed to get them out unharmed. But this is only the beginning."

O'Malley didn't waste another second. He could sense the storm gathering on the horizon, the kind that called for swift and decisive action. "I'll have a combat team assembled and on the road within the hour."

"Thank you, Major," Leonard said in relief.

O'Malley's jaw clenched as he prepared to hang up, but not before throwing out a final warning. "This better not be some wild goose chase, Doctor. Or you'll have more than just a few angry animals to deal with." Then, with a sharp click, he ended the call, already moving to mobilize his men for whatever nightmare awaited them in the dark.

***

Ashton had just finished inspecting the last of the containment tubes. The sterile, clinical air of the lab felt unusually heavy tonight, as if the walls themselves were holding their breath in anticipation of the marvels that would soon be revealed to the world. As he moved toward the main computer terminal, preparing to run a system diagnosis one last time, a sudden vibration in his pocket broke the silence. His hand instinctively shot down, pulling out his phone.

Darcey's message flashed on the screen. His brow furrowed, the words seeping into his mind like poison. *The military? Already?* His heart skipped a beat. This was bad — very bad. The military showing up on the scene so soon could unravel everything. Ashton's mind raced, calculating the potential fallout. The only way to avoid a disastrous confrontation was to get the team out before the unit arrived.

His fingers flew across the screen, sending a terse, urgent text to Clause. The message was clear: *Get out. Now.*

Shoving the phone back into his pocket, Ashton took a deep breath, forcing a smile that barely touched the edges of his lips. The room, filled with its cold, methodical hum, felt like it was closing in around him. He needed to stay calm, keep his wits about him. The truck would be there soon, delivering his two new specimens—specimens that could change everything.

Ashton's gaze swept over the lab, a twisted sense of satisfaction bubbling beneath his anxiety. He was ready. Whatever was coming, whatever chaos was about to unfold, he was ready. But the thought of the military closing in lingered in his mind like a storm cloud on the horizon. He couldn't afford any slip-ups. Not now. Not when he was this close.

CHAPTER 19

Sergeant James Anderson couldn't believe the mission laid out before him. His Marines—hardened men and women who had faced the unrelenting heat of the Afghan desert—were now being sent on what seemed like a wild goose chase in the middle of Southern California. He clenched his jaw, trying to tamper down the rising irritation, and strode into the barracks of 1st Platoon, Company A. His voice thundered through the room, cutting through the quiet, "Rise and shine, ladies!"

The response was immediate, a chorus of groans and rustling sheets as the Marines shook off the last vestiges of sleep. Anderson's voice came again, more forceful, "I said, off your asses, now!"

The order snapped every Marine to attention. In seconds, all fifteen members of the platoon were on their feet, the remnants of sleep replaced by the cold, stern gaze of their Sergeant. Anderson's eyes swept the room, daring anyone to utter another sound.

"Listen up," he barked. "Bravo Squad, I need everyone ready to move out in twenty."

Antawn Fisher, a towering, muscular figure who

commanded respect as the unofficial leader of the squad, spoke up. "What's going on, Sergeant?"

Anderson's face was unreadable as he answered, "We have a situation in La Quinta that needs your assistance."

Peter Jackson, a Marine with a reputation for speaking his mind, grumbled, "La Quinta? Really? What the hell kind of mission is that?"

In a flash, Anderson was in Jackson's face, his voice low and dangerous, "You got a problem, Jackson?"

Jackson stiffened under Anderson's glare. "No, Sir."

"Good," Anderson growled. "Seems there's a serious animal control problem down there, and they need our help keeping the residents safe."

Fisher, still not satisfied, pressed on. "So, this is a dog-chasing assignment?"

"Not quite," Anderson replied, his tone growing even grimmer. "Intel says something's affected nearly all the wildlife in the area. It's like a massive rabies outbreak on steroids."

Guerera, the lone female in the squad with arms that could outmatch most men, asked, "What could cause something like that?"

Anderson's voice was hard, almost mechanical. "All I know is that some rock fell from the sky, crashed into the ground, and then the animals started going ape-shit crazy. Your job is to protect those civilians just like you would in any other god-forsaken hole. Got it?"

"Yes, Sir!" The squad echoed back in unison, the seriousness of the mission sinking in.

As Anderson turned to leave, he shouted over his shoulder, "Twenty minutes! Not a second later!"

As soon as the Sergeant was out of sight, Fisher spun

around, barking orders. "You heard the man, let's move!"

Bravo Squad leaped into action, moving with practiced efficiency. In record time, they were geared up and outside, the cool night air biting at their skin. Two Humvee s waited for them, engines idling like beasts ready to be unleashed. Anderson stood by the vehicles, holding a manila envelope that he handed to Fisher as the squad approached.

"Everything you need to know is inside. I expect to be kept in radio contact at all times."

Fisher nodded. "Yes, sir."

Anderson's eyes narrowed. "Remember, Fisher, civilians must be protected at all costs. Use any force necessary."

A dark grin spread across Fisher's face as he jumped into the passenger seat of the nearest Humvee. Guerera slid into the driver's seat, while Jackson climbed into the back. The rest of the squad boarded the second vehicle, and within moments, both Humvee s were tearing down CA-62, the base shrinking in the rear-view mirror.

Fisher opened the envelope, a small flashlight in hand, and began sifting through the documents inside. His heart skipped a beat when he saw the satellite photos. The images were grainy, but the carnage was unmistakable. In all his tours, he had never seen anything so grotesque.

"Holy shit," he muttered under his breath, eyes wide with disbelief.

Jackson, noticing Fisher's reaction, leaned forward. "What you got there, Fisher?"

Without a word, Fisher passed the photos back. The moment Jackson's eyes landed on them, he let out a low whistle. "Man, that's some seriously fucked up shit."

Guerera glanced in the rear-view mirror. "I thought nothing creeped you out, Jackson."

Jackson shook his head. "I didn't say it creeped me out,

Jaz. Just said it was fucked up. Big difference."

As Jackson studied the photos, Fisher turned his attention back to the remaining documents. There was a map of the area, a detailed route to the crash site, and dossiers on each member of the research team. But one stood out—Clause's file. Aside from his name, it was completely blank, a ghost in the system.

Fisher suddenly grew uneasy. Whatever they were heading into, he had a terrible feeling it was going to be far more dangerous than he had first imagined.

CHAPTER 20

The mysterious rescuers had barely finished patching their wounds before vanishing into the darkness, leaving Nancy and Josh alone in a world that had spiraled into madness. The night around them buzzed with an eerie stillness, broken only by the distant, echoing growls of the beasts outside. Laying together in the cramped space of the van, they fought to keep their breathing shallow, barely able to keep their fear in check.

The low, guttural snarls grew closer, a spine-chilling reminder that the nightmare wasn't over. The beasts were prowling nearby, their heavy footsteps crunching on the gravel as they circled the van. Each second stretched into an eternity as Nancy and Josh strained to remain silent, their hearts pounding in unison with the ominous thuds outside.

Then, as if by some miracle, the growls began to fade, the monstrous presence receding into the night. A breath of relief escaped each of them, but it was short-lived. Without warning, their bodies convulsed violently, like marionettes yanked by invisible strings. Eyes wide in terror, they both began to shake uncontrollably, their limbs thrashing against the van's metal floor.

Josh's head snapped back, his eyes rolling into his skull as his teeth clamped down hard enough to draw blood. Nancy's nails dug into her palms, her vision blurring as the seizures tore through them both, relentless and merciless. Just when it seemed the violent tremors would never cease, their bodies stilled, falling limp as if the life had been sucked out of them.

The silence was broken by a soft, sickening sound, as thick, black ooze began to trickle from their mouths, its foul stench filling the air. The inky liquid moved with a mind of its own, slithering away into the shadows, vanishing into the dark corners of the van.

Nancy's eyelids fluttered, her consciousness slipping away, but before the darkness claimed her, she caught a glimpse of movement. Two figures, ghostly in the dim light, loomed over them. Dressed in hazmat suits, their faces hidden behind reflective visors, they moved with clinical precision. Cold metal pricked her arm, and a moment later, the same happened to Josh. The needle's sting was brief, followed by a strange numbness spreading through her veins.

The door slammed shut, and the van jerked, the sensation of being lifted onto a flatbed unmistakable. The world outside was swallowed by the sound of machinery, the vibrations humming through the vehicle's frame. Nancy's vision tunneled, the edges darkening until the last remnants of consciousness slipped away, plunging her into the abyss.

***

A torrent of black ooze hammered against the van like a relentless hailstorm, each impact sending a shudder through the metal frame. The alien substance splattered across the roof and windows, but the most terrifying sight was watching it slither down the windshield. It was alive—an unearthly mass teeming with a life-force that defied everything the scientists knew.

Samuel's gaze was locked on the writhing sludge, his mind grappling with the impossibility of what he was seeing. So, when the phone in his pocket vibrated, he nearly jumped out of his skin. He fought to stay composed, but out of the corner of his eye, he noticed Clause's sharp glance. It was the briefest of moments, yet it was enough to remind Samuel of the danger the man presented.

Everyone's attention was completely riveted on the bizarre alien substance until Kelvin finally broke the silence. "What the hell is this stuff? I've never seen anything like it." He turned to Simon, "Simon, get your camera! We need to document this!"

Simon nodded, pulling his camera from his bag with shaky hands. As he powered it on, the camera's light cast an eerie, unnatural glow inside the van. But when Simon aimed the lens at the windshield, the light's reflection turned the outside world into a blur.

"I can't see anything through the glare," Simon muttered. "I'll have to go outside for a better shot."

Andrea's eyes widened. "Are you sure that's a good idea?"

"No, it's not," Simon replied nervously. "But it's the only way to get this on record."

"Be careful," Samuel said.

Simon managed a faint smile before he reached for the door handle. With a deep breath, he flung the door open and leaped out, sliding it shut behind him with a decisive thud. He told himself it was just a trick of the light, a mass of insects perhaps—but deep down, he knew better. They were dealing with something far beyond their worst nightmares.

Simon crept forward, camera in hand, every nerve on edge. The second the camera's light hit the ooze, it reacted violently, undulating and merging into a pulsating, monstrous mass. It clung to the windshield like some primordial beast, alive with a dangerous intelligence.

The ground trembled beneath his feet, and Samuel's heart pounded as he watched the terrifying scene unfold through a tiny clear patch on the glass. From the depths of the crater, another massive form began to rise, a dark entity emerging from the black pool, towering over them like a specter of doom. Samuel threw the door open, shouting, "Simon, get back in here, now!"

But his warning came too late. The mass hurtled forward, a churning wave of insects that swarmed the van in the blink of an eye. They moved as one, a hive of ravenous creatures that descended upon Simon with horrifying speed. His scream was a gut-wrenching cry of agony as the swarm engulfed him, stripping flesh from bone in mere seconds. The sound of his bones cracking under the onslaught was drowned out by the relentless buzzing.

And then, as quickly as it had come, the swarm moved on, a black cloud racing into the woods, joining the legion of undead creatures in their march toward civilization. The van was left eerily silent, the only sound the ragged breathing of its occupants, all paralyzed with shock—except for Clause, who remained unsettlingly calm.

Minutes passed before Clause opened his door and stepped out of the van.

"What are you doing?" Andrea asked, trembling visibly.

Clause's reply was cold, detached. "I'm checking if the threat has passed. Unless you'd prefer to do it?"

Andrea didn't reply and dropped her head in defeat. Clause stepped out, closing the door behind him with a finality that sent a shiver down Samuel's spine.

The moment Clause was outside, Samuel seized the

opportunity. His hands trembled as he yanked Clause's phone from his pocket, quickly scrolling through the messages. What he found left him reeling, his heart thudding in his chest. A message from Ashton, as chilling as the swarm that had just taken Simon: *Recovery team mobilized. Will be there soon. Military on its way. Secure specimens. Begin Stage 2.*

Before Samuel could react, the door flew open, and Clause was back. He snatched the phone from Samuel's hand, his expression unreadable. "I'll take that," Clause said coolly, tossing Simon's camera into Samuel's lap. "Maybe you'll find something more interesting on that."

Samuel sat frozen in his seat, unable to move, but a moment later, Clause was already back behind the wheel, the van rumbling to life.

"But... what about Simon?" Andrea's voice was barely a whisper.

Clause didn't even look at her as he replied, "Simon's dead."

Andrea gasped in horror, her face crumpling. "No... no, he can't be. Are you sure?"

Clause turned, his eyes cold and unforgiving. "You're welcome to check for yourself."

Andrea buried her face in her hands, the tears flowing freely.

***

The swarm moved like a living shadow, a monstrous tide of insects and arachnids pouring out from the depths of the crater. The black mass surged through the forest, spreading with a sinister intelligence, each creature within it driven by a singular, terrifying purpose. Trees shuddered and cracked as the swarm passed, the forest alive with the sound of snapping branches, rustling leaves, and the panicked cries of animals fleeing the oncoming darkness.

The forest was quickly overrun when the rest of the local wildlife succumbed to the swarm's savage attack. The creatures that emerged were grotesque parodies of life, their eyes glowing with an unnatural light, their movements jerky and unnatural. They turned as one, following the swarm's path out of the park and toward the city, where the distant hum of traffic signaled the presence of fresh prey.

The occupants of the car speeding down the I-10 were completely unaware of the nightmare they were barreling into. Music thumped from the speakers, bass shaking the windows as they passed a joint around, their laughter mingling with the acrid scent of weed and the tang of cheap liquor.

"Man, I'm telling you, they should just legalize everything," Mike argued from the back, his voice rising over the noise as he brushed the hair out of his eyes. "People are gonna do what they want, anyway. Just regulate it and make it safe."

Sarah, sitting next to him, frowned as she passed the joint back. She shook her head emphatically. "Are you serious? You want the government controlling even more? They'd mess it up, just like everything else they touch."

Tyler glanced in the rear-view mirror while trying to keep his focus on the road in his impaired state, his grip on the wheel tightening subconsciously. "It's not about control. It's about reducing harm. Look at what prohibition did back in the day — it only made things worse."

Melissa, in the passenger seat, was half-listening, her phone in hand as she took a bunch of blurry photos of the group. She pulled the neck of her shirt out and snapped a quick picture of her boobs and snickered as she turned the phone toward Tyler, who dared a glance at the screen and immediately had to jerk the car back onto the road when he went onto the shoulder.

"Watch what you're doing up there!" Sarah demanded, "or you're gonna get us killed."

"Hey, it's not my fault," Tyler answered. "Blame the phone queen up here."

Melissa chuckled and turned in her seat toward the back, "You guys are so naive. It's all about money. The second they figure out how to make bank on it, they'll flip the switch, and suddenly it's all 'safe and legal.' But it's not really about us."

"Exactly!" Mike chimed in, leaning forward. "It's all a game to them, and we're just the pieces. We might as well play by our own rules, then."

Sarah rolled her eyes. "Playing by your own rules is what gets you in trouble, Mike. Just because the system's flawed doesn't mean anarchy's the answer."

"Anarchy's not what I'm talking about," Mike shot back before taking another hit. "I'm talking about personal freedom, responsibility, you know?"

Tyler replied, "Listen, freedom's great, but not if it means everyone's out for themselves. There's gotta be some kinda balance."

The debate continued passionately for some time, with everyone oblivious to the dark clouds gathering in the distance. Outside, the desert was eerily silent, the only sound the rush of wind against the car and the thumping bass inside. But then, Tyler saw something—movement in the corner of his eye.

"What the...?" he muttered, leaning forward to get a better look.

Suddenly, the car jolted violently, as if struck by something massive. "Holy shit!" Tyler yelled, as he yanked the wheel to keep the vehicle under control.

"What the hell was that?" Melissa shrieked, clutching at the dashboard. "Did we hit another car?"

"I don't know! Something's out there!" Tyler shouted back, his heart pounding as he gripped the steering wheel tight.

In the distance, the road ahead seemed to shimmer, an undulating wave of blackness that surged into the car's headlights. Before anyone could react, a swarm of writhing, churning creatures swept across the asphalt, a living river of beetles, scorpions, and spiders, all moving with terrifying coordination. Above them, a whirlwind of flying insects rocketed toward the vehicle, flying in parallel to wave of death approaching on the ground. The creatures slammed into the car like an unholy force of nature. The windshield was instantly obscured by the seething mass.

"Oh my God, what's happening?" Sarah screamed, clawing at the door as the insects began to seep through the vents and the cracks in the windows.

Tyler slammed on the brakes, the tires screeching as the car skidded across the slick road. But it was too late—the swarm engulfed the vehicle, the sound of thousands of tiny bodies slamming against metal and glass drowning out their screams.

Outside the car, a hundred yards from the freeway, a coyote scavenging through the desert had been caught in the chaos, its frantic yelps cut short as the swarm overtook it, the infection spreading through its veins, twisting it into something monstrous.

The infected coyote, its eyes glowing with unnatural light, leaped onto the freeway, its snarl echoing across the desert. Other creatures, now twisted and rabid, emerged from the shadows—owls, snakes, even a lone mountain lion, all driven by the same dark hunger.

On the freeway ahead, the chaos began to spread with the speed of a wildfire. A convoy of cars, driving home late at night, suddenly found themselves caught in a nightmare as the infected animals launched themselves at the vehicles. Drivers slammed on their brakes, tires screeching as cars swerved and collided, the freeway becoming a tangled mess of metal and glass. Horns blared, and panicked voices filled the air as the traffic jam grew, the blocked lanes stretching back for miles.

Tyler's car, still in the thick of the swarm, was caught in the chaos as it smashed into the back of an SUV, the impact jolting everyone inside. The windshield cracked under the weight of the seething mass, the glass splintering as the creatures continued their assault.

"Get them off! Get them off!" Sarah yelled, frantically swatting at the insects that crawled over her, their bites stinging as she tried to fend them off. The rest of the group echoed her frantic yells for a brief moment before their voices were choked silent.

Suddenly, the car was rocked by another impact as a semi, unable to stop in time, plowed into the side of the pileup. The sound of metal crunching and glass shattering filled the air, mingling with the roars and snarls of the infected animals.

In the midst of the chaos, the swarm began to move on, their dark work done. The black cloud of insects surged over the cars, leaving behind a trail of devastation as they headed toward civilization, infecting every creature in their path. The once-vibrant desert night was now filled with the sounds of panic and destruction, the freeway a twisted, smoking ruin.

As the dust settled, the group of college kids lay silent in their car, their bodies torn apart by the wrath of the swarm. Outside, the infected creatures prowled among the wrecked vehicles, their eyes glowing in the dark as they sought out their next victims. The swarm raced onward, its hunger unquenched, leaving behind a trail of terror as it continued its relentless march.

CHAPTER 21

Guerera merged the Humvee onto I-10 E, the vehicle's thick tires gripping the pavement with the low hum of raw power. Bryant followed close behind in the second unit, their caravan moving swiftly through the dark desert. The moon was low, casting long shadows over the highway as they carved their way eastward. For the first hour, things were steady, almost routine—until it wasn't.

The screeching halt came out of nowhere, the convoy lurching to a dead stop near the Palm Springs exit. A sea of red brake lights stretched out ahead, taillights flickering as far as the eye could see.

"Shit," Fisher muttered as he reached for the radio. "Sergeant Anderson, we've hit a wall here. Traffic's backed up as far as I can see."

There was a tense pause before Anderson's voice crackled through the static. "N. Indian Canyon exit's just up ahead. If you can make that, you'll bypass this mess and take HWY 111 toward La Quinta. Should keep you moving."

Out of habit, Fisher nodded, even though Anderson couldn't see him. "Roger that."

He turned to Guerera, but she was already edging the

Humvee onto the shoulder, threading her way past the grid locked cars.

"We're not sitting in this cluster-fuck all night," she said, inching along with mere inches separating them from the vehicles to their left.

The exit was only half a mile ahead, but it felt like miles as they crawled forward. The tension in the vehicle grew thick, punctuated only by the rhythmic thrum of the engine and the faint chatter over the radio. After what seemed like an eternity, they finally reached the exit and veered off the freeway. The relief was palpable, but short-lived.

Traffic was still backed up on the surface streets. The long line of cars snaked its way down Vista Chino, filled with frustrated drivers looking for their own escape routes. Guerera's hands clenched the wheel. "At least we're moving, though barely," she grumbled, though her patience was wearing thin.

Jackson, in the back seat, groaned. "Knew this mission was gonna be a pain in the ass from the start."

"We're not out of it yet," Fisher shot back. "Focus on the job."

After making a few turns, they found themselves on Gene Autry, cruising through Palm Springs with relative ease—until they hit Ramon Road. Construction cones blocked their path like a cruel joke, cutting traffic down to one lane, and Guerera slammed her hands against the wheel.

"You've got to be shitting me!" she yelled.

Jackson leaned forward, smirking. "I swear, nothing goes easy with you around, Guerera."

She shot him a glare. "You think I'm enjoying this?"

Fisher interjected, "Enough. Jackson, what's the next best route?"

Jackson pointed ahead. "Take Ramon down to Date Palm,

cut right. That'll get us on 111."

They turned, moving through the quieter side streets. The glow of fast-food joints and gas stations passed by, casting flickering neon light on the pavement. As they cruised past a Jack In The Box, Jackson couldn't help himself. "Man, I could go for a burger right now."

Guerera snickered. "When aren't you hungry?"

"Hey, I'm a growing boy. Gotta keep this manly figure in shape."

"Boy sounds about right," she shot back with a grin.

***

The scent of cheap cologne mixed with the faint stench of beer and sweat, and the steady thrum of hip-hop rattled the speakers inside the black BMW, setting a dark pulse to the night. Luis gripped the steering wheel tightly, his tattoos glinting in the light of the dashboard as his knuckles whitened.

"Yo, Luis, you sure this route's cool?" Benny asked from the backseat, nervously tapping his foot on the floor. His shaved head reflected the dim glow of the passing streetlights. "Cops been thick on this side lately."

Luis scoffed. "We ain't got time to worry about cops, man. We're good. Just keep it cool." He flicked his fingers toward the glove compartment, where a half-empty bottle of tequila sloshed. "Take a swig, you'll chill out."

Benny hesitated, but Chuy, sitting in the passenger seat, was already reaching for it, laughing as he tipped it back. "Benny always scared. That's why he's in the back, huh?" Chuy sneered, his gold teeth flashing as he handed the bottle to Benny. "Take it, man. Ain't no one messin' with us tonight."

Benny reluctantly took a sip, his gaze flicking from the road ahead to Luis. "I'm just sayin', shit feels weird out tonight."

Luis's grip tightened as he turned onto a dark stretch of highway. The desert sprawled on either side of them, eerily quiet beneath the moonlight. His eyes scanned the road, sharp as ever, but he also felt like something was off, although he'd never admit it to the others. He couldn't shake the creeping unease curling at the back of his mind.

"You think too much, Benny. That's your problem," Luis said, trying to keep his voice cold and steady. "Ain't nothing out here but sand and stars."

The car was silent for a beat, save for the low rumble of the music. Then, from the back seat next to Benny, Rico, the quietest of the crew, finally spoke. "I don't like it either. This shit's got a vibe tonight, man."

Luis glanced over at him, brow raised. Rico wasn't the type to get spooked easily, and if even he was feeling it, maybe something was up. He was about to say something when they rolled up behind a military Humvee. The heavy vehicle crawled down the road, blocking the BMW's path, and Luis's mood darkened.

"Look at this fool," Luis muttered under his breath, annoyance flickering in his eyes. He stepped on the gas and swerved around the vehicle as they approached an intersection, coming to a stop next to the Humvee as the traffic light turned red.

The boys in the back leaned forward. Benny's nervousness was replaced by excitement as he grinned. "Yo, think they'd take us on? Let's see what this ride can do against the army, huh?"

Luis's lips curled into a smirk. "Hell yeah, let's go." He revved the engine repeatedly, the sound cutting through the desert silence like a knife.

***

The light ahead turned red just as the Humvee pulled up to the intersection. A black BMW slid into place beside them, its driver revving the engine obnoxiously. Guerera glanced over, her expression unreadable. The BMW's driver—barely twenty, if that, with a cocky grin plastered on his face—gave them a challenging look, the kind that begged for trouble.

"Oh, come on," Guerera sighed. Fisher shrugged. When the light turned green, she slammed the gas pedal down hard, the Humvee growling as it surged forward. The BMW shot ahead, weaving in and out of lanes with reckless abandon, but Guerera stuck to her course, eyes on the road.

The BMW pulled ahead, its taillights flickering as it sped down the stretch of road. Then it happened—a violent swerve, tires screeching as the car collided with something unseen in the darkness. The BMW spun out of control, crashing to a stop, while something large and mangled flew through the air and landed directly in the path of the Humvee.

"Fuck!" Guerera shouted as she slammed the brakes. The Humvee jerked forward, but it was too late. They hit whatever it was, the vehicle bouncing as it ran over the object with a sickening thud.

Fisher's voice cut through the chaos. "What the fuck did we just hit?"

Guerera's knuckles were white on the wheel. "I think it was an animal, but I couldn't tell what it was."

"We need to check it out," Fisher said, unbuckling his seatbelt. "Jackson, go see if the car's occupants are okay."

The Humvee rolled to a stop as Fisher, Guerera, and

Madison jumped out, their flashlights cutting through the dark desert night. Bryant pulled up behind them, the second Humvee's headlights illuminating the wreckage ahead.

As they scanned the road, Madison's beam caught something grotesque. "Holy shit!" he called out. "Over here!"

The others joined him, their lights revealing the mangled remains of a coyote—or what was left of it. Its body was twisted beyond recognition, entrails strewn across the road, its head nearly severed but still connected by a thin string of flesh. And then—against all reason—the head twitched.

"What the hell?" Guerera muttered, taking a step back.

The coyote's eyes flickered open, glowing eerily in the beam of the flashlight, and it let out a low, menacing growl. The jaws snapped wildly, even though most of its body was destroyed.

Bryant's voice was tight with disbelief. "How in the flying fuck is that thing still alive?"

Before anyone could react, Guerera stepped forward and plunged her knife into the coyote's skull, ending its twisted second life with a sickening crunch. Silence fell, broken only by their heavy breathing and the distant hum of traffic.

"What the hell is going on here?" Madison whispered, his face pale in the moonlight.

Fisher, grim-faced, stared down at the coyote's lifeless body. "That's what we're here to figure out. Let's move."

But before they could regroup, a sound cut through the night—an eerie howl, not far off. The group froze, the desert air suddenly feeling colder, thicker.

Fisher's skin prickled. He didn't know what they were dealing with, but one thing was certain: something far worse was lurking in the shadows.

As Jackson reached the black BMW, he found it hunched against the curb, its front bumper smashed and its sleek body marred by the crash. The engine was still running, coughing smoke into the night air. The headlights flickered erratically, casting long, distorted shadows against the nearby bushes.

Jackson banged on the driver's side window, trying to see through the smoke. "Hey, you alright in there? Open up!"

The window cracked open just a sliver, and a voice came from inside, shaky but defensive. "What the hell, man! You just gonna run me off the road?"

Jackson blinked, caught off-guard by the aggression. "Run you off the road? You swerved and hit something! We're here to help."

The door creaked open, and Luis stumbled out, his face slick with sweat and blood trickling from a minor cut above his eyebrow. He looked rattled, but tried to play it off with a cocky grin.

"I'm fine, man. It was just... it happened so fast. I don't know what it was."

Jackson glanced at the dented front of the car. "Whatever it was, you hit it hard. Anyone else in the car?"

From the back seat, a muffled voice piped up, "Can we just go, already? I'm not trying to sit here all night waiting for Animal Control."

Jackson crouched down and peered inside. Three more passengers sat slumped in their seats. The guy in the passenger seat was rubbing his temples, eyes squinting against the harsh glare of the flickering headlights. He looked high as a kite.

The driver shook his head, trying to focus. "We're good, we're good. We'll get outta here. Just—"

"You're not driving anywhere," Jackson cut him off. "Your car's beat to shit, and something way bigger is happening. Just stay put while we figure things out."

Luis scowled. "Who the hell do you think you are you,

anyway?"

Jackson stepped back with smirk. "Just a bunch of Marines on a mission."

Benny raised an eyebrow. "Wait, why's the military involved? What the hell did we hit?"

Jackson didn't have an answer that would make sense, so he ignored the question and glanced back at Fisher, who was waving him over. "Just stay here, alright? We're calling in backup, and you don't wanna be driving when they get here. Trust me."

The driver opened his mouth to argue, but his words were cut short by a sudden, gut-wrenching sound—a howl, so loud it seemed to rattle the car windows. This wasn't like any coyote howl they'd ever heard. It was deeper, more primal, and echoed across the desert like a death knell.

Chuy exclaimed, "What the fuck was that?"

Luis' bravado instantly vanished, replaced with wide-eyed fear. "It's just an animal, right? Coyotes or some shit?"

Jackson's hand instinctively went to his sidearm as he took a step back, scanning the darkness. He couldn't see anything, but the air had changed. There was a thickness to it now, a tension that made the hair on the back of his neck stand up.

"Stay in the car," he ordered, backing away toward the Humvee. "Lock the doors."

Luis hesitated, looking like he wanted to argue, but the howl came again—closer this time—and he scrambled back into the car, slamming the door.

Jackson turned and jogged back to Guerera and Fisher, his heart racing.

"What the hell is going on?" Fisher asked, his voice low but tense.

Jackson shook his head, glancing back at the BMW. "They're fine, but that howl... We gotta move. Something's out there."

Fisher nodded, turning to Guerera. "Get ready to move out, but keep an eye on that car. We might need to get them out of here if things get worse."

Suddenly, they heard a rustling sound nearby, followed by a low, guttural growl. It seemed to come from the side of the road, hidden in the brush.

Luis's voice echoed from the car. "Man, this is really fucked up! You're not leaving us out here like this, are you?"

Jackson called back, "Sorry, we're on a strict time-line. But we've already called for help. Just stay in the car and you'll be safe."

But in the pit of his stomach, Jackson knew there was no such thing as "safe" anymore—not out here in the dark, not with whatever was out there hunting them.

CHAPTER 22

After a few agonizing minutes, Andrea managed to pull herself together. She wiped away the last of her tears, her breath coming in shallow, controlled bursts as she tried to bury her grief beneath layers of scientific reasoning. The horror of what had just transpired lingered, thick in the air, but she forced her mind to focus on the bizarre reality they now faced. She couldn't let the sorrow consume her, even though it tugged at her relentlessly, like an invisible weight pressing against her chest. Losing Simon had ripped something vital from her—a part of her soul. They had shared so much, developed a bond that transcended anything she had ever known. Confidant, lover, friend—he had been everything to her. And now he was gone, torn from her in the most horrific way imaginable.

The van's engine rumbled beneath her, a mechanical growl cutting through the otherwise deafening silence. Clause was in the driver's seat, his face set in a grim, unreadable mask as he maneuvered the vehicle carefully through the wreckage-strewn forest. Samuel turned Simon's camera over in his hands, the cool metal sending a chill through his fingers. His hand hovered over the power button, hesitant, knowing the weight of what he was about to witness. Finally, he clicked it on, the small screen flickering to life, casting a ghostly light over his face.

The footage jolted him instantly. Simon's final moments showed a frenetic blur as the swarm descended. It wasn't just locusts or some coordinated hive—this was worse, far worse. Samuel squinted at the screen, his eyes narrowing as the image steadied. The swarm was made of a nightmarish mix: insects of all kinds—beetles, ants, flies—whirling together with spiders, worms, even scorpions, all coalescing into a seething, pulsating mass. They moved like one organism, as though driven by a singular, malevolent consciousness. The buzzing filled his ears even through the low volume, a sound that sent a shiver racing up his spine.

Samuel's heart raced as the swarm grew denser, blotting out the background of trees and sky until all that remained was that black, undulating cloud. The camera shook, jerked violently, then fell. For one horrible second, Simon's face appeared in frame, fleshless and skeletal, staring directly into the lens with dead eyes. Samuel's stomach lurched. His thumb slammed the camera off.

He hadn't realized how loudly he had gasped until Andrea glanced over with a mix of suspicion and concern. Her voice was quiet, trembling with exhaustion but firm, "What did you see?"

Samuel's throat tightened. How could he tell her? How could he describe the horror, the way Simon had been consumed? He took a breath, trying to steady his voice. "You don't want to know," he said, his words clipped.

"We need to know," she insisted, her eyes sharp. "To figure this out. We can't fix this unless we understand it."

Reluctantly, Samuel exhaled and recounted what he had seen, choosing his words carefully. "It wasn't just one type of insect. The whole mass... it was a combination. Insects, spiders, worms—all acting together. Like... like they were all part of a single mind." He paused, fighting the image that still haunted his vision. "They weren't even all flying creatures. It was like something was propelling them."

Kelvin, seated nearby, turned his head toward Samuel, frowning. "That doesn't make sense. Different species don't cooperate like that. Not naturally."

Andrea nodded in agreement. "A queen bee can control a hive," she offered, though her tone was uncertain.

Samuel shook his head. "This was different. Arachnids, worms... insects. All moving as one. It's like something external was forcing them."

Kelvin rubbed his temples. "But what could do that? It's not in their DNA. Insects don't behave like that."

Clause, steering the van through the dense foliage, grunted, his eyes never leaving the dark road ahead. "That's what you're all here for. Now buckle up and let me get us the hell out of here."

The van rocked gently as it rolled over uneven terrain, the headlights illuminating the carnage left behind by the swarm. Andrea's hand trembled as she gripped the seat, her mind racing.

As they neared the area where the officers had been attacked, Samuel noticed something strange. The media van was gone. There were faint tire marks leading away, but it was as if the van had vanished into thin air. He narrowed his eyes, focusing on the faint glow of taillights far ahead. "Where's the van?" he asked, his voice low.

Clause didn't hesitate, his tone casual, almost dismissive. "Taken in for examination."

"Taken where?" Samuel pressed.

Clause shot him a sideways glance, the expression on his

face hard and uninviting. "You ask too many questions. Eisenhower Regional, if you must know."

Samuel fell silent, biting back his frustration. He didn't trust Clause but he had no choice but to follow his lead.

Suddenly, a low growl filled the air. The van slowed as a pair of bloodied, mangled dogs staggered into the beam of the headlights. Their once-beautiful fur was matted with gore, their eyes empty, glowing with an unnatural hunger. They were part of the undead horde now, too, though they didn't attack. Instead, they watched with dead, glassy stares as the van rolled by, their bodies jerking with spasms as they limped away into the night. The rest of the horde had clearly moved on, toward the heart of the city, toward civilization.

They drove in heavy silence down Jefferson Street, passing by more packs of infected animals. The undead beasts shuffled along the roadside, grotesque shadows cast by the van's headlights.

Clause brought the van to a halt at a bend where Jefferson turned into 58th Street. The headlights illuminated a grisly scene ahead. A dozen undead animals—coyotes, dogs, and birds—were feasting on the remains of three human bodies, their dead eyes gleaming in the pale light. Clause immediately killed the lights, plunging them into darkness.

"Let's not attract attention," he whispered. "We're almost out of here."

The van crawled forward, weaving slowly past the feasting horde, the sound of tearing flesh and snapping bones filling the quiet night.

Once they were clear of the carnage, Clause turned the headlights back on. The lights fell this time on a single large dog, a Golden Retriever, with half of its face ripped off. The red collar told Samuel that it was someone's pet at one time, when it had still been alive. He prayed that the pet's owner would never have to see it in such a state.

As they neared the intersection to Madison Street, loud buzzing started to fill the van. Samuel turned on the overhead light so they could get a look at the culprit. Things were already stressful enough without some pesky fly driving them crazy. But as soon as the light filled the cab, they were terrified to see dozens of insects scurrying about.

Andrea cried out as she promptly jumped up and started stomping on anything that moved. Kelvin followed her example.

"They must have come in through the A/C vents," Samuel shouted. "We have to get out of here, now!"

Although the prospects of facing the zombie animals outside was frightening, at least the group knew that the beasts could be killed. The insect swarm was another matter. And it wasn't just the alien consciousness controlling them that was horrifying. They weren't in a position to treat a bite or sting by anything poisonous.

Clause tried to bring the van to a halt, but he was too busy swatting away a mob of insects himself. The vehicle swerved from side to side as it flew through the intersection. They almost made it through unscathed, but at the last second a northbound driver which had slammed on his brakes to avoid a collision clipped the rear passenger's side, sending the van spinning until it came to a sudden stop when it crashed headlong into a telephone pole.

The force of the collision shattered the windshield and sent the group all crashing forward. The insects instantly gathered as one and flew out of the opening to reunite with the rest of the swarm.

CHAPTER 23

In all his twenty years on the force, Captain Gerald Harrison had seen more than his share of horrors, but nothing could have prepared him for the waking nightmare unfolding around him. He had cut his teeth as a fresh-faced patrol officer, working the streets with a sense of purpose, chasing down petty criminals, and breaking up bar fights. From there, he climbed the ranks—detective, then homicide, each promotion stripping away a bit of his innocence, hardening him. He thought he'd seen it all. Drug busts gone wrong, the aftermath of gang violence, the raw brutality of human nature revealed in the worst kinds of murders. But what he had just witnessed... it was something beyond comprehension.

Those... things outside the door, they weren't animals. Not anymore. They were grotesque imitations of life, mutilated and twisted by some dark force he couldn't understand. They should have been dead—by all rights, they were dead—and yet they moved with a frenzied hunger, their bloodshot eyes glowing with a hellish light. The memory of them ripping through his squad sent a cold, nauseating shiver through him, and he clenched his fists in helpless fury.

Harrison's gaze drifted to Jerry Durant, slumped against the far wall, his chest heaving as he fought to keep his composure. The kid had been by his side since day one, since that fresh academy graduate had nervously shuffled into the precinct and taken the desk next to his. Harrison had taken him under his wing, showing him the ropes, helping him grow into the kind of cop you wanted by your side when the shit hit the fan. Now, looking at Durant, Harrison saw none of the bright-eyed enthusiasm that had once defined the young officer. Instead, there was only fear—raw, suffocating fear—and a weariness that seemed to age him ten years in mere hours.

Harrison swallowed hard. He prayed the rookie-turned-seasoned cop had the strength to survive this, but deep down, he wondered if any of them would.

They huddled together in the cramped room, the walls closing in around them, as the sounds of death prowled just outside. The snarling, growling, and bone-chilling scratches on the door seemed to echo endlessly. Minutes stretched into an eternity as the creatures—whatever they were—continued their hunt, their claws scraping against the wood, their foul breath heavy in the air. Harrison kept his gun steady, but he knew damn well it wouldn't be enough if they broke through. His heart pounded in his chest, each beat like a drum of impending doom.

Then, after what felt like a lifetime, the sounds began to fade. The growling turned into distant snarls, the shuffling claws into eerie silence. For the first time in what felt like hours, Harrison allowed himself to breathe. But the relief was fleeting. They weren't safe. Not yet.

He fumbled for his phone, his hands shaking, pulling it from his pocket with the same sense of urgency that had become second nature in this nightmare. He punched in Dr.

Leonard's number, hoping against hope that NASA had some kind of explanation—something to help them make sense of the impossible. But when the line picked up, it wasn't Leonard's voice that answered.

"NASA's Near-Earth Object Program. Darcey speaking," came the familiar, professional voice.

Harrison lowered his voice, speaking in a hushed but urgent tone. "I need to speak to Dr. Leonard right away. It's Captain Harrison again. This is an emergency."

There was a brief pause, and he could hear the faint tapping of computer keys on the other end. Darcey's reply came, polite but maddeningly detached. "I'm sorry, Captain. Dr. Leonard stepped out for a few minutes. I can take a message and have him call you as soon as possible."

A wave of frustration surged through Harrison, hot and sharp. He gritted his teeth, feeling his blood pressure spike. The situation was spiraling out of control, and the woman on the other end of the line couldn't grasp the gravity of what was happening. He fought to keep his temper in check, knowing that a lapse in control could get them all killed. He needed to stay calm.

"Tell him the situation has gotten worse," he said, his voice tight with restrained anger. "We need emergency assistance right away."

There was another brief pause, and then Darcey replied, her tone unchanged. "I'll be sure to tell him, Captain."

The line went dead.

Harrison stared at his phone, the silence in the room now more suffocating than the chaos outside. The creatures might have moved on, but they were still out there. Somewhere. Waiting.

***

* * *

Just as Darcey hung up the phone, Dr. Leonard strode by her desk, his usual air of authority evident in the sharpness of his step. He glanced at her, a frown tugging at his brow. "If Captain Harrison happens to call back, make sure you put him through to me right away."

Darcey smiled, a little too quickly. "Yes, Doctor. I'll be sure to do that."

Leonard lingered for a second longer, studying her as if sensing something wasn't quite right. She kept her expression steady, her hands folded neatly in front of her, hiding the slight tremor in her fingers. After a brief pause, he gave a nod and returned to his office.

As soon as his door clicked shut, Darcey's smile faded. Her eyes flickered to the phone, and she exhaled softly. She had no intention of letting that call go through—not until she knew more. Something was happening, something bigger than what Leonard was telling her... and she intended to figure out exactly what.

***

A deep sigh escaped Harrison's lips as he slid his phone back into his pocket. The weight of everything pressed on him, a suffocating cloak of dread, heavier than the stench of death that clung to the air. Jerry's eyes flickered toward him, pale and wide, a ghost of the once bright rookie he had been.

"What now?" Jerry asked in a hollow voice that had been drained of all hope.

Harrison shook his head slowly, staring at the darkened ceiling as if it might offer answers. "I don't know. Leonard wasn't in. Maybe... maybe they'll send more help." His words felt empty.

Jerry looked at him with eyes filled with fear. "What do we do until then?"

It tore at Harrison. He had been Jerry's mentor, had promised to show him the ropes, prepare him for anything the world could throw their way. But nothing could've prepared them for this. The broken world outside their hiding place was no longer bound by the rules they had spent their careers following. Now, survival was all that mattered. If he couldn't pull Jerry from the brink, Harrison feared the kid would unravel completely, just as the world had.

With a forced smile, Harrison tried to lighten the mood. "Hey, remember that time you pulled over that little old Chinese lady for reckless driving?"

Jerry blinked, confusion flashing across his face before the memory hit. A ghost of a smile tugged at his lips. "Yeah," he whispered, "She was like four feet tall, about sixty-five, ornery as hell, and drunker than a skunk."

Harrison let out a chuckle, the sound hollow in the tense air. "I remember pulling up behind you, laughing so fucking hard I nearly pissed my pants. That old lady had her finger in your face, screaming who-knows-what in some language I didn't understand, and you were trying to make her take a sobriety test."

Jerry's smile widened, the weight lifting just a little. "I thought she was gonna take my head off with that damn purse of hers. I'm glad you showed up when you did."

For a moment, the memory wrapped them in a fragile bubble, separating them from the madness just beyond the door. But then Harrison's smile faded. "And don't forget, Jerry. I'll always be there when you need me."

Jerry glanced at him. "Thanks, Captain. I appreciate it."

Harrison clapped a reassuring hand on his shoulder, giving it a firm squeeze. "Now," he said, his voice low, "let's see if it's safe to finally get the fuck out of here."

They both strained to listen for movement outside the room. Silence. No more growling, no more shuffling. Harrison moved to the door, every nerve on edge. Slowly, he turned the handle, the creak of the hinge sounding impossibly loud in the eerie quiet.

With guns drawn, the two crept out of the records room. The hallway was dark, lit only by the faint, flickering light of an emergency lamp down the corridor. They moved cautiously, their steps echoing off the cold tile floor, weaving between the lifeless bodies of their comrades and the mangled remains of animals—once faithful pets, now turned into monsters.

Jerry's breath caught in his throat as they passed by one body—Officer Kelley, his face frozen in a mask of terror, his chest torn open. The sight turned Jerry's stomach. He looked away, trying to breathe through the wave of nausea, only to step over the lifeless husk of what had once been a Siberian Husky. Its white fur was now slick with blood, eyes clouded and vacant.

Suddenly, the dog's jaws snapped open with a feral snarl. Jerry reacted without thinking, bringing his boot down hard. Bone crunched beneath his heel, silencing the beast with one final, brutal stomp. The sound echoed through the corridor, making them both freeze.

At the end of the hall, they heard a sound, different from the groans of the undead beasts—a low moaning and shuffling.

"Jesus..." Jerry whispered, gripping his gun tighter.

The sounds filtered out from a janitor's closet on their right. The urge to run was overwhelming. Every instinct screamed to keep moving, to get out before the horrors found them. But loyalty ran deep. They couldn't abandon anyone, not when there was a chance they were still alive.

Jerry nodded at Harrison, both of them understanding without words. Repeating the same maneuver as before, Jerry yanked open the door, and Harrison sprang forward, weapon raised.

Inside, slumped against the wall, was Jeremiah Dooling—a man who had been with the force longer than both of them combined. His white hair shone like a beacon in the dim light. Harrison's heart sank at the sight.

"Jeremiah?" Harrison whispered.

The man was trembling, his body jerking in painful spasms. Blood oozed from his mangled arm, the flesh torn as if something had ripped it apart. Two of his fingers were gone. Worse yet, a black, oily substance seeped from the corner of his mouth, slithering across the floor toward a drain like it had a mind of its own.

"What the shit is that?" Jerry gasped, stepping back.

Harrison kneeled beside Jeremiah to get a closer look at the stuff. "I don't know, but it's not good." A large section of shelving against the far wall held a vast array of supplies. "Grab some towels," he said urgently. "We need to stop this bleeding."

As Jerry rushed to grab supplies, Harrison leaned closer to Jeremiah, whose eyes were fluttering open. "Cap'n..." he whispered, his voice barely a rasp. "They wouldn't die... they just kept coming."

"Shh," Harrison said softly as he tied a make-shift bandage around Jeremiah's arm. "We'll get you out of here. Just hang on."

They were almost at the door when a low growl filled the air. Harrison turned just in time to see a Rottweiler—black as midnight, its insides spilling from a gash in its side—lurch toward them. Without hesitating, Harrison fired. The bullet hit between the dog's dead, glassy eyes, and it crumpled to the ground with a sickening thud.

Before they could catch their breath, a chorus of growls rose throughout the rest of the precinct. The pounding of claws scraping against the blood-soaked floors echoed down the hall, growing louder with each passing second.

Then came the buzzing.

It started as a faint hum, but quickly swelled into a deafening roar. An instant later, an endless stream of insects scurried under the door and poured through the ceiling vents, flooding the room like a living tide of death.

"Use the spray cans!" Harrison shouted over the noise, fumbling for his lighter.

Jerry grabbed a can of cleaner and tossed it to him just as Harrison ignited the chemical spray into a blazing inferno. Screeches, accompanied by the crackling and popping of burning insects, filled the air as the fire engulfed the swarm, turning the room into a scene from hell.

In the meantime, Jerry did his best to keep himself from being eaten alive. He grabbed another can of cleaner and began spraying anything that moved. The chemicals were effective in dropping the flying insects to the ground so he could stomp on them. After a couple of frantic minutes, the swarm was reduced to a handful of stranglers.

Both men looked at each other despairingly. Each one had numerous stings and bites on their arms and faces, but for the most part seemed none the worse for wear. Then they looked at Jeremiah and their hearts sank.

Already weak from his previous injuries, he wasn't able to fend off the swarm. He was slumped over with his back against the wall. When Jerry reached down and leaned him back, Jeremiah's head lolled to one side and he looked at them through dead eyes. His face had dozens of blisters forming from the venom of the crazed swarm. His mouth was slightly ajar and white foam drizzled down his chin. Both men jumped back as they watched a large spider crawl from his mouth and scurry off into the shadows.

A second later, Jerry dropped to his knees and began shaking violently, as the venom from numerous insects overloaded his system. His stomach started to heave and then he vomited uncontrollably. It was a mixture of green bile and the same black oily substance Jeremiah had running down his chin when they found him earlier.

A moment later, Harrison followed Jerry's example and found himself in the same throes of agony. Both men lay there on the floor of the small room, perilously hanging onto life as their bodies worked to fight off the poison. As darkness closed in, the last thing they saw were three figures stepping through the smoke, dressed in hazmat suits.

CHAPTER 24

Everything seemed unnervingly calm as the squad cruised down Highway 111. The desert stretched out like an endless graveyard under the moon's pale gaze. No zombie dogs ambushed them from the shadows, no black birds tore flesh from lifeless bodies, and no chilling howls echoed through the stillness. It was almost as if the world held its breath, waiting.

But as they neared Monterey Avenue in Palm Desert, the calm shattered. Flashing lights flickered ahead, red and blue strobing through the night. A fire truck and police cars blocked the northbound lane, right in front of the Westfield Mall, creating a tangled mess of traffic. At first glance, it looked like a standard accident—a brutal one, maybe, but just a crash. That is, until the squad noticed the bodies.

When Guerera brought the vehicle to a stop, the scene hit them like a punch to the gut. People were running in blind terror, chased by frenzied animals that looked more like demons than creatures of this world. Bloodied hands clawed at the air as the night filled with their cries for help in a symphony of horror.

"Holy shit!" Jackson's voice trembled, his face drained of

color as he stared at the chaos.

Fisher snapped his head toward him. "Get on that spotlight! Now!"

Without hesitation, Jackson jumped up and threw open the roof hatch. His hands shook as he powered on the five-thousand-watt spotlight, sweeping it toward the mall. In an instant, the second vehicle followed suit, the searing beams flooding the area with harsh, unforgiving light.

What the light revealed was far worse than any of them expected.

Bodies littered the streets, their faces frozen in masks of pain and terror. Hungry animals tore into the dead with ravenous delight. Police and rescue workers who had come to help were among the fallen, their uniforms now soaked with their own blood.

The chaos was relentless. Panicked civilians abandoned their cars, desperately trying to outrun the nightmare, but the beasts—some wild, others once domesticated—moved with terrifying speed. Screams filled the air, joining the guttural growls of the undead animals. It was a chorus of death.

In Afghanistan, the Marines had seen plenty of horror. But nothing had ever been this savage, this surreal. For a moment, they were frozen, as if the ground beneath them had turned to quicksand. Then Fisher's voice cut through the paralysis, sharp and commanding.

"Jackson, you and Bryant stay up top! Keep those lights on!" Fisher barked into the com-link. "The rest of us, fan out. Shoot anything that moves and isn't human. I don't care what it is. If it's got more than two legs, I want it dead."

The response was instantaneous. "Yes, Sir!" they all echoed, the fear in their voices barely concealed.

Fisher and Guerera leaped from their vehicle as Madison and Thomas followed suit from the second one. Then the night exploded into gunfire.

The animals surged toward them, a grotesque blend of household pets and wild predators, all snarling, teeth gnashing, eyes gleaming with unnatural hunger. A volley of bullets met the charging beasts, dropping several of them to the pavement. But as the Marines began to breathe a sigh of relief, the horror deepened.

The animals didn't stay down.

With sickening, jerking movements, the fallen creatures began to rise, their bodies twitching and contorting, blood still gushing from mortal wounds.

"What the fuck?" Madison screamed, his voice cracking. "Why aren't they dying?"

Fisher didn't hesitate. "Head shots! Only way to stop 'em."

They switched to their sidearms, the M16s too unreliable for the precision needed. One by one, they put bullets through the skulls of the rising dead. The stench of death mixed with gunpowder burned their nostrils. But within moments, the horde was down—for now.

Fisher's voice crackled through the com again. "Jackson, keep those lights steady. Madison, cover us while we search for survivors."

The Marines spread out, their boots crunching over broken glass and scattered debris. The ground was littered with the remains of both humans and animals, displaying a battlefield of the macabre. Fisher's eyes scanned the wreckage. His heart pounded against his ribs, each beat louder than the last. Then, faint and desperate, he heard it—a soft sob, cutting through the carnage like a knife.

A blue Honda Civic sat skewed on the side of the road. Fisher motioned to Guerera, his hand steady but his voice low. "Over there."

They approached cautiously, the sobs growing louder, more distinct. It wasn't coming from inside the car—it was from beneath it.

Guerera crouched, peering into the darkness. A small, terrified face stared back at her. A child, barely six, curled up and trembling.

"It's okay, sweetheart," Guerera said gently, her voice cracking slightly. "We're here to help."

The little girl whimpered, pulling back. "What about the monsters?"

Guerera's chest tightened, memories of her own childhood flashing through her mind. "What's your name, honey?"

The girl sniffled. "Ashley."

"Ashley, that's a beautiful name. Can you come out? We need to get you somewhere safe."

Ashley's lip quivered. "You can't. The monsters already got Mommy and Daddy, and they're gonna get you too."

Guerera's heart broke. She swallowed hard, pushing back the emotions rising in her throat. Before she could respond, a loud crash echoed from behind. The spotlight above them flickered wildly as Jackson screamed. A dozen black birds had descended on him, their talons clawing at his face, their beaks piercing his skin.

Bryant's body lay slumped against the other vehicle, one of the birds still flapping its wings frantically as it tried to pull its beak free from his skull.

The air erupted with more gunfire. Madison and Thomas unleashed a hailstorm of bullets into the flock, but the birds moved like shadows—fast and nearly impossible to hit.

Fisher's voice was frantic through the com. "Fall back! Now!"

Guerera didn't hesitate. She grabbed Ashley, pulling her from under the car. "We've gotta go. Now."

The girl didn't argue, her small hand gripping Guerera's tightly. They sprinted toward the Humvee, the sound of flapping wings and screeching birds growing louder. Then came the growl—a deep, menacing rumble that froze them in place.

A leopard, sleek and powerful, blocked their path. Its eyes gleamed with hunger, blood dripping from its teeth.

But Fisher was already there. He didn't give the beast a chance. One clean shot to the head, and it collapsed in a heap.

"Move!" Jackson's voice rang out from the Humvee as he swung his rifle like a bat, knocking birds to the ground—only to watch in horror as they crawled toward him, broken but still hungry.

Guerera shoved Ashley into the vehicle and climbed in after her. Fisher and Jackson followed, slamming their doors in unison. Inside, the soldiers sat in stunned silence, their bodies trembling from a mixture of adrenaline and fear.

Ashley's voice, small and fragile, broke the silence. "Are we safe now?"

The howls of the dead rose in the distance, answering her question with chilling finality.

CHAPTER 25

The black sky was beginning to bleed into gray, with a faint, bruised hint of purple hovering over the San Jacinto Mountains as Samuel groggily came to. His head throbbed, a dull ache that exploded into dizzying pain when he tried to move. Slowly, disoriented, he turned his head, gripping the edge of the seat to steady himself. The world outside the van hadn't changed—if anything, it had only grown worse. The nightmare was still alive, and it was rapidly closing in.

Kelvin's body lay crumpled on the floor, his lifeless form surrounded by a thick, dark pool of blood, glistening under the weak morning light. It spread out beneath him, seeping into every crevice of the van, its coppery stench filling the air. Andrea was slumped over the seat, her head hanging limply, strands of her hair brushing the blood-streaked floor.

Clause was gone—vanished without a trace—and that filled Samuel with a cold, gnawing dread almost as much as seeing Kelvin's unmoving form. His heart raced. With shaky hands, he reached for his coat pockets. Empty. Clause had taken the samples. *Of course he had.*

A sharp pain jolted him back to the present. He winced, bringing his hand to his right temple. Warm, sticky blood clung to his fingers, its metallic scent mixing with the dirt and sweat on his skin. The dizziness began to fade, replaced by the raw sting of his head wound.

Movement stirred beside him. Samuel twisted precariously around just in time to see Andrea stirring, her eyes fluttering open. She sat up slowly, groggy, her face pale. "What... what happened?" she asked, her voice thick with confusion.

"We crashed," Samuel replied, his voice rough. "We were hit by another car at the intersection."

Andrea rubbed her head, blinking against the rising light. "How long have we been out?"

"About an hour, by the looks of it." Samuel's eyes drifted down to Kelvin's body.

Andrea followed his gaze. Panic immediately seized her. "Is he—?"

Samuel didn't need to check. The stillness of Kelvin's body told him everything. But out of duty, or perhaps denial, he reached down and pressed his fingers to Kelvin's neck. The skin was cold, the pulse absent. Samuel shook his head, a heaviness settling into his bones.

Andrea choked back a sob, her hands shaking as she gripped the seat for support. "And... what about Clause?"

"I don't know." Samuel's voice was tight. "He was gone when I came to. Took my samples with him."

Andrea's breathing quickened. Her voice cracked with fear. "You mean we're alone? Samuel, what are we going to do?"

"Listen to me," Samuel said, forcing his voice to stay calm, though the pounding in his head made it difficult. "We're going to figure this out. I'll call Leonard, update him on the situation. Maybe he can send help."

Andrea nodded, her eyes fixed on Kelvin's body, as if looking anywhere else would make the situation worse. The sight of their fallen comrade weighed on both of them, but there was no time for grief.

Samuel turned back toward the front of the van, his fingers trembling as he fumbled for his phone. The screen flickered to life, showing several missed calls from NASA. Ignoring them for now, he scrolled through his contacts until he found Dr. Leonard's private number. His fingers hesitated for a moment before he pressed dial.

Leonard picked up almost immediately, his voice thick with concern. "Samuel! Thank God, you're okay. We've been trying to reach you for nearly an hour."

Samuel clenched his jaw, his chest tightening. "Far from okay, Pat. We've lost Kelvin and Simon. And Clause is missing."

There was a pause on the other end, a silence heavy with disbelief. "What do you mean, 'lost'?"

Samuel swallowed hard, the words catching in his throat. He had known these men for years, shared missions, risks, and laughter with them. Now they were gone, and it hardly felt real. "They're dead, Pat," he said quietly, the weight of the words sinking in.

Leonard's sharp breath crackled through the line. "My God. What happened?"

"We don't have time to get into it," Samuel replied, his voice strained. "Things have gone to hell fast, and it's only getting worse."

Leonard's voice steadied. "Tell me what you need."

"We need reinforcements, and I need the address of Subject Zero—the one who made first contact with the meteor."

"There should be a Marine squad already on-site. Haven't they arrived?"

Samuel's gut twisted. "No sign of them. What about the

local police?"

"We lost contact with them a long time ago. It's been chaos over here."

"Shit." Samuel's mind raced. "Alright, give me the address."

Leonard rattled off the details, and Samuel scrawled them down. "The police checked in on him earlier, but that was right before the lines went dark."

"Let's hope he still has something we can use," Samuel muttered. "Clause took my specimens when he bailed. Where's the nearest lab I can work with?"

Leonard paused for a moment, and then said, "There's an Eisenhower Medical facility off 111 near Washington. I'll call ahead and have them prepped for your arrival, if I can get through, that is."

"Thanks, Pat," Samuel said. Then, before he hung up, he added, "One more thing. Be careful what you say. It looks like your employee named Darcey is working with Ashton."

Leonard's breath hitched. "What—"

Samuel didn't wait for a response. He ended the call, a sinking feeling in his gut, knowing they were walking a razor-thin line between survival and disaster.

****

Leonard slammed his phone into its case, fuming as he stood from his desk. Rage coursed through him, not just at Darcey but at himself for falling for her lies. Her long legs, charming smile, and air of innocence had been her weapons, and he'd allowed them to work. He clenched his fists, feeling the bitterness of betrayal creep up his spine.

He took a deep breath, trying to regain control. Now wasn't the time for an outburst. He needed to handle this quietly. If Darcey even suspected that he knew the truth, she'd bolt, and there was no telling what kind of damage she could cause in the process. Ashton's reach was already too close.

Leonard adjusted his tie, steeling himself, and walked out of his office with feigned calmness. He made his way down the hall, ignoring the tightening in his gut. As he walked, he recalled every interaction he'd had with Darcey since she'd been hired a few months ago. She had been too perfect, too sweet, and too eager to help. Now, the whole operation was compromised because he'd been too blind to see it.

He entered the control room, his eyes scanning the rows of workstations. His stomach dropped when he saw her station empty chair. She was gone.

"Where's Darcey?" Leonard's voice was too sharp as he turned to Justin, who was hunched over his own console, headphones halfway on.

Justin, without lifting his head, shrugged. "She said she was taking a break about twenty minutes ago. Haven't seen her since."

Leonard's pulse quickened. She was already far enough ahead to evade him. He cursed under his breath, turning abruptly and stalking back toward his office, leaving Justin staring after him in confusion.

***

Darcey moved swiftly down the dim corridor leading to the back exit. To any observer, she was just an employee taking a routine break. She resisted the urge to glance over her shoulder, knowing full well that suspicion would make her stand out. Her heart raced, but her face remained calm.

She slipped through a side door that led to an isolated

hallway, her footsteps quickening once she was out of sight. She couldn't shake the feeling that Leonard had started piecing things together. She'd seen the way he had looked at her earlier—too thoughtful, too guarded. He was no fool, and if he was on to her, Ashton wouldn't tolerate any missteps. She needed to leave, fast.

Darcey made it to the staff exit, a sharp gust of wind hitting her face as she stepped outside. A sleek black car idled at the far end of the parking lot, lights off, barely noticeable in the pre-dawn gloom. She hurried toward it. As she neared, the passenger door opened just enough for her to slip inside.

The driver was a man she knew only as Cole, one of Ashton's best operatives. He gave her a quick nod as she shut the door behind her. Without a word, the car pulled away from the facility, blending into the shadowed streets.

Darcey exhaled, her heart slowly returning to a steady rhythm. She'd escaped, but the game was far from over. Now it was up to Ashton to finish what they had started. As they sped away, Darcey glanced back at the facility, her lips curling into a small, satisfied smile. Leonard had never seen it coming.

***

While Samuel spoke with Leonard, Andrea rummaged through the back of the van, her hands trembling as she searched for something—anything—that could provide some sense of order in the chaos. Her fingers brushed against a large, rough material, and with a sinking heart, she pulled out a black tarp. She hesitated for a moment, glancing at Kelvin's still, bloodied form on the floor. She knew what she had to do, but covering him felt like the ultimate betrayal, like erasing his presence from the world. Gritting her teeth, she draped the tarp over his body. Out of sight didn't mean out of mind, though. The image of his lifeless face lingered like a ghost in the van, and she knew going forward it would forever haunt her thoughts, however brief they may be.

As she stood there, the silence pressed in, broken only by Samuel's low voice. When he finally hung up, Andrea's gaze darted to him, desperate for reassurance that never seemed to come. "What did Leonard say?" she asked weakly.

Samuel took a long, shaky breath. How could he tell her the truth? That they were fucked, stranded in a city overrun by undead creatures? That the Marines hadn't shown up, the police were MIA, and their one chance at stopping this nightmare had disappeared when Clause had run off with their only research samples? And worst of all, Ashton was playing them all in some twisted savage apocalyptic game.

He ran a hand through his hair, trying to steady his thoughts. "Leonard gave me the address of the subject who had first contact with the meteor. There's a chance we can gather new samples there. He's also contacting a medical center nearby to get us access to their labs."

Andrea's eyes widened. "But that means we have to go out there, where those... things are waiting for us!"

Samuel pulled out his phone and punched the address into the GPS, praying it wasn't too far. A brief glimmer of relief crossed his face as the map displayed it a quarter mile away. But given the current nightmare they were in, it might as well have been a hundred miles. "His house is only a short distance from here. If we move fast, we can probably be there in fifteen minutes."

Andrea's face paled. "I—I don't know, Samuel. What if the creature's find us? Maybe we should stay here and wait for help. We're safer in the van."

Samuel turned to her, trying hard to disguise his own fear.

"Andrea, we don't know if help's coming. And even if it does, this thing—whatever it is—it's spreading like wildfire. We can't just sit here. If we wait too long, there might not be anything left to save."

She opened her mouth to argue, but stopped, chewing on her bottom lip. He was right. She hated that he was right. Finally, she nodded, though her fear was evident in the way her hands trembled at her sides. "Okay. But if we run into any crazed monsters, you're first on the menu."

Samuel managed a weak chuckle. "Fair enough." But he wasn't laughing. He knew the danger they were walking into. He turned his attention back to Kelvin's lifeless form under the tarp and kneeled down beside him, his hand reaching into Kelvin's pants pocket.

Andrea watched, her brow furrowing. "What are you doing?"

Samuel's fingers fumbled through the fabric until he found what he was looking for. He pulled out a long, well-worn pocket knife and flicked open the four-inch blade. "Kelvin carried this everywhere. Said it was a gift from his grandfather." He stared at the knife for a moment, the weight of its history pressing down on him. "It's not much, but it's better than nothing."

They both climbed out of the van, moving cautiously, each step deliberate. The world around them was eerily quiet, too quiet. The city, once full of life, now felt like a hushed tomb. The sky, which had been a deep purple moments ago, had shifted into a violent burst of red and orange as the sun began its slow rise. It painted the deserted streets in a blood-soaked glow, as if the sky itself was bleeding.

Samuel's grip tightened around the knife, his heart pounding in his chest. Every shadow, every rustle of the wind, felt like a threat lurking just out of sight. They walked in tense silence, their senses on high alert, knowing that at any moment, something could lunge at them from any direction.

"I hate this," Andrea whispered, her voice barely audible over the pounding in her ears. "I hate everything about this."

"Me too," Samuel muttered. His eyes scanned the street ahead, the crumbling remains of civilization casting long, jagged shadows. He could only hope the day would be kinder than the night had been.

But deep down, he knew hope was a luxury they couldn't afford anymore.

CHAPTER 26

Tommy woke with a start, his head throbbing like someone had driven nails into his temples. A dull ache spread through his skull, growing worse with every second he tried to move. It was like his brain was too big for his head, swelling and pressing against the bone, threatening to burst. His stomach churned, a deep, twisting pain, as though someone had tied his insides in knots and yanked them tight. He groaned, turning on his side, and for a split second thought he was going to puke right there in bed.

The room spun as he forced himself to sit up, sheets tangling around his legs like dead weight. The air was thick, humid, with a strange scent clinging to it—something sour, metallic, decaying. He sat there for a moment, head in his hands, trying to steady the pounding. His breath came in shallow gasps, his body drenched in a cold sweat.

What is wrong with me? Is this because of the meteor last night? Am I changing into some kind of alien monster?

Slowly, Tommy shook the thoughts from his head and pushed himself out of bed, his legs wobbling like they didn't belong to him. The floor seemed farther away than usual, like he was floating in some strange, twisted version of his bedroom. He tried to steady himself, gripping the edge of the nightstand for support. His mind flashed back to the night before—the meteor, the strange goo that had dripped from the sky. That inky black substance that had coated his skin, clinging to him like tar.

God, is it still inside me?

A wave of nausea hit him, harder this time, and he lurched toward the bathroom, barely making it in time. He leaned over the toilet, waiting for the bile to rise, but nothing came. His stomach twisted again, though, the pain stabbing deep into his gut. Sweat dripped from his forehead, stinging his eyes, and he wiped it away with the back of his hand, panting.

As he stood there, something caught his eye. He glanced toward the bathtub, where a towel lay crumpled in a heap by the drain. But now, the towel wasn't just a towel anymore. It was smeared with patches of black—inky, oily stains.

His mind raced, spiraling into a thousand dark places. Images of his own body mutating flashed before his eyes— extra limbs sprouting from his torso, skin bubbling and splitting open to reveal slick, alien appendages. A scorpion tail curling up from his spine, poised to strike.

He shook his head hard, trying to clear the horrific visions. *Don't be stupid, Tommy. It's just a towel.* But the thought of that alien goo coursing through his veins gnawed at him. He had to be infected. There was no other explanation for the way he felt. His gut twisted again, and for a moment, he thought his insides might rip apart right there.

He quickly flushed the toilet and staggered out of the bathroom, gripping the walls for balance. He needed fresh air. But before he made it to the front door, he almost ran straight into Kate.

She stood in the hallway, her small frame bathed in the faint morning light that leaked through the windows. Her face was pale, her eyes wide, pupils dilated as if she hadn't slept at all.

"What are you doing up so early?" Tommy asked, his voice hoarse, rough like sandpaper.

Kate blinked at him. "I couldn't sleep." Her voice was soft. "I kept having these bad dreams... about monsters and aliens. And Dad snores like crazy."

Tommy forced a laugh. "Yeah, he does that, doesn't he?"

But Kate wasn't laughing. She stared at him, her eyes flicking across his face, studying him like she didn't recognize him. "How do you feel?"

Tommy hesitated, rubbing his aching temples. "I dunno... my head's killing me. And my stomach feels weird."

Kate bit her lip. "Do you feel anything else? Like... like something's wrong inside you?"

Her words sent a chill racing down his spine. *Like something's wrong inside you.* The image of his body splitting open, of that alien goo crawling through his veins, flashed back into his mind. His heart skipped a beat, and he quickly shook the thought away. "No. Why?"

She shrugged, glancing at the floor. "I dunno... That space goo from last night. You were covered in it. What if it's, like, doing something to you?"

Tommy felt his pulse quicken again, the fear creeping up his throat like bile. He forced a smile. "Nah. I'm fine. It's probably just the flu or something."

Before Kate could respond, a low, mournful howl echoed from somewhere outside. Both of them froze.

Kate shivered. "That sounds... spooky."

Tommy nodded, the knot in his stomach tightening. "We need to check on King!" he said quickly.

Immediately, Tommy ran for the front door, with Kate close behind. The howls were louder now, a chorus of them echoing across the desert. His hand shook as he grabbed the doorknob and flung it open.

A wave of stench hit him like a brick wall—thick, sour, and rotten, like something long dead and festering in the sun. He gagged, covering his nose with his sleeve. "What the hell is that smell?"

Kate coughed, her eyes watering. "It smells like Grandpa's chili night, but worse."

Tommy tried to laugh, but the stench was overpowering. And then, through the haze of rot and decay, he saw movement at the edge of the yard.

"King!" he shouted in relief.

The dog was there, limping toward them, but something was wrong. Tommy's heart dropped as the details came into focus. King's fur was matted with blood—dark, wet patches that glistened in the faint light. His body was torn open in multiple places, skin hanging in ragged strips. His left front leg dangled uselessly, barely attached to his body.

But worst of all were his eyes.

They weren't King's eyes anymore. They were black and hollow, filled with a seething rage that chilled Tommy to the core. There was no recognition in them, no spark of life. Just... hate.

"What's wrong with him?" Kate asked, her voice trembling.

Tommy swallowed hard, trying to keep his voice steady. "He... he just got into a fight, is all. Just don't move, okay? He's scared."

But it wasn't fear in King's eyes. It was something far worse. He let out a low, guttural growl, his lips curling back to reveal bloodstained teeth. Tommy's pulse raced as the dog's gaze locked onto him, the growl growing louder.

Kate took a step forward, her hand outstretched. "Come here, boy. It's okay. We'll help you—"

Before Tommy could react, King lunged.

A blur of teeth and claws, a snarling mass of fury, and then Kate was on the ground, screaming as King tore into her, his jaws snapping at her face.

"No! King, NO!" Tommy screamed as he hurled himself at the dog, slamming into him with all the strength he had.

They hit the ground hard, Tommy's shoulder smashing into the dirt. King scrambled to his feet, blood dripping from his mouth, his black eyes filled with hatred. He snarled, teeth bared, ready to pounce again.

Tommy stood frozen, his heart hammering in his chest. But before King could lunge again, a deafening gunshot rang out, echoing through the desert morning. King's body crumpled to the ground, motionless.

Tommy spun around and saw his dad standing on the porch with his shotgun still raised, smoke curling from the barrel.

"Dad..." Tommy whispered, but his voice was drowned out by his mom's scream.

She rushed past him, dropping to her knees beside Kate, who lay unmoving in the dirt. "Oh my God, Kate!" she sobbed, frantically checking her daughter's wounds.

Tommy collapsed beside them, tears streaming down his face. Kate's arm was shredded, deep gashes running down her flesh, and her face was scratched, streaked with blood. He stared at her, guilt washing over him in waves. He thought of all the times he'd teased her, all the dumb fights they'd had. Now, all he could think was, *Please, don't die. Please, be okay.*

"Is she gonna be okay?" he asked, his voice barely a whisper.

Melinda's lips trembled. "I don't know."

William rushed down from the porch to join them, dropping his shotgun on the ground. He was just about to check her pulse when she bolted upright and let out a terrible scream. When she realized where she was, she collapsed into their mom's arms, sobbing uncontrollably.

Melinda held her tight, rocking her gently to calm her down. "It's okay, sweetie. Everything's over now."

Kate sobbed, "But King—"

"I know. You're safe now."

Kate turned her head so she could see. Blood was smeared on the side of her face, causing thick strands of hair to stick to her skin. After a minute, her crying calmed to a whimper. She closed her eyes tight in an attempt to forget the nightmare she had just seen.

But when she opened them again the nightmare was alive and stronger than ever. King—bloodied, mangled King—was back on his feet, growling, his black, hate-filled eyes fixed on them once more.

Kate tried to scream again, but when she opened her mouth only a gargled noise came out. Melinda tried to calm her down again, assuring her that the threat was over. Then she heard the horrible growl behind her and her body stiffened.

William heard it too, his mind racing with the idea that there was no way King should still be alive. His shot had hit the dog squarely in the chest and should have killed him instantly. A terrible thought came to him about the Last Days. Maybe the dead that the Book of Revelations foretold actually walked on four legs instead of two?

He quickly reached behind him for his shotgun, but found a handful of grass instead. Then he heard another shot ring out, and this time King fell to the ground and stayed there.

Tommy's head whipped around to see a middle-aged man with his dad's shotgun in his hands and a grim expression on his face. A woman stood nervously behind him, trying unsuccessfully to appear strong.

"You've got to hit them in the head," the man said, his voice calm, too calm. "It's the only way to keep them down."

William yanked his gun back from the man's grip, eyes narrowing. "And you are?"

The man raised his hands in a gesture of surrender, then cleared his throat. "Sorry. My name is Samuel Greenburg. I'm the head of the Space Biosciences Division at NASA's Ames Research Facility." His voice was clipped, urgent, as though they didn't have the luxury of time. He extended his hand, but William hesitated for a moment before grasping it firmly.

William's brow furrowed as the weight of the situation began to settle. "This has something to do with the meteor last night, doesn't it?"

Samuel's eyes locked with his, tense and unblinking. "Yes, it does. And if I'm not mistaken, you're William Patterson?"

William nodded, unease settling deeper into his gut.

Samuel glanced over William's shoulder at Tommy, whose face was pale and streaked with sweat. "And this is your son, Tommy?"

Another nod. William didn't trust himself to speak. The air between them felt thick, like the silence carried an unspeakable truth.

Samuel wasted no time. "Good. We don't have much time. The situation is growing more desperate by the minute. Can we go inside? The gunshots... they're bound to attract more of them."

The word "them" hit William like a cold slap. He didn't want to ask. He wasn't sure he could handle the answer. Instead, he nodded once more, pushing open the door. His mind was racing, thoughts tumbling over each other like a violent storm, each one darker than the last. What was happening to them?

As soon as they stepped inside, the door barely latched when Kate collapsed to the floor, convulsing violently.

"Kate!" William shouted, dropping to his knees. Melinda was already there, trying to keep Kate's arms pinned so she wouldn't hurt herself, her face a mask of desperation and terror.

"Hold on, baby. Just hold on," Melinda whispered, her voice breaking, eyes wide with fear as Kate's body jerked uncontrollably on the cold wooden floor.

Seconds dragged like hours before the seizure finally subsided, leaving Kate limp, her tiny chest heaving with shallow, ragged breaths. For a brief, hopeful moment, Melinda's shoulders relaxed, but then her breath caught in her throat as thick, black liquid oozed from Kate's mouth. It glistened in the dim light, like tar, pooling at the corners of her lips and dripping slowly down her chin.

"Oh, God," Melinda gasped, her voice barely above a whisper. "No... no, no."

Samuel stepped forward, his expression turning grim. "Quick! We need a sample. Now."

Andrea, who had been standing in the background like a shadow, swiftly dropped to her knees beside Kate. She fumbled inside her coat and pulled out a small vial. With practiced precision, she held it beneath Kate's chin, catching the slow, thick drip of the black substance. The liquid hit the glass with a sickening splat, sliding down the sides like a thread of glistening slime.

Halfway through filling the vial, Andrea's face twisted with alarm. "It's... moving," she whispered, yanking the vial back and clamping a stopper on it.

"What's wrong?" Samuel asked, eyes darting between the vial and Kate's unconscious body.

Andrea's voice trembled slightly, despite her effort to stay calm. "Whatever this stuff is, it's alive. It's like it's trying to break free."

William stood up and looked at them in confusion. "What the hell are you talking about?"

Samuel's gaze shifted, his expression darkening as if the implications of this revelation had just dawned on him. "I thought we were dealing with a viral outbreak... but this..." He paused, studying the black ooze as it wriggled within the glass. "This is more like a parasite. A living organism, one capable of replicating itself—fast."

William felt the ground shift beneath him. "A parasite? Are you saying this thing is inside my daughter?"

Before Samuel could respond, a soft moan came from Kate.

Melinda held her in her lap, brushing damp hair from her forehead. "Kate? Sweetie, can you hear me?"

Kate's voice was a weak whisper, barely audible. "Mommy... my head hurts... and my arm too."

"I know, dear," Melinda said, stroking her daughter's cheek with trembling fingers. "Let's get you cleaned up, okay? We'll take care of those wounds."

Kate nodded weakly, her small frame shivering. Then, as Melinda helped her to her feet, Kate turned and looked up with wide, terrified eyes. "Mommy?"

"Yes, dear?"

"Is King dead now?"

The question cut through the room like a knife. Melinda's face tightened, her lips pressing into a thin line. She didn't want to answer, didn't want to face the reality of it. But how could she lie to her daughter in this moment? "Yes," she finally whispered, her voice breaking. "King's dead."

For a moment, Kate said nothing, her eyes glazed over as if trying to process what that meant. Then, in a small, trembling voice, she asked, "Is the same thing going to happen to us?"

Melinda blinked, taken aback. "What? What do you mean?"

"The black goo," Kate mumbled. "It turned King into a monster. Now Tommy, Daddy, and me... we're all 'fected, aren't we?"

Melinda's heart broke. "No, baby, no." She pulled Kate into her arms, holding her close, trying to smother the trembling that had overtaken her own body. "You're not turning into a monster. None of you are. I won't let anything happen to you. I promise."

But as she scooped Kate up and carried her out of the room, she threw a glance over her shoulder at William. A look filled with fear—fear that her promise, no matter how much she wanted it to be true, might be impossible to keep.

CHAPTER 27

At first, Clause had seethed with rage. He was furious at the idiot who had run the red light, barreling through the intersection like his life meant nothing. Furious at Ashton, whose terrible planning had led him to this disastrous mission. Furious at Samuel, that slippery bastard, for swiping his phone and throwing everything off balance. But mostly, Clause was furious at himself—at his arrogance, his miscalculation, his assumption that this whole mess would go down smoothly.

As he sat there, trying to regain his composure while reliving the impact, something shifted. His anger faded, replaced by the cold, calculating realization that maybe—just maybe—the crash had been a stroke of luck. A dark smile tugged at the corner of his mouth. His instincts, honed over years of survival in this grim world, had kicked in at the exact right moment. He'd managed to escape the wreck virtually without a scratch.

He looked around the cabin and saw with sadistic delight that Samuel and Andrea had both been knocked unconscious from the impact, while the blood pooling around Kelvin's head indicated that he hadn't been so lucky. Carefully, he reached over and pulled the vials from Samuel's coat, before he slipped outside and crept toward the back of the van. As luck would have it, the rear door stood ajar, inviting him to take what was his, anyway.

Sliding the small vials into the inside pocket of his jacket, Clause hefted the large case from the back of the van. Its weight was reassuring in his hands, solid, real. He glanced back at the wreckage once, making sure no one had seen him, and then vanished into the shadows, finally free of the pathetic group.

A hundred yards down Madison Street, Clause spotted his new ride: a sleek, black BMW X3 SUV with Canadian plates, sitting like a prize waiting to be claimed. Next to the vehicle, the owner—a 'Snowbird' from up north—lay sprawled in a heap. The shredded remains barely resembled anything human, a mangled lump of blood and sinew torn apart by something feral. The sight didn't even make Clause flinch.

"Poor bastard," he muttered under his breath, climbing into the driver's seat. The interior still smelled faintly of leather, untouched by the carnage outside. As he turned the key, the engine purred to life—a comforting sound in a world gone mad. The gas gauge read half a tank. "More than enough," he mumbled.

He buckled himself in before dialing Ashton's number. The line clicked, and Ashton's cool voice crackled through the speaker.

"What the hell happened, Clause?"

Clause took a deep breath, hiding his disdain. "Had a little accident. Some moron ran a light. Van's totaled, but the specimens are safe."

There was a pause on the other end, and then Ashton's sigh of relief was unmistakable. "Good. Don't lose them."

Clause clenched his jaw as he ended the call. "What a

dick," he muttered, tossing the phone onto the passenger seat. He hated Ashton's smug, self-assured tone, hated the way the guy treated him like some disposable asset. But money was money, and Ashton was paying well—too well to walk away from. And, it gave Clause the excuse he needed to stay close to his sister, to protect her from the chaos Ashton had unleashed.

He shifted into gear, pulling away from the curb. The roads were eerily quiet, almost desolate. Clause knew these streets—he had worked private security in La Quinta for a couple of years after the Marines, and this area was as familiar as the back of his hand. His plan was simple: stay on Madison for a few miles, catch Highway 111, and get the hell out of this nightmare.

But as he approached Avenue 54, Clause's breath caught in his throat. The intersection was choked with movement— hundreds of undead animals, a writhing mass of fur and teeth, all surging northward like a plague. They moved as one, a grotesque tide of death. And above them, like a dark cloud, was the unmistakable buzz of the insect swarm, leading the charge.

Clause slowed the car to a crawl, hoping to slip past the horde unnoticed. For a moment, it seemed to be working— until a mangled coyote, half its face hanging off in strips, turned its rotting eyes toward him. It let out a blood-curdling howl, a sound straight out of a nightmare, and in an instant, the horde surged toward him like a wave of hungry mouths.

"Shit!" Clause slammed the gas pedal down and the BMW roared to life, tearing down Avenue 54 as the swarm of creatures gave chase. He swerved, dodging abandoned cars and debris, glancing in the rear-view mirror. Even though they were falling behind, their twisted, broken bodies too slow to keep up, he knew better than to let his guard down.

He knew the beasts would be relentless.

Finally, he hit Jefferson Street and floored it, racing toward Highway 111. As the sun began to creep over the mountains in the east, he got his first real look at the world in the daylight—a world forever changed by the savage apocalypse that had been unleashed by the otherworldly meteor crash. Bodies littered the road like discarded trash, some still twitching as undead animals feasted on them. Dogs, coyotes, even cats—all twisted into ravenous creatures of death. A cougar-sized beast ripped into a carcass with such fury that it barely noticed the car until Clause swerved to avoid it. Its head snapped up, eyes gleaming with hunger as it let out a snarl that echoed in his bones.

Clause kept his speed just fast enough to stay out of reach but slow enough not to attract more attention. The road was a minefield of bodies, twisted metal, and the occasional undead beast. As he passed the Indian Wells Tennis Garden, something massive slammed into the side of the SUV, sending it spinning wildly across the lanes. Metal screamed, rubber burned, and the car lurched into the median with a violent crash.

Dazed from the impact, Clause fought feverishly to regain control of the vehicle, his fingers tightening on the wheel. He glanced in the rear-view mirror, expecting to see a truck or another car spinning likewise out of control. Instead, what he saw sent a chill down his spine.

Charging toward him was a black horse, or at least what used to be a horse. Its flesh hung in tatters, the muscle and bone of its left side exposed like something out of a slaughterhouse. Its mane was nothing but a tangled mess of stiff, matted hair, its eyes glowing with an unnatural fury. It was a creature straight from hell, a nightmarish beast that looked like it had risen from the depths of Satan's own stable.

"Holy fuck!" Clause stomped on the gas, weaving through the wreckage as the horse charged again. He couldn't afford another hit—if that thousand-pound beast struck the SUV again, he'd be done for.

The beat of the undead horse's hooves pounded in his ears as the sun continued its slow crawl over a world that would never be the same again. A score of undead beasts nearby, drawn by the sound, turned their twisted, hungry heads in unison. Clause glimpsed them in the rear-view mirror—mangled, slavering, racing to close the distance—but he pressed harder on the gas.

Even in their frenzied state, the creatures were too slow, their decaying bodies no match for the car's power. Clause allowed himself a fleeting smile. For a brief moment, he felt invincible, like nothing in this hellish world could touch him. He was faster, smarter—better than the evil closing in around him.

The road ahead was clear, untouched by the carnage that had swallowed everything else. Clause thought maybe, just maybe, he had outrun the threat. The miles of devastation and death faded in the rear-view, replaced by a slim hope that he'd escaped.

But as he neared the intersection at Portola, his optimism shattered.

The road ahead was a war zone. Cars piled on top of each other in a snarled wreck of twisted metal and broken glass. People ran screaming, their faces masks of terror, chased by the nightmare beasts that hunted them. The creatures moved with terrifying efficiency, cutting down their prey like sickle through wheat. Clause slowed, eyes scanning the carnage. His hands tightened on the wheel, the pulse in his ears quickening.

Calmly, almost too calmly, Clause pulled to the side of the

road, sinking low in his seat. From here, he could watch undetected. He was no stranger to death, but the savagery of what he saw gnawed at something deep inside. A young woman screamed, her voice cutting through the chaos like a knife. An undead Akita, its fur matted with dried blood, leaped at her, its jaws snapping shut with a sickening crunch as it tore through her neck. The head came off clean, rolling across the pavement while the body collapsed in a twitching heap. The beast was on her before the corpse hit the ground, ripping and tearing, sending splatters of blood across the asphalt.

Everywhere Clause looked, the same brutal scene played out—people reduced to meat, torn apart by the maddened creatures in a savage morning massacre.

And then, as if on some unspoken command, the beasts paused. Their heads snapped up, ears twitching, listening to something only they could hear. For a second, the street went unnervingly still. Then, a collective howl rose from the throats of the creatures—a bone-chilling sound that sent a shiver down Clause's spine. In unison, they turned and raced down Highway 111, heading toward Palm Desert like a tide of death.

Clause leaned back in his seat, intrigued. There was something about their synchronized behavior, a chilling intelligence guiding them. He decided to follow, keeping a safe distance, of course. Whatever had triggered that reaction, he wanted to see it for himself.

Half a mile down the road, the source of the excitement came into view. A squadron of Marines was holding the line at the intersection of Monterey and 111, their guns blazing, a hailstorm of bullets raining down on the horde. Clause pulled his car to a stop in the middle of the street, watching the battle unfold. A wicked smile crept across his face. Bravo

Squad, he thought. That meant Fisher was down there, and if Fisher was fighting those things, maybe—just maybe—Clause would get to see the bastard torn apart.

Fisher had been the reason Clause was no longer a Marine. Him, and that bitch, Guerera. The thought of them both dying here, in this hellhole, brought a sick sense of satisfaction. Clause's grin widened as he considered the possibility of taking their bodies back to Ashton, handing them over for his twisted experiments. The ADAR Initiative didn't care about ethics—anything in the name of science, anything to learn more about the alien menace. Fisher and Guerera would make fine specimens.

As Clause sat there, waiting for the inevitable carnage, the fight on the ground intensified. The Marines were focused on the undead swarming around them, unaware of the death descending from above. A dark mass of crows—huge, rotting things—swooped down on rotting wings, their talons slashing through flesh and bone. The first soldier went down in a spray of sparks as his head slammed into the spotlight of the second Humvee. The light flickered wildly before cutting out, casting strange, twitching shadows over the battlefield.

Clause's eyes narrowed as two Marines dragged a little girl from beneath a wrecked car. The light flicker caught one of the soldiers' attention, and when they turned, Clause's heart lurched. *Guerera!* She was right there, close enough to kill if he wanted to. Every muscle in his body screamed for him to pull the gun from his belt, to end her life right here, right now. But something held him back—a tiny shred of control.

He gripped the steering wheel tighter, white-knuckled, forcing himself to stay focused. There was a job to do. Guerera would have to wait.

But when a rotting leopard streaked across the battlefield, aiming straight for her, Clause's mouth went dry. He watched with gleeful anticipation as the feline closed in on its prey. He could already see Guerera's blood spilling across the pavement. And then, to his disappointment, a shot rang out, dropping the cat just inches from her feet.

Clause's heart sank, his moment of triumph stolen. He waited, hoping the creature would rise again, that it would finish the job. But it stayed dead, its body motionless on the ground.

Frustration boiled over, and Clause slammed his fist into the steering wheel, a move he instantly regretted. The sound caught the attention of the crows overhead. A split second later, they descended on his car like missiles, their rotting bodies smashing into the roof and the windshield, clawing and screeching as they tried to get inside. He could see them up close—their hollow eyes, their twisted beaks scraping against the glass. Clause knew he had seconds before they broke through.

He slammed the car into gear and tore down the street, weaving through the wreckage, narrowly avoiding bodies and abandoned vehicles. The crows screeched in pursuit, but he managed to break free.

As he neared the first Humvee, Clause's eyes locked with Guerera's. His stare was ice-cold, filled with a hatred that burned deep. She looked back, unaware of the dark thoughts running through his mind. One day, he promised himself. One day, she'd pay.

The second Humvee sat motionless in the middle of the road, which struck Clause as odd. When he drew closer, the reason became evident. The Marines inside were dead, their bodies torn apart by the same fate that had befallen so many others. He recognized one of them—Stephen Madison, a cocky young recruit from back in the day. Now, he was nothing more than a meal for two rotting dogs.

Twenty yards away, the second soldier lay face down, convulsing violently.

Without thinking, Clause swerved next to the man, threw open the rear hatch, and jumped out. He had seconds, maybe less, before the horde was on him. He grabbed the soldier, slinging him over his shoulder in a fireman's carry, and threw him into the back of the SUV.

As Clause reached for the door, a low growl rumbled from the front of the car. He turned, eyes widening as a black jaguar—its face half-chewed, one eye missing—rounded the hood.

With lightning speed, Clause pulled the gun from his waist and fired, the bullet finding the creature's remaining eye. The cat dropped dead at his feet.

As his adrenaline surged, Clause leaped into the car and sped away, the rear tires kicking up gravel as he fled down 111. In the rear-view mirror, he could just make out the writhing mass of undead, moving relentlessly toward Palm Desert. A wave of death for anyone still left alive.

CHAPTER 28

Guerera slammed the Humvee door shut, her hands shaking as she turned to check on Ashley, who was huddled tightly into herself on the back seat. "Are you okay, Sweetie?"

The little girl nodded, her lips pressed together tightly, fighting back tears with a bravery that seemed out of place in someone so young.

Guerera's eyes flicked to Fisher. His jaw was set, his expression hard. She knew he didn't like having the girl with them—it was an unnecessary risk, and Fisher was a man of strategy. But what was she supposed to do? Leave a child behind to be torn apart by those monsters? Not a chance.

Suddenly, it hit her—Madison and Thomas. They were still out there, in the chaos! Without thinking, she reached for the door handle, ready to jump out and run back into the fray.

Fisher's hand clamped around her arm, yanking her back into the seat with surprising force. "Where do you think you're going?"

"Madison and Thomas!" Guerera's voice was desperate. "We have to get them!"

Fisher clenched his jaw, visibly struggling to keep his emotions in check. He hadn't expected to lose anyone, not like this, not so soon. The anger was rising inside him like a storm, threatening to pull him under. But he knew if he lost control now, they'd all be dead before sunrise. "They're gone, Guerera. We can't do anything for them now."

Guerera froze. She had seen Bryant go down, but everything had been happening so fast, so violently, she hadn't noticed Madison and Thomas fall. Her throat tightened, and tears welled in her eyes. "Are you sure?"

Fisher's face softened just enough to show his pain. He nodded, his voice quieter than before. "I saw them go down. There's no coming back from that."

She bit down on her lip, forcing herself not to cry. Madison and Thomas were more than just soldiers—they were family. And now they were gone, just like that, ripped away by the horror surrounding them. She turned away from Fisher, her eyes staring blankly out the windshield, her mind trying to process the loss.

In the distance, the eerie howls of the undead echoed through the early morning air, their haunting cries carried on the wind as the faint light of dawn began to creep over the horizon.

After what felt like an eternity, Guerera broke the silence. Her voice was low and steady. "Okay, now what?"

Fisher was already on his phone, his face turned away from her as he updated Sergeant Anderson on the situation. His conversation was short, his voice rough around the edges until he spoke the names of the fallen. Then it softened. The weight of each name hung in the air like a death sentence. A moment later, he hung up and turned back to Guerera.

"So?" she asked, her voice carrying a sharp edge.

Fisher's gaze hardened. "We keep moving. Stay on mission. Find those scientists and pray they know how to stop this nightmare before it spreads any further."

Guerera nodded, steeling herself. She wouldn't let the grief consume her, not now. There was too much at stake, and she would make damn sure these hellish creatures would pay for what they'd done. With a deep breath, she shifted the Humvee into drive, her hands steady on the wheel as she pressed forward.

As they cleared the intersection, something caught her eye. She glanced out her window and froze. There, in the opposite lane, was Clause, driving a battered, blood-splattered SUV, heading the other way.

Her heart skipped a beat. *What the hell is he doing here?*

***

Melinda carefully carried Kate into the master bedroom, the weight of the world pressing down on her with every step. Her little girl felt light in her arms, almost too fragile, and as Melinda laid her gently onto the king-size bed, she couldn't help but feel like everything was crumbling around her.

She bent down and kissed Kate's forehead, her lips trembling as they brushed against her daughter's cool skin. "How are you doing, kiddo?" she asked in a soft but strained voice.

Kate whispered weakly, "I'm okay, Mommy. My arm and my face and my head hurts. And I'm sad about King."

Melinda's heart broke all over again. "I know, sweetie. Me too. Try not to think about it right now, okay?"

Melinda stood up and stepped into the bathroom, averting her gaze from the shower stall, where the red stain on the white tile wall seemed to pulse with a haunting presence. It was a grim reminder of the nightmare that had unfolded just hours earlier. She shook the image from her head and forced herself to focus, opening the medicine cabinet and pulling out a tube of antibiotic cream and a box of Band-Aids. She grabbed a washcloth from the drawer beneath the vanity and ran it under cold water, the icy sensation briefly numbing the flood of emotions threatening to overwhelm her.

When she returned to the bedroom, she found Kate's eyelids drooping, her small body struggling to stay awake. Melinda worked quickly to clean the cuts and scratches on her daughter's arm and face. Each swipe of the cloth felt like a futile attempt to wash away not just the dirt, but the horror of what had happened. By the time she secured the last bandage, Kate had drifted into a deep sleep.

Melinda stood there for a moment, watching her daughter's chest rise and fall, trying to gather a sense of calm from the sight, but the storm inside her still raged on. Quietly, she crept out of the room, pulling the door shut behind her with a soft click. When she returned to the living room, the reality of their current situation hit her hard once more. The two scientists were huddled in the corner with grim faces as they talked on the phone in hush, urgent tones. Across the room, Tommy was curled up on the couch, his tear-streaked face buried in his arms.

William entered the room with a cup of coffee in each hand, his expression a mix of exhaustion and worry. He handed her a cup, his fingers briefly brushing hers in a gesture of comfort.

"Thanks," Melinda murmured, taking a sip, though the taste of it barely registered. "How's he holding up?" Her eyes flicked to Tommy, who hadn't moved since she came in.

William sighed. "Not very well. Him and King... they were really close."

Melinda nodded, her throat tightening as more tears threatened to spill. "We all were. King was family." Her voice cracked, and she swallowed hard, her mind racing. "What's happening, William? What in the world is going on?"

Before William could answer, the two scientists approached, their faces filled with uncertainty.

"I think I can explain," Samuel said. "At first, we thought it was a virus—maybe a mutated rabies strain. But now..." He paused, glancing at Andrea before continuing. "Now, we believe it's something far more dangerous. We think it's more like a dynamic, replicating microorganism, probably of alien origin. It seems to attack the brain stem, altering the victim's behavior, turning the infected into something... monstrous."

William grimaced. "That's an understatement," he said sadly.

Samuel's eyes softened with genuine sympathy. "I'm truly sorry for your loss. But we need to act fast. This... thing is spreading quickly."

"What about people?" Melinda asked as she glanced at the couch, her heart crumbling even more as she watched Tommy sobbing softly.

"So far," Andrea said, "we haven't seen any people that have been affected by the organism. Our theory is that human DNA possesses certain traits that makes the alien organism incompatible with a human host."

"Well, that's a little comforting, I guess," Melinda replied. "So, what's the next step? What can we do?"

Samuel took a deep breath. "We need to get to the Eisenhower Medical Center on Highway 111. NASA has already arranged access to their labs. We have to analyze this microorganism, figure out what it is, and find a way to neutralize it."

"Just how big is this threat?" William asked.

Samuel's face darkened. "From what we've observed in the last few hours, the infection has already affected hundreds, maybe even thousands of animals. If we don't move fast, the entire Coachella Valley will soon be overrun."

Andrea, her voice firm, added, "We have to go now, before it's too late. Can you get us to the medical center?"

William's gaze shifted to Melinda. She could see the determination in his eyes, the same determination she'd fallen in love with. But now, it terrified her. She knew there was no changing his mind. Reluctantly, she nodded, trying to keep her lips steady and her eyes clear.

"I can get us there," William said, turning to Samuel. "It's only a few miles away. We should be able to get there pretty quickly."

Samuel nodded. "Good. Because time is running out faster than we could imagine."

CHAPTER 29

Sergeant Anderson stood outside Major Thomas O'Malley's office, drawing in a breath so deep it felt like it might be his last. His chest tightened with the weight of what was about to come. The Major wasn't just demanding—he was a force of nature, a tempest in human form with a temper that had scorched more men than Anderson cared to count. And nothing stoked that fire like failure. Unfortunately, today Anderson had no choice. What he was about to say would make anyone's blood boil.

The soft rap on the door seemed to echo unusually loud in the silence, and a deep, throaty grunt followed. "Come in."

Anderson stepped inside, his boots clacking against the cold tile as he snapped a salute. Behind the desk, Major O'Malley was a hulking brute of a man whose mere presence was enough to make a grown man feel like a scared kid. Six-foot-six, well over two hundred and fifty pounds of pure muscle—O'Malley looked like he'd been carved from granite. His eyes, sharp and intense, flicked up from the papers on his desk. "At ease," he muttered, his voice a low rumble.

Anderson shifted his stance, hands clasped tightly behind his back as he stood like a man condemned. The words he was about to speak tasted like bile, and he knew no matter how he said it, the explosion was inevitable. "Sir, we have a problem with the squad in La Quinta."

O'Malley's head jerked up quickly. "What kind of problem?"

Anderson swallowed hard. "I'm afraid the situation's much worse than we anticipated. We've lost three members of Bravo Squad, sir. The others... they're in serious danger."

The Major's chair creaked ominously as he sat up, his eyes narrowing into slits. "Lost? What in the hell are you talking about, Sergeant? How do we lose three of our best soldiers on a routine animal control mission in fucking La Quinta?"

Anderson braced himself. "Fisher reported in about twenty minutes ago, sir. Said the whole area is crawling with crazed animals. They barely made it to Palm Desert before everything went sideways. Traffic was backed up. When they got out to assess the situation, they were ambushed. It's bad, sir. Real bad. And... the Living Desert Zoo has been compromised."

O'Malley's eyes blazed. "Compromised? What the fuck does that even mean? How does a damn zoo get compromised?"

Anderson could feel the fuse burning dangerously low. His voice remained steady, though inside, every nerve felt raw. "We don't know, sir. It looks like a rabies-like virus. It's spreading, and fast."

The Major's face darkened. "How fast?"

Anderson hesitated. "We estimate it'll reach Palm Springs to the west and Coachella to the east within the hour."

For a moment, O'Malley was stunned into silence, his eyes widening in disbelief. "Holy shit," he breathed. "What are the expected casualties?"

Anderson's voice dropped. "It's hard to say, sir. We've lost contact with local emergency response teams. La Quinta PD went dark hours ago. Casualties could already be in the hundreds... maybe even thousands."

O'Malley had always prided himself on keeping a tight lid on his emotions, but Anderson could see that control slipping, like water spilling from a broken dam. The Major slammed his fist down onto the desk with a thunderous crack, scattering the papers he'd been sifting through. "I don't care what it takes or who you have to send, Sergeant, but you'd better get a fucking lid on this, and fast!"

Anderson snapped to attention. "Yes, sir!" He knew he had barely walked out of the lion's den with his head still attached, but this wasn't over. Not by a long shot.

O'Malley was already reaching for the intercom as he dismissed Anderson. "Janet, get me Governor Davidson on the line. Now."

"Right away, sir," came the secretary's voice, cool and efficient, as if the world weren't about to tear itself apart.

Anderson turned on his heel, heart pounding, and made his way back across the base toward his office, pulling his phone from his pocket. His fingers trembled with adrenaline as he dialed Dr. Leonard's number. The phone barely rang before the doctor picked up.

"Leonard," the voice on the other end sounded hollow, stretched thin.

Anderson didn't waste a beat. "Please tell me you've got news."

Leonard hesitated. "A little. My team's located the civilian. We're escorting them to a local medical center. We're hoping to identify what we're dealing with there soon."

Anderson barked into the phone, barely containing his frustration. "Well, you'd better work fast or we're all going to be dog meat. Literally. I've got three soldiers heading your way now. Be ready."

Leonard's voice cracked with disbelief. "You only sent three soldiers?"

Anderson's temper flared. "No, dumbass. I sent a whole squad. Three are all that's left. Get the point? Figure it out. Now!" He hung up, rage seething beneath his skin.

As he neared his office, the sun vanished, casting the base in an eerie shadow. Anderson glanced up, thinking it was just a passing cloud. But the sky wasn't dark from clouds—it was alive, a mass of black wings blotting out the light.

The realization hit him like a sledgehammer. Birds. Hundreds, maybe thousands of them. A murder of crows, a flock of hawks—an unnatural swarm.

Then came the sound. A cacophony of unholy screeches and cackles, like something torn straight from Hell. Anderson's pulse quickened as the birds descended, their forms twisting in the air like a living storm. He watched in horror as they plummeted down on unsuspecting soldiers below, talons slicing, beaks tearing into flesh. The screams of his comrades ripped through the air, soldiers falling like rag dolls under the assault.

Anderson sprinted the last few yards to his office door, shoving it open just as a hawk collided with the steel frame, its blood-red eyes burning with hellish fury. The bird thrashed and clawed at the door, desperate to get at him.

Without thinking, Anderson slammed his hand on the control panel, punching in the code and smashing the button to trigger the base-wide alarm. The piercing wail of sirens filled the air as chaos erupted outside.

His heart pounded in his ears as the hawk's frenzied shrieks pierced through the walls. He knew, deep in his bones, that this was only the beginning.

* * *

***

O'Malley slammed the phone down so hard it nearly cracked. Nothing on Earth disgusted him more than politicians. They were all disgusting bastards, only looking out for themselves while the world around them went to hell. They only cared about their image and their precious reputations. To them, people were just pawns and completely expendable.

But O'Malley knew the game. He'd learned long ago that sometimes you just had to smile when you wanted to spit and nod when you wanted to scream. Now was one of those moments he wanted to scream. Trying to get the governor to understand the severity of the situation had been one of the most pathetic conversations he'd ever been engaged in.

He let out a growl of frustration, running a hand through his hair. His eyes drifted to the cup of coffee sitting on his desk. It had long gone cold, but he didn't care. He needed something to distract himself from the rage growing inside him.

With the cup in his hand, he stalked over to the window, hoping that staring out at the base might calm his nerves.

But the second he neared the glass, the sharp wail of sirens ripped through the air. The sound was so jarring that O'Malley's hand jerked, sending the cup crashing to the floor, coffee splattering across the tile.

"What the hell?" he exclaimed. "I didn't authorize any damn tests!"

He looked down at the shattered mug for just a second, but then something outside drew his eye—something wrong, something that froze him in his tracks. His eyes snapped up to the window, and all at once, the world shifted.

This wasn't a drill!

Soldiers were scattering in a blind panic across the base. It wasn't just chaos; it was carnage. And then he saw them, descending from the sky like nightmares with wings—black, sleek, and deadly.

Death had come to his base on raven wings, a storm of dark, screeching terror. The sinister undead flock swooped down in droves, their beaks flashing like knives, talons shredding flesh from bone with horrifying efficiency. Soldiers screamed as their bodies crumpled to the ground while they died a savage death.

O'Malley stood frozen, gripping the windowsill so tightly his knuckles turned white as he watched his men being ripped apart. One soldier tried to make a run for it, only to be caught by a black-winged demon that latched onto his back and savagely impaled its beak deep into his skull over and over again. The man screamed—a sound so terrifying it made O'Malley's stomach turn—before collapsing under the weight of the attack. It was like watching a scene from Hell, but Hell wasn't a distant concept anymore.

The sirens screamed on, louder and more insistent, but they barely registered. All O'Malley could hear was the savage cawing of the birds, the frantic cries of his men. His jaw clenched, teeth grinding together as rage began to bubble up deep inside him.

With a sudden, explosive fury, O'Malley turned away from the window, grabbing the nearest phone to call the command center. His voice was a growl as he barked into the receiver, "Every unit on high alert! We're under attack!"

A second later, the message rang out over the PA system that the savage apocalypse was upon them.

CHAPTER 30

Melinda's heart sank as she watched William move toward the door, joining the two scientists with a grim expression that mirrored her own. The terror twisted inside her, coiling tighter with every step he took. She didn't want him to go—not out there, not into the jaws of whatever nightmare awaited them. The world was falling apart, crumbling under the weight of horrors she couldn't even begin to understand. And if something happened to him, if he didn't come back... *No. Don't think like that.* She threw the thought from her mind, hoping to bury it deep, but knowing it could resurface at any moment, just like the dead outside coming back to life.

She swallowed the rising lump in her throat, knowing deep down there wasn't another choice. William's police training made him their best shot at survival. But that knowledge did little to soothe the gnawing fear in her chest.

He walked over to her, his expression softening for just a moment as he wrapped her in a tight hug. The kind of hug that said a thousand things—goodbye, I love you, don't let go—all without saying a word. His arms were firm around her, his breath hot against her neck, and she could feel the tension in his body, the weight of what was coming. When he finally

197

pulled away, his hands lingered on her shoulders for a beat longer than usual. His eyes bore into hers, filled with a kind of desperation she'd never seen before.

"Whatever happens, you stay inside and keep the door locked. Got it?" His voice was calm, the result of years of training under extreme circumstances, but underneath she knew he was just as scared.

Melinda nodded, not trusting herself to speak. If she opened her mouth, her voice would crack, and she didn't want him leaving with her fear hanging in the air. He kissed her, soft but lingering, and then turned away, leading the scientists out into the unforgiving nightmare world beyond the door.

The moment the door clicked shut behind him, she locked it. Her knees buckled, and she slid down to the floor, her body shaking as silent sobs racked her chest. This time, she didn't hold back the tears. She let them fall, knowing that it might be the last time she'd ever get to cry for him.

***

William took a deep breath, the stench of death hitting him like a physical blow. The desert heat only made it worse. Rotting flesh was cooking under the relentless sun, and the acrid scent of it clawed at the back of his throat, thick and choking.

The dead were out there, prowling the streets on four legs, hunting with a ferocity that chilled his bones. William forced the thoughts from his mind, letting his police training take over. *Focus, William. Stay sharp.* That was the only way they were going to survive this.

The truck was parked in the driveway, only twenty yards away, but in the current landscape, it might as well have been a mile. The sound of raspy howls filled the air—a haunting, unearthly chorus that signaled the dead were close.

They were just a few feet from the truck when William's eyes caught movement down the street—a coyote, or what was left of one, barreling toward them, its flesh hanging in ragged, rotting strips, eyes glowing with savage hunger.

"Everyone in the truck, now!" William barked.

The three of them charged forward, scrambling into the truck just as the undead coyote leaped onto the hood. Its snarls filled the cab, black blood and bile dripping from its mouth as it clawed at the windshield, leaving streaks of filth in its wake. William's heart pounded in his chest, but his hands moved on instinct. He twisted the key and the engine roared to life. When he slammed the truck into reverse, the sudden jolt sent the coyote flying off the hood, its body crashing into the pavement with a sickening thud. Flesh and tissue splattered across the driveway as the creature hit the ground.

Without missing a beat, William threw the truck into drive and gunned it down the street. The tires screeched, rubber burning against asphalt, and when he glanced in the rear-view mirror, his stomach clenched. A pack of the undead was chasing them, their twisted, grotesque bodies moving with unnatural speed.

Good, he thought grimly. *Let them follow. At least it keeps them away from the house.*

He pushed the truck harder, barely slowing as he took the turn onto 58th. Then another left, and they were on Madison Street. William suddenly slammed on the brakes, his breath catching in his throat as he took in the sight ahead. A hundred yards up the road, a horde of undead creatures swarmed in a sickening mass—canines, felines, birds, bats— every kind of nightmare he could imagine. And they moved with terrifying precision, like a single, bloodthirsty organism.

Above them, the flying beasts circled in formation, black shadows blotting out the rising sun as they surged forward. *Scouts*, William thought. *They're hunting—searching ahead for fresh prey.*

"Is there another way around?" Samuel asked nervously.

"Not really," William replied, eyes still fixed on the horde. "This is the most direct route to the medical center."

"They haven't seen us yet," Andrea whispered. "Maybe we can follow behind? It'll be slower, but... safer?"

"Safer," Samuel echoed. "As long as that pack by your house stays away."

William nodded, his grip tightening on the wheel. "Stay sharp. If this goes sideways, we'll need to move fast."

They crept behind the horde with every nerve on edge. For a while, it seemed to work—they kept their distance, undetected, until they passed Airport Boulevard. Then, as if some invisible signal had been sent, the creatures howled and cried as one, surging forward, their hunger driving them toward some other unfortunate soul.

For a moment, the road ahead was clear. But it didn't last. As they neared Jefferson Street, William gasped. The road was a graveyard of vehicles—cars and trucks piled on top of each other, semis overturned, and in the center of it all, a Sunbus lying on its side with its hazard lights blinking in a slow, mocking rhythm.

"Holy shit!" William muttered. "What could have caused all this?"

Samuel's eyes were cold. "Not anything of this world, William. That's for sure."

"I know that. But what kind of force...?"

"That's what we have to find out."

The devastation stretched on as far as the eye could see, a

testament to the raw, unstoppable power they were up against. William scanned the chaos, looking for a way through. His hands clenched the wheel so hard his knuckles were white.

"There's no way through," he muttered, more to himself than anyone else. "We have to go back and double around."

With a sinking feeling, he realized: if Madison wasn't clear, they were done for.

CHAPTER 31

Immediately, Guerera's mind yanked her back to that day, nearly six years ago, when Clause—once a friend, maybe even something more—turned into something dark, something rotten. It was like a switch had flipped, and in an instant, the man she trusted had morphed into her worst nightmare. She had always been wary of men, the shadow of her past clinging to her like smoke—growing up in a house where her mother was a punching bag for her father's rage had made sure of that. Verbal abuse, physical torment—every night it was the same. Guerera had learned early on to keep her guard up, never to let anyone too close. But Clause had slipped through her defenses, and that had cost her.

What happened with him wasn't just a betrayal—it was a violation. She had told him no, and he'd laughed, as if her boundaries were a joke. He touched her anyway, his fingers crawling over her like spiders. She shoved him off, made it clear that he'd crossed a line, but Clause wasn't the type to take rejection quietly. When it all came out to the Sergeant, Clause spun the story like a madman, throwing wild accusations and painting her as the instigator. The lies were venomous, scandalous, designed to destroy her. But justice had prevailed, at least that time, and Clause had been dishonorably discharged. She thought that would be the end of it—that she'd never have to see his face again.

But hope is a fragile thing. It had crumbled now, replaced by cold fear, because she knew exactly what Clause was capable of. He was a man who thrived on revenge, and with the world coming apart at the seams, the thought of running into him again had become a twisted reality. Amid all this chaos, Clause had reappeared like a demon from her past, lurking on the edge of her nightmares. She could almost feel his eyes on her, like a predator stalking its prey.

She snapped her head back to the road, gripping the steering wheel harder than necessary. Her voice was tight, edged with the simmering panic she tried so hard to suppress. "I just saw Clause."

Fisher coughed in surprise, his face twisting in disbelief. "Say what?"

Her voice was sharp. "In the next lane, heading the opposite way."

Fisher's jaw tightened as he processed what she'd said. "You're sure it was him?"

Guerera turned her head slowly, locking eyes with him. The look she gave him was enough to silence any further doubts. "I'm sure." Her voice had an edge to it, steel beneath the surface.

Fisher knew better than to argue. He rubbed his chin thoughtfully. "Maybe it's just a coincidence? If I remember right, he had family in this area."

"Maybe," she said, but the word came out flat and hollow. She didn't believe it. Coincidence? In this hell? No, she'd see Clause again—soon—and it wasn't going to be a reunion of old friends.

She refocused on the road ahead, her heart hammering in

her chest, every muscle in her body tensing as she scanned the landscape. Death was everywhere. Corpses rotted in the sun, twisted, mutilated—some human, some not. The air was thick with decay, the kind that clung to your skin like it wanted to become part of you. And then she saw her a woman, terrified, running across the road like a cornered animal.

Guerera's foot hit the brake, the vehicle lurching to a stop. She was halfway out of the door, her instincts screaming at her to help, to do something, when Fisher's hand clamped down on her arm, pulling her back.

"Where do you think you're going?" His voice was stern, laced with the authority of someone who knew better than to leave the safety of the truck.

"We have to help her!" Guerera shot back, her voice tinged with desperation.

Fisher shook his head, his grip tightening. "You heard our orders. Our mission is plain and simple: find these scientists and get them to the medical center. That's it. No detours, no distractions."

The woman was closer now, her eyes wide with terror, her hands outstretched toward them as she screamed for help. Guerera's heart ached at the sight of her, every instinct screaming to act. But Fisher's words echoed in her head—stay on mission, stay alive.

And then the decision was made for her. Out of nowhere, a mountain lion—what was left of one, anyway—lunged from the shadows. Its flesh hung in tatters, patches of fur clinging to exposed muscle and bone. In one swift, savage motion, it tore into the woman's throat, silencing her pleas in a gurgle of blood. Guerera froze as the mountain lion gnawed at the corpse, the wet sound of tearing flesh filling the air.

For a long moment, Guerera just sat there, paralyzed. The

woman had been alive mere seconds ago. And now... now she was just meat. Meat for something dead that shouldn't even be walking. Guerera's hands started to tremble, her whole body shaking as the image of the woman's death burned itself into her brain.

Fisher's voice cut through the fog, pulling her back from the brink. "You okay?"

Guerera didn't answer. She couldn't. The horror was too much. Too real. She felt like she was drowning in it.

From the back seat, Jackson's voice broke the silence. "You want me to drive, Jaz?"

The sound of her name pulled her back from the abyss. She turned, meeting Jackson's concerned gaze. He was her closest friend, the one who'd always had her back. She saw the strength in his eyes, the same strength that had been there when he pulled her from darker places in the past. She nodded, not trusting herself to speak, and crawled into the backseat, trading places with him.

Once Guerera was settled in, Ashley laid her head on her lap and looked up through eyes filled with fear. "Are we gonna be okay?"

Guerera ran a hand through Ashley's hair, pushing it away from her face. "I'm going to do everything I can to make sure we are," she said, though her voice was barely above a whisper.

Fisher exchanged a look with Jackson. Both men were thinking the same thing: Something had cracked inside Guerera. She wasn't the same. And if they had any hope of surviving this nightmare, they needed the old Guerera back. Fast.

***

* * *

William gripped the steering wheel tight enough that his knuckles turned white, his jaw clenched as if it would hold back the fear gnawing at the back of his mind. The truck's engine roared to life as he made a hard U-turn, tires squealing, gravel kicking up from the road. The air felt heavy —as if the world itself was holding its breath. Above them, a dark cloud rolled across the sky, blotting out the sun like a sudden eclipse.

Samuel leaned forward, eyes squinting through the windshield. He shouldn't have looked, but something about the sky felt... wrong. He craned his neck, focusing on the darkness above, and his stomach knotted as he realized the truth. What he thought was just a shadow wasn't some fleeting cloud—it was alive. A massive flock of birds moved in a swirling, chaotic formation, their wings beating like war drums. But it wasn't just birds. Samuel's breath caught in his throat when he noticed the strange shapes intermingling with the flock. Bats, hundreds of them, flitted erratically, their leathery wings slapping through the air as they merged with the avian swarm.

The sight was almost too much to take in. The animals were moving together—birds and bats—like something out of a nightmare, as if they were being driven by the same dark force.

"Jesus..." Samuel whispered under his breath before snapping back to reality. His voice was tight, urgent. "We need to move. Now." He didn't try to mask the fear. "Step on it, William! Whatever's coming, we're running out of time faster than I thought."

William shot a glance upward, and when his eyes met the churning mass of winged creatures blotting out the sky, he felt his gut twist. A sinking feeling rooted itself deep inside him. His foot immediately slammed down on the gas pedal, and the truck lurched forward, speeding back onto Route 54.

The road stretched before them like a gauntlet, littered with debris and corpses, transforming the narrower road into an obstacle course of wreckage and abandoned cars. William's training instantly kicked in. He gritted his teeth, weaving through the wreckage and navigating the chaos like he was in a high-speed chase.

Along the sides of the road, the horror was everywhere. Undead creatures, their flesh rotting and their eyes vacant, feasted on the dead with a ravenous hunger that sent shivers down Samuel's spine. What had once been gentle house pets were now twisted abominations, their mouths dripping with gore. They snapped at the air, charging toward the truck with mindless aggression, their growls deep and guttural. William didn't flinch. He floored the gas, plowing through them without hesitation. The truck's tires crunched bones, spit flesh from beneath its wheels. He didn't think of them as animals anymore, certainly not as someone's beloved pets. They were just a threat that needed to be eliminated.

They drove up Madison like this for nearly twenty minutes, the tension mounting with every passing second. Samuel kept glancing out the window, his nerves stretched tight. The road felt longer than it ever had before.

When they approached the intersection at Avenue 52, William considered taking a left, a shortcut that might bring them closer to their destination. His eyes flicked to the side, seeing the clogged traffic choking Jefferson. It was chaos—cars jammed in every direction, people out of their vehicles, shouting, some fighting, others just running. *No way we can make it through there.* He had no choice but to stick to his route and pray that Avenue 50 would offer them some kind of relief.

But the further they went, the more hopeless it seemed. His

heart sank when they passed the Eldorado Polo Club, now nothing more than a funeral pyre. Flames licked at the sky, consuming everything in their path. The once-pristine grounds were a blackened wasteland, smoke pouring mercilessly into the sky. It felt like they were driving through hell itself.

William's grip tightened on the wheel again, his knuckles popping as his foot pressed harder on the gas. They had to get through this. He had to get his family through this. His mind raced with grim scenarios, but he pushed them away, focusing only on the road ahead. He didn't have time for fear.

"We'll make it," William muttered under his breath, though he wasn't sure if he was saying it for Samuel's sake, or to convince himself.

Samuel remained silent, his mind working furiously to figure out a way to stop this nightmare. He kept his eyes on the road, but now and then he would glance up at the sky, watching the swarm, feeling the weight of impending doom pressing in from all sides.

The truck roared down the road, as William prayed for an open stretch of highway ahead. All they could do now was drive, as fast and as far as they could, and hope that the darkness chasing them wouldn't swallow them whole.

***

Guerera sat in the back seat, cradling Ashley's small head in her lap, the girl's soft, fragile weight pulling her back into memories she had spent years trying to bury. Her mind drifted against her will, and suddenly, she was no longer in this hellish nightmare, but in the living room of her childhood home, with her sister Caroline curled up beside her on the couch. They'd sit there for hours, the flicker of the

TV bathing them in its soft glow, sharing inside jokes, making plans for a future that would never come. It felt like a lifetime ago—a life she would never get back.

Tears stung her eyes, uninvited and fierce. Caroline's face, so clear in her mind, twisted into that final day. The day it had all shattered. It had been so fast. Too fast. One moment, they were together. The next, Caroline was gone, ripped away by a senseless accident that had left Guerera standing alone in the wreckage of her own heart.

She couldn't stop the guilt from clawing at her soul, eating her alive from the inside out. Even though everyone said it wasn't her fault, even though they called it an accident, Guerera couldn't believe them. She couldn't forgive herself. Not for the way she'd hesitated, not for the seconds she'd lost. And she knew those were the moments that made the difference between life and death.

The weight of that guilt was a chain she carried every day, wrapped around her neck, tightening with every breath. She had long accepted that it would never loosen, that she would be a prisoner to it until the day she died herself. Only then, maybe, would she be able to face Caroline, look into her eyes, and beg for the forgiveness she'd never be able to give herself. Maybe then, she could say the words that had haunted her every night since: "I'm sorry."

Caroline's death had torn her apart, shattered her into something unrecognizable. All the pain, all the grief—they were too much to face. So, she didn't. Instead, she let rage take over, anger filling the cracks in her soul where love and joy used to be. Anger was easier. Anger gave her purpose. And it was safer than drowning in sorrow.

Her mother, already broken by years of abuse, couldn't handle the force of Guerera's fury. She didn't have room for another storm in their house. So, she sent Guerera away—

handed her over to the Marines, where someone else could deal with the angry, shattered girl she had become. The moment Guerera walked into the recruiter's office, she knew she wasn't coming back. The girl she used to be had died with Caroline. But the Marines built her back up, piece by hardened piece. They took Jasmine, the weak and terrified child who couldn't save her sister, and forged Guerera—the unstoppable soldier who would never fail again.

She became a force, a legend, the fiercest fighter 29Palms had ever seen. She wore her toughness like armor, unbreakable. No one would ever see the scared girl beneath the surface. No one could ever hurt her again, because she wouldn't let them close enough to try.

Now, sitting in that Humvee, with the chaos of the world collapsing around her, she looked down at Ashley resting in her lap, and she felt the weight of the past slam into her chest like a punch. Ashley needed her—needed the fighter, the protector, the unbreakable Guerera. And in that moment, she resolved to be that soldier again. Even though she wasn't able to save Caroline, she damn well wasn't going to lose Ashley. Not today. Not ever.

Jackson suddenly stepped on the gas and launched the Humvee forward, apparently trying to declare to her that he was a better a driver, but she wasn't in the mood for his antics, and instead just sat there ignoring him.

Realizing that he wasn't going to get any kind of reaction from her, Jackson shifted his focus onto the road ahead. He figured she'd come around, eventually.

Periodically, undead creatures charged at the hulking vehicle, and Jackson responded by swerving so he could hit them head on. The Humvee bounced as it ran over their mutilated bodies.

Fisher wasn't amused. "What the hell are you doing?" he

exclaimed.

Jackson turned and grinned. "I'm bowling for monsters."

Fisher rolled his eyes. "Stop fucking around and focus, or you're going to get us all killed."

Jackson responded by sulking for a minute, but did as instructed, and focused straight ahead. Then, just as they crossed the intersection at Cook Street, they saw an enormous mass flying overhead.

Something massive and dark blotted out the sky above them. A rolling, churning mass that was descending—too fast, too erratic. It wasn't dust. It wasn't anything natural.

They all jumped as the first few splats hit the windshield, leaving yellow and green puss on the glass. Fisher exclaimed, "What the hell was that?"

"Insects... big ones," Jackson muttered, flipping on the wipers. But the more he tried to clear the mess, the worse it got. The wipers smeared the goo, reducing visibility to nothing but streaks of slime and horror.

Fisher frowned at him. "Good going, shit-head."

Jackson opened his mouth to respond, but was silenced when a barrage of insects hit the windshield. "Holy shit!" He jerked the wheel, narrowly avoiding an oncoming car, but it wasn't enough. The smaller vehicle spun out of control, flipping over the highway median in a blur of twisted metal.

The full fury of the swarm now rocketed against the windshield of the Humvee with such force that it sounded like a Howitzer.

Ashley's terrified screams cut through the chaos. Guerera wrapped her arms around the girl, pulling her close, trying to block out the terror with her body. "It's going to be okay," she whispered. "Cover your ears. Close your eyes. Think of something good, something safe."

But Ashley couldn't. Her tiny body trembled

uncontrollably, and Guerera could feel it—the same hopelessness she had fought for years. The world was a nightmare now, and there was no escaping it.

Fisher was shocked to see the thick glass, built to withstand gunfire and shrapnel, began to spiderweb under the relentless assault.

In response to the onslaught, Jackson started to pull the vehicle toward what he thought was the side of the road, but Fisher quickly stopped him. "We have to keep going! If we stop, who knows what these insects will do to the engine? Then we'll be sitting ducks for God knows what'll come next."

Jackson protested, "But I can't see a damn thing!"

Fisher pressed his cheek tightly against the side window and could just barely make out the landscape ahead. "I can try to guide you forward until this is over. Just keep the wheel steady."

"That's all fine and good as long as it's clear in front of me."

Then Guerera spoke, her voice hard. "We need Freddy."

Fisher turned to her. "As soon as we open that hatch the whole swarm is gonna be on our asses! We won't last a minute."

"We're dead anyway if we don't," Guerera shot back. "This isn't going to stop on its own."

Before Fisher could argue, the Humvee lurched as it collided with another car, sending the unknown vehicle spinning into the darkness. He sighed, knowing this was their only chance. "Ashley, come up front. Now."

The girl hesitated, her wide eyes darting to Guerera.

"Go," Guerera urged, softer this time. "I'll be right behind you."

Ashley crawled into the front seat, trembling. Guerera

wasted no time. She stretched a tarp across the back of the seats, creating a makeshift barrier. Then, she quickly strapped on her flame-retardant gear—heavy jacket, gloves, and a helmet that swallowed her entire head. She hefted the flamethrower, its weight familiar and comforting in her hands.

"Try not to blow us up," Jackson muttered.

"Thanks for the vote of confidence," Guerera growled, igniting the flamethrower. A tiny flame sparked at the nozzle. "On my count."

She took a deep breath to prepare herself, then a moment later she clenched her jaws tight and nodded toward Jackson. "Okay, now!"

Jackson slammed on the brakes, and the Humvee screeched to a halt. Guerera swung the roof hatch open and pushed herself through, the roar of the swarm hitting her like a physical force. It was madness—a swirling, buzzing tempest that blotted out the sky and the earth, everything alive and hungry.

Without a savage fury, she unleashed the flames.

The fire exploded from the nozzle, arcing through the swarm in a wide, violent spray. The insects shrieked as they burned, their bodies crackling and disintegrating in mid-air. The stench was unbearable—burning flesh, chemicals, death. But no matter how many she took down, hundreds more came to take their place. The swarm was relentless.

The flamethrower roared, and Guerera could feel the heat searing through her jacket and the strain in her muscles as she fought against the overwhelming force. For a moment, she faltered—*What the hell am I doing?* They were going to die out here, all of them. This was suicide.

But then she gritted her teeth and pressed on. Too many people were counting on her. She couldn't fail. Not now.

With a scream of pure defiance, she focused the flamethrower's blast toward the heart of the swarm, pushing with everything she had.

And then it happened—a piercing, high-pitched screech from within the swarm. The insects hesitated, then gathered together in a pulsating mass. For one terrifying second, the swarm hung there, suspended in mid-air. And then, just as quickly, it shot upward, disappearing into the night sky.

Guerera stood there dumbfounded for a moment before she dropped back down into the Humvee and closed the hatch.

Jackson turned to her. "Whatever you did seems to have worked."

Guerera replied, "Then why are we still here? We need to get going."

"We have a problem." Then he pulled the tarp away from Ashley, who was lying across Fisher's lap, unmoving. A series of large red spots had formed on the side of her neck where multiple creatures had stung her.

CHAPTER 32

With every passing mile, Clause's hatred thickened, boiling up like molten lava ready to erupt. The rage inside him was raw, primal, barbaric—an unrelenting fury that consumed every rational thought. All he could see was her face, that smug, manipulative bitch who had ripped his life apart, piece by piece. He cursed her with venomous hatred, wishing her a thousand different kinds of hell. And then, he cursed himself —for his weakness, for allowing her to destroy him.

His grip tightened on the wheel. He barely noticed the undead canine that darted across the road as he roared past Date Palm, heading toward Palm Springs. Rotting animals littered the area, but only a few—he was ahead of the horde. Still, that dark cloud of doom was coming, and he knew it wouldn't be long.

A grim smile twisted his lips as a savage thought flickered through his mind. He imagined the cursed flock descending on the very same Marine base that had betrayed him, tearing it apart like vultures feasting on a carcass. The image filled him with a sick sense of satisfaction, fueling his hatred even more.

With newfound urgency, he slammed his foot on the gas

and flew down Highway 111, the car screaming beneath him. As he passed the I-Max Theater, his eyes caught sight of something massive perched on the roof—a bird, enormous, like a goddamn pterodactyl. Its hollow, dead eyes locked onto him for a second, but it didn't move. Good. He didn't have time for more bullshit.

Minutes later, Clause veered off onto Ramon Road, the airport coming into view, but his temper flared again as he spotted the gridlock ahead. Traffic was backed up, crawling, a line of cars stretching toward the horizon. He cursed under his breath. A rent-a-cop was making his rounds, talking to each driver. Clause's heartbeat quickened as the burly security officer approached his car. Not only was the vehicle a beat-up piece of junk—one that wasn't even his—it also had a body in the back, and the last thing Clause needed was some wannabe cop with too much authority and too little sense.

The officer tapped on the window, and Clause rolled it down just enough to remain unassuming. "What's the holdup?" Clause asked, his voice cold and measured.

"All outgoing flights are grounded until further notice," the guard said flatly. "Incoming flights are being rerouted to LAX."

Clause's patience snapped, but he kept his face neutral. He pulled a business card from his pocket, flashing his NASA credentials. "I need access to our private jet. This is urgent."

The security guard glanced at the card, then nodded. "I can let you through to the hangar, but no planes are getting off the ground."

"How long?" Clause snapped.

The man shrugged. "I'm just the messenger, man. No clue what's going on."

I do, Clause thought. He gave a gruff thanks and pulled out of line, maneuvering the car through the maze of vehicles. Other drivers threw him dirty looks, while some flipped him off and hurled curses through their windows. He found their outrage amusing, a dark grin tugging at the corners of his mouth. *Idiots. If they only knew what was really going on.*

Finally, he reached the junction leading to NASA's private hangar. Ashton had sent him a message—the pilot was already expecting him. As Clause pulled in, the pilot descended the stairs from the cockpit. When Clause got out of the vehicle, the man was shocked to see that Clause was alone.

"Where's the rest of the crew?" the pilot asked warily.

Clause ignored the question. "Where's the helicopter?"

The pilot blinked, then pointed across the airfield. "About a hundred yards that way. 'Dedicated Helicopters.' You can't miss it."

Without acknowledging the pilot further, Clause stalked back toward the car. His frustration boiled over as he pounded the steering wheel. Time was fleeting fast, his window of opportunity closing, his moment of revenge slipping away.

He floored the gas, the engine roaring as he tore away from the hangar and sped toward the helicopter service. His mind raced with dark thoughts. Delays. Always delays. Everything was dragging him down, and the world around him was crumbling. But he was determined to push through the chaos and claim that which belonged to him. Claim her.

As he approached the entrance to the helicopter rental, his lips curled into a sneer. The sign read "Dedicated Helicopters," but all Clause could think was, *How dedicated are they, really? And how far would they go to keep a man like me happy?*

* * *

***

Guerera stared down at Ashley, her body sprawled motionless on Fisher's lap, and a familiar dread seized her heart with cold, icy fingers. *Not again!* Her mind screamed, echoing the painful memory she'd never shake. Her sister. The way she had died, her small body convulsing, helpless. Guerera had failed her, hadn't known what to do. And now this little girl was lying there, her skin pale as death, breathing in ragged, shallow gasps. It was happening all over again.

She refused to let history repeat itself.

"We have to do something!" Guerera's voice cracked as she tore her eyes from Ashley's face. Her hands hovered helplessly over the girl, trembling. "What about the anti-venom in the med-kit?"

Fisher's face was grim. "We don't know what bit her," he said, too calm for the situation. "If we give her the wrong med, it could make things worse."

"We can't just sit here!" Guerera's desperation erupted as tears streamed down her face. "We have to do something, Fisher!"

Jackson twisted around in the driver's seat, his gaze darting between Guerera and the unconscious girl. "Lay her down on the floorboard. I need more room to work."

They moved quickly, Guerera cradling Ashley's limp form as gently as she could while Jackson cleared space on the floor. While the interior of the Humvee was spacious, it felt like a coffin in that moment. Ashley's tiny chest was barely moving, her breaths so faint Guerera feared they'd stop any second.

"Med-kit," Jackson ordered, his Marine training kicking in with a force that steadied the others. Fisher handed him the kit without a word, knowing that Jackson's EMT training made him their best shot. The second Jackson popped open the kit, the small compartment filled with the harsh scent of rubbing alcohol.

Ashley's breathing became more labored, her chest heaving like it took all her strength just to draw in another breath. Jackson worked quickly as he slipped an oxygen mask over her mouth and nose, trying to coax her lungs back to life.

Then, as if conjured by some unspeakable nightmare, something moved in Ashley's hair. Guerera's eyes watched in horror as a group of large black spiders, their legs twitching in an unholy manner, crawled out. The creature's bulbous bodies gleamed under the dim light, a trio of Black Widows, each one swollen with venom, and each one as big as a half-dollar. The sight of them, skittering along the floor, made Guerera's stomach turn.

With a savage yell, she stomped her boot down hard on the spiders, her foot crushing the life out of them with a series of sickening crunches. The sounds echoed in the small space, like the final exhale of a dying thing. Fisher didn't flinch. Instead, his hands were already moving, grabbing the anti-venom vial from the kit. He thrust it into Jackson's waiting hands.

Jackson quickly jabbed the needle into Ashley's neck, near the swollen spider bites, his jaw clenched tight. The silence that followed was suffocating. They all waited, hearts in their throats, as if the universe itself had paused to see if this tiny girl would survive the venom coursing through her veins.

Then, slowly, Ashley's breathing began to change. Her shallow gasps grew deeper, steadier. A collective sigh of relief rippled through the Humvee. Even Fisher, who never let emotion crack through his hardened exterior, allowed himself the faintest exhale of relief. He knew how much this girl meant to Guerera, even if they had barely known each other long. That was enough for him. If she mattered to Guerera, she mattered to him.

Jackson gently placed a cold compress on Ashley's forehead, his fingers lingering for just a moment, as if grounding himself in the task at hand. Guerera squeezed the girl's hand tight as she whispered a silent prayer—though she'd long given up on believing in anything like God, she found herself begging someone to listen, to save this little girl that had suddenly given her a purpose beyond her own existence.

But then, just when it seemed like things were turning around, Ashley's body jerked. A violent tremor shot through her, and her tiny frame began to convulse. The seizure hit fast, too fast. Guerera's heart raced. She leaned forward, holding Ashley's shoulders down as she tried to keep the girl from hurting herself.

And then came the horror.

From the wounds on Ashley's neck, thin streams of black liquid oozed out, slow at first, then quicker, dripping to the floor of the Humvee in thick, inky splatters. Guerera's eyes widened as she watched the jelly-like secretion join together to form one large blob and then wriggle quickly through a crack in the floorboard of the vehicle, disappearing into the darkness. "Holy fuck! What the hell was that?" she cried.

Both men looked at her in shock, but before they could respond, Ashley's seizures stopped. As quickly as they'd begun, Ashley's body stilled, her chest rising and falling in a steady rhythm. Her eyes fluttered open, soft and unfocused.

"I'm thirsty," she rasped, her voice barely audible.

Guerera let out a breath she hadn't realized she was holding, a sound that was half a sob and half a laugh. With shaky hands, she helped Ashley up. She grabbed a bottle of water from her pack, unscrewed the cap with trembling fingers, and handed it to the girl.

Ashley took a long drink, the water trickling down her chin. She turned to Guerera, her face pale but alive. "Thank you."

Guerera's throat tightened. "It's okay. Drink as much as you need."

But Ashley shook her head, her expression softening. "Not for the water, silly," she whispered. "Thank you for saving me... for saving all of us."

Guerera's heart cracked wide open. She pulled Ashley into a tight hug, her eyes stinging with unshed tears. She couldn't lose this girl. Not her. Not after everything. She glanced up at Jackson and Fisher, who were both watching her, quiet smiles playing on their lips. They understood.

But then Guerera wiped her eyes, refusing to show them any further emotion. Her face hardened as she tried to hide behind her mask once more. "Let's get the hell out of here," she growled, "before something else decides to try to kill us."

CHAPTER 33

For a fleeting moment, Clause considered doing the logical thing—flying straight back to the research facility and handing his grim cargo over to Ashton. That would've been the smart move, the one any sane man would make. But Clause wasn't feeling sane. His mind was a storm of fury, and reason had long since been drowned in the tide of vengeful thoughts that swirled in his head. No, logic wasn't in control anymore. The only thing he could focus on was a single burning question: *Should he put a knife through Guerera's heart, or a bullet in her brain?*

The thought electrified him as he paced around the hangar, his hands shaking with barely contained rage. Guerera had crossed a line and now that Clause had a second chance at vindication, he wasn't going to let that slide. Not this time.

His lips curled into a tight sneer as he grabbed a couple of tarps and a roll of duct tape from the management office at Dedicated Helicopters. He wrapped his cargo—the bodies—carefully, ensuring the tarps were tight enough to obscure what was inside but loose enough that the surviving Marine could still breathe. *The guy has guts, I'll give him that.* Bleeding out, barely conscious, and yet clinging to life with a stubbornness only a Marine could muster. How long the man would last was anyone's guess.

Clause's mind snapped back to the task at hand. He hauled the body bags to the helicopter, the pilot watching him with a wary eye. "This is it," Clause muttered to himself as he loaded the first one in, the Marine letting out a weak groan as he was hoisted into the back. Clause shoved the second body in, followed by the case with the samples, then wiped his hands on his pants, as if he were attempting to cleanse himself of the atrocities he had committed.

The pilot, a grizzled man with a scruffy beard and sunglasses, leaned back against the side of the chopper with his arms crossed. "Just so you know, I'm no damn delivery boy. If you need someone to fly this stuff for you, find another guy."

Clause stopped in his tracks. His eyes narrowed, and for a second, he considered whether killing this man would make his day any better. But violence wasn't the answer at the moment. He needed this guy alive.

Without missing a beat, Clause pulled a wad of cash from his jacket pocket, crisp hundred-dollar bills folded neatly together. He peeled off a few notes with deliberate slowness, watching the pilot's expression shift from defiance to something more pliable. The man's eyes flicked to the money, then back to Clause, who dangled the bills in front of him like bait.

"Five hundred bucks," Clause said, his voice cold as steel. "Easy money for a short flight. Get this stuff to where it needs to be, and this is yours."

The pilot hesitated, his jaw tightening. "This ain't about the money, pal. I'm not risking my neck—"

Clause stepped closer, his voice dropping to a low, dangerous murmur as doubled the amount of bills in his hand and stuffed them inside the man's shirt pocket. "You're not risking anything. Just fly the damn helicopter and keep your mouth shut. No one needs to know what you're carrying. Hell, no one will even see you."

The pilot's mouth twitched as he considered the offer. After a beat, the man let out a low sigh. "Fine," he muttered. "But if this goes south, it's on you. I don't know what you've got back there, and I don't want to know. I'm just the guy flying the bird."

"Exactly," Clause replied, his lips curling into a smile that didn't reach his eyes. "You don't need to know anything."

With the deal sealed, Clause sent a quick text to Ashton, explaining the change in plans. He wouldn't be on the helicopter, not yet. He had unfinished business to attend to first.

The helicopter's engine roared to life as the rotors began to spin, and the ground trembled beneath Clause's feet. He watched the chopper lift off, the tarps flapping slightly in the back, the Marine hopefully still groaning softly beneath them. The helicopter rose into the air, a dark silhouette against the bright desert sky, carrying its grisly cargo toward its clandestine destination.

Clause turned, his eyes narrowing as he slid back into the driver's seat. His thoughts were already miles away, focused on the betrayal that burned in his veins like poison. This wasn't about the mission anymore. It wasn't even about Ashton, or the cargo, or the research facility. This was personal. Guerera had to pay, and Clause had already decided how.

He slammed his foot on the gas, the tires screeching against the asphalt as he sped away from the airport.

***

* * *

Ashton's fingers clenched around his phone, the plastic casing creaking under the pressure. He wanted to hurl it against the wall, let it shatter into pieces, just to feel some kind of release. The urge was so strong his arm twitched. But then, with a hiss of breath, he stayed his hand. Destroying his only reliable means of communication wasn't just foolish—it was dangerous. His frustration didn't ease, though. In fact, it grew even hotter as Clause's message flashed across the screen again.

The little bastard had gone rogue, chasing his personal demons, jeopardizing everything in the process.

Ashton paced around the room like a restless spirit, his agitation manifesting itself in tight, sharp steps that echoed through the room. His fingers flexed at his sides, itching to wrap themselves around something, or someone, just to feel the satisfying crack of bones under pressure.

Clause had always been unpredictable, but this... this was reckless, insubordination at the worst possible moment. The stakes were too high. They were on the precipice of something monumental—world-changing, no less. The object, the facility, the alien technology... everything hinged on careful execution. And now, the weakest link in Ashton's meticulously crafted chain had snapped.

Damn him!

Then, Ashton suddenly stopped, as a cold clarity swept over him. His eyes narrowed as the flicker of an idea surfaced from beneath the storm of rage. Maybe Clause's rogue actions could be turned to his advantage somehow. Ashton wasn't one to abandon an opportunity, even one born of disobedience.

Clause's vendetta might actually be of use. If he succeeded in his foolhardy mission, that would mean the Marines would be removed from the equation, thus solving one of

Ashton's problems. Clause would eliminate the opposition. And once he had served his purpose, well... it wouldn't be too hard to cut him loose.

He returned to his desk and settled into his chair, his fingers drumming rhythmically against the polished wood. Samuel's silence was concerning, but Ashton knew better than to let fear take root. Samuel was resourceful, perhaps too much so. And that made him another liability. Ashton would have to tighten his grip there, too—soon.

He glanced down at the screen again, the text from Clause staring back at him like a taunt. But this time, he didn't allow anger to cloud his mind. The disaster was moving faster than expected, but Ashton knew how to adapt. He would bend this catastrophe to his will, reshape it into the perfect opportunity.

Clause might think he was acting on his own, chasing revenge in the name of some personal justice. But in the end, it was Ashton who pulled the strings. He always did.

And when the dust settled, when the blood had dried and the last pieces of the puzzle fell into place, Ashton would stand at the top, looking down at the world he had remade.

He smiled, dark and cold, a smile devoid of warmth or humanity, as he thought about the future and the world he would rule.

After a moment of reflection, he dialed Leonard's number, already rehearsing the dance of half-truths in his mind that he'd have to use. When Leonard picked up, Ashton immediately cut to the chase. "I need an update," he barked.

To his disappointment, Leonard didn't offer him anything useful. His responses were too vague to be of any actual use, and Ashton's suspicions immediately sharpened like knives. *He's hiding something. I know it*, Ashton thought. Samuel and Leonard had spoken recently—he could feel it—and the good doctor was lying through his teeth.

Fine, Ashton thought, a bitter smile touching his lips. *I'll deal with Leonard later.*

For now, he had bigger concerns. The situation in Coachella Valley was unraveling faster than even he had anticipated. The alien object—its nature, its power—was far beyond what they had imagined. Ashton cursed under his breath, a rare admission of miscalculation. He was too smart for this, too damn careful to be caught unprepared. He swore that it would never happen again.

The disaster spreading across the valley was no longer just a blip on the radar—it was a full-blown catastrophe. And if he didn't act swiftly, it would devour everything in its path. Including him.

Ashton's mind shifted, recalibrating his strategy. The goal hadn't changed—he would still seize control of the research facility, take their resources for himself, and solidify his power. But the means to achieve that goal was evolving. What was once a calculated rise to scientific glory, a chance to stand at the pinnacle of human discovery, now demanded something far more theatrical. Far more... heroic.

If he was going to survive this, he needed to become more than just the mastermind. He needed to be the savior. The man who vanquished the chaos, who brought peace to a land ravaged by terror. The hero of the hour. And once the dust settled, the world would fall at his feet, begging for leadership. For protection. For order.

Then, Ashton mused, his lips curling into a dark smile, *then I'll finally get what I deserve.*

He chuckled softly, his mood lifting as the plan took shape in his mind. Let Clause play the executioner. Let Samuel's group be the fools who stumbled upon salvation, only to be swallowed by it in the end.

And when it was over, Ashton would stand victorious, the sole architect of the world's survival.

And they'll never see it coming.

***

Clause had barely made it a mile down the road when his phone rang, the shrill sound cutting through the low hum of the engine. He glanced at the screen, saw Ashton's name, and cursed under his breath. Of all the people he didn't want to hear from right now, that self-righteous, manipulative bastard topped the list. His fingers hovered over the 'decline' button, tempted to ignore the call altogether. But he hesitated. He might despise Ashton, but the man was paying him—and paying him well. With a deep, frustrated sigh, Clause answered.

"Ashton," he muttered, barely concealing his irritation.

Ashton's voice, sharp and commanding, came through immediately. "Clause, whatever personal vendetta you're chasing, I need you to put it on hold."

Clause's grip tightened on the steering wheel, his knuckles turning white. He clenched his teeth, forcing himself to stay silent.

"Did you hear me, Clause?" Ashton continued impatiently. "I need you to meet up with the research team again. Help them. Do whatever it takes to keep them moving forward. If they find a solution—anything that can stop this chaos—I need you to secure it. Bring it directly to me. No detours."

Clause could almost see Ashton's smug face through the phone, could imagine him pacing in his office, safe from the horrors in the valley. Safe, while he sent him to do the dirty work. Clause's jaw tightened, but he kept his voice steady. "And then?"

There was a pause on the line, a calculated one, before Ashton responded. "Once you've secured the weapon, you can do whatever you want. Tie up any loose ends, settle your scores. Hell, kill them all if that's what you want. Just bring me the weapon first, and I'll double your fee."

Then, the line went dead.

Clause threw the phone into the passenger seat, his eyes narrowing as the road stretched out ahead of him. For a moment, he just drove, his thoughts swirling in a dangerous mix of frustration, rage, and something darker. Ashton's orders were explicit—help the scientists, play nice, and then secure whatever weapon they managed to scrape together.

The thought of going back to those spineless researchers turned his stomach. He didn't owe them anything, didn't care about their noble pursuit of saving the world. All they were to him were obstacles, and he'd spent enough time pretending to be on their side.

But... if Ashton was offering double his fee, that meant this situation was more dire than even Clause had realized. The chaos spreading through the valley wasn't just another outbreak. This was something else. Something big. If Ashton wanted the weapon so badly, it had to be powerful—game-changing. The kind of thing that could reshape the world, if not destroy it.

Clause's lips curled into a slow, sinister smile. He didn't need Ashton's permission to do what he was already planning—kill every last one of those scientists and take the prize for himself. He could still play along, bide his time, and when the moment was right... the weapon would be his.

And so would the fate of this world.

A wicked glint flashed in his eyes as he imagined the possibilities, his mind wandering to all the gruesome ways he could dispose of those sniveling scientists. The idea of watching the light leave their eyes as he pulled the trigger or watching them squirm as the blade went in... It brought a dark, sadistic joy that spread through him like wildfire.

He grinned wide, his foot pressing harder on the gas as the car roared down the road. Ashton thought he was in control, pulling the strings from his ivory tower. But Clause knew better. Ashton might be the one giving orders, but Clause was the one on the ground, the one with blood on his hands.

And when the dust settled, Clause had no intention of sharing the spoils.

"Whatever you say, Ashton," he muttered to himself, the dark grin still etched on his face. "But this time... I'm the one calling the shots."

***

Leonard felt a chill crawl up his spine the moment he hung up the phone. Something wasn't right. Ashton had sounded off—his voice sharp, desperate, like a man clutching at straws. Leonard knew that tone all too well. He'd seen it in Ashton before, during the early days of their work together. Back then, he had witnessed the man's unsettling willingness to cross any line, sacrifice anyone or anything, to achieve his ends. And that ruthlessness terrified Leonard now more than ever.

His mind raced, replaying every word of their brief, cryptic conversation. Ashton hadn't just been fishing for information—he was hunting, prowling, trying to gauge what Leonard knew, or worse, what he was hiding. Leonard had spent too much time with Ashton to be naive about his intentions. A man like Ashton didn't get desperate unless the stakes were sky high.

And that's what scared him most. Ashton was capable of

doing anything when his back was against the wall.

Without wasting another second, Leonard grabbed his phone and dialed Samuel's number, his fingers shaking just a bit more than he would've liked. After the third ring, Samuel's familiar voice came through. Leonard exhaled a breath he didn't realize he'd been holding.

"Thank God you're still alive," Leonard blurted out.

"What's up, Leonard?" Samuel's voice was cool and collected, but you could sense the hidden tension.

"Where are you?" Leonard asked, trying to keep the urgency out of his voice but failing miserably.

"About two miles from the medical center. Why?"

Leonard glanced out the window, the landscape suddenly appearing desolate and bleak though the nightmare they were facing was thousands of miles away. He lowered his voice, as if Ashton might somehow overhear him. "Watch your back, Sam. I just got off the phone with Ashton... and something's not right. He's up to something, I can feel it. He sounded... off."

There was a brief pause on the other end of the line before Samuel replied, "Well, we both know he's not exactly a trustworthy guy."

Leonard swallowed, the taste of fear bitter on his tongue. "You don't get it, Sam. You don't know him like I do. In this situation, he's capable of anything. If he thinks for a second that you're a threat to his plan... he'll bury you."

Samuel was quiet for a moment. "I've dealt with men like Ashton before. But if he's really that desperate, it makes him dangerous. I'll keep my eyes peeled for anything out of the ordinary."

Leonard shook his head, a hollow chuckle escaping his lips. "At this point, I don't think anyone knows what ordinary is anymore."

A tense silence fell between them, both men aware of the storm brewing around them. Leonard could almost feel the weight of it pressing down on his chest. Ashton wasn't just a man chasing power—he was a man cornered by his own ambitions, and that made him lethal.

"Stay safe, Sam," Leonard said finally.

"I will," Samuel assured him.

As the line went dead, Leonard couldn't shake the gnawing feeling building in his gut. Ashton was planning something—something bigger than either of them realized.

And Leonard knew, deep down, that whatever it was... they might not be ready for it.

CHAPTER 34

Samuel hung up the phone, muttering under his breath, "That's just great."

"What was that all about?" Andrea asked from the backseat.

Samuel sighed, rubbing his temples as if trying to massage the stress out of his skull. "Leonard," he said. "Called to warn us about more of Ashton's bullshit."

William cocked his head. "Who's Ashton?"

"Deputy-Director at Ames," Samuel huffed. "Supposed to be our point of contact for this mission. Only problem is, it looks like he's got his own agenda, and it sure as hell doesn't include making sure we stay alive."

William snorted, a dark chuckle escaping his lips. "Sounds like a real stand-up guy."

Samuel couldn't help but laugh bitterly. "You have no idea. Classic scientific egomaniac. Thinks he's the smartest guy in every room, dead or alive. But the real danger isn't him—it's Clause. He's ex-military or something, built like a tank, and meaner than a snake on amphetamines. I didn't like the guy from the moment I saw him. He's not just dangerous—he's unhinged."

William looked at Samuel with a fierce and determined gaze. "Don't worry about Clause. If he shows up, I'll deal with him."

Samuel nodded, though William's confidence didn't ease his mind. He had seen Clause in action, watched him rip through these unholy threats with a cold, efficient violence that left no room for mercy. He could only hope William's bravado matched his skill because if Clause decided to come after them, he knew there'd be no easy way out.

The sooner they got to the medical center, the better. "How much further?" Samuel asked as he glanced anxiously out the window.

"Barring any disaster, we'll be there in a few minutes," William replied.

Samuel was about to respond when a sudden thud rocked the truck. His heart lurched into his throat, and his eyes darted to the side mirror. In the fading twilight, he caught sight of a Golden Retriever, its once-soft fur now matted and patchy, bouncing grotesquely across the asphalt. Its legs, shattered from the impact, twisted at unnatural angles as it tried to stand again, jaws snapping mindlessly at the air. The dog's eyes—clouded, dead—locked onto the truck as it stumbled toward them, dragging its broken limbs behind it.

"Jesus Christ," William whispered. The sight dredged up an image he had been trying to bury—King, lying on their front lawn in a pool of blood, a twisted abomination that no longer resembling their beloved canine. He slammed his foot on the gas, the engine roaring as they sped down Route 111, trying to outrun the horrors chasing them, both literal and imagined.

Minutes later, they screeched into the parking lot of the medical center. Immediately behind them, a military Humvee made the same turn from the opposite direction. Samuel breathed in relief when he saw the vehicle. Leonard had said that help was coming, but until he actually saw them, he had held out much hope. Now maybe they'd have a chance to put a stop to this madness.

"This must be the backup Leonard was talking about," Samuel muttered, though his voice betrayed his lack of confidence. Even as he hoped for salvation, a gnawing feeling told him it wouldn't be that simple.

The moment they stepped out of the truck, any hope he had evaporated like morning mist under the unforgiving desert sun. The scene before them was a nightmare come to life. Bodies littered the parking lot, charred and swollen under the sweltering heat. The air was thick with the nauseating stench of rot and decay, a foul mix of putrid flesh and scorched earth. Flies buzzed in dense clouds, feasting on the decomposing remains scattered across the ground. Samuel gagged, pulling his shirt over his nose as his eyes watered from the acrid stench.

Andrea and William did the same, each one recoiling from the grotesque spectacle of death surrounding them. As they staggered toward the building, the Humvee skidded to a stop a few feet away. Three Marines spilled out, weapons drawn, and a small girl followed close behind, wide-eyed and pale.

"You must be the squad from 29Palms?" Samuel asked, approaching cautiously.

Fisher nodded. "Yeah, what's left of us," he grunted.

Samuel's heart sank. "How many?"

"We lost three back at the mall. Got swarmed by those... things." Fisher spat on the ground. "Where's the rest of your group?"

"Same story here," Samuel replied, his voice hollow. "We lost two. And our driver—Clause—disappeared after a wreck."

At the mention of Clause's name, Guerera stepped forward. "Did you say Clause? Stocky build, Russian-looking' bastard?"

Samuel's gut clenched. "Yeah... you know him?"

Guerera, exchanged a dark glance with Fisher. "Yeah, we know him. Bad news. You'd be smart to stay as far away from that psycho as possible."

"You don't have to tell us twice," Samuel muttered. The memory of Clause's cold eyes flickered through his mind, sending a chill down his spine.

Suddenly, a chorus of distant howls pierced the air—low, guttural, and filled with an unholy hunger. The dead were approaching.

Fisher snapped to attention. "Time to move. Jackson, take the rear. Rest of you, stay tight."

As the group moved toward the medical center entrance, the howls grew louder, closer. Rounding the corner, they came upon a medical van, its doors hanging open. A thud from beneath the vehicle made Fisher freeze.

Then, out of nowhere, a hand shot out and grabbed Fisher's ankle. He jerked back, eyes wide, staring down at the emaciated form of a woman crawling from the shadows. Her skin was pale, translucent, as if all the life had been drained from her. A gaping hole in her side was crawling with insects, beetles and maggots spilling from her wound like water from a cracked dam. Her bulging eyes locked on Fisher's.

"Help... me..." she rasped, her voice barely audible over the buzzing of the flies.

Fisher's face hardened, his jaw clenching as he glanced at William. A nod passed between them. Fisher raised his gun, the barrel gleaming in the dim light, and fired. The bullet tore through the woman's skull, silencing her plea forever. Her body crumpled into the dirt, a lifeless heap.

But the insects weren't finished. With the woman gone, they turned toward the group, a wave of skittering legs and snapping mandibles rushing across the ground like a living flood.

"Move! Everyone inside, now!" William barked, shoving the others toward the entrance.

The automatic doors jammed, refusing to open. Fisher, with a grunt of exertion, pried them apart just enough for everyone to squeeze through. As the doors slammed shut behind them, the group panted, slapping at the insects clinging to their clothes and hair.

When they finally looked up, a fresh horror awaited them. The lobby resembled a slaughterhouse, bodies littering the floor, each one hollowed out by the swarm. Blood pooled on the floor, congealing into thick, syrupy puddles beneath their feet. The scent of copper and decay filled the air, so thick it stuck to the back of their throats.

They moved in stunned silence, stepping over the remains of doctors, nurses, and patients, every step accompanied by a sickening squelch as their boots pulled free from the sticky floor. The walls crawled with more insects, their tiny legs tapping against the tiles like raindrops on a tin roof.

"Dear God," Andrea whispered. But she knew there was no God here—not anymore. Only death.

The group moved cautiously down the hallway, every step a reminder of the nightmare they were trapped in. They tried not to look at the bodies, or what was left of them, strewn haphazardly along the corridor. Some which didn't have faces anymore.

Insects buzzed and scurried in the shadows, their tiny legs making faint scratching sounds as they moved, like nails on a chalkboard. Centipedes, fat with gore, wriggled along the walls, and spiders the size of fists dangled from overhead fixtures, their beady eyes glinting in the dim light. Occasionally, someone would flinch or slap at something crawling too close to their skin, their nerves frayed to the breaking point.

After a number of twists and turns, they reached an intersection. The dull red glow of the emergency lights reflected off the blood-streaked tiles, casting everything in a sickly hue.

William's voice was barely a whisper. "Left."

Fisher nodded and led the group down the left passage, their footsteps growing quieter even as the sound of their breathing grew louder and more ragged. After a few yards, they stopped in front of two doors, side by side, with faded metal plaques hanging above them: Clinical Pathology and Anatomic Pathology.

Fisher's voice was low but tense, his eyes darting between the doors. "Which one?"

Andrea nervously pointed to the left. "That one."

The moment she spoke, a scream ripped through the air from the other side of the door—a high, piercing wail, filled with terror. William's heart lurched in his chest, and his hand flew to the doorknob without thinking. He looked at Fisher, who gave a quick nod.

William yanked the door open, and Fisher charged inside, gun raised.

The sight that met them was a snapshot of madness. A young woman in her mid-twenties, her white lab coat splattered with something that wasn't just blood, was crouched on top of a desk, her body trembling violently as she screamed. Her eyes were wide with horror, locked on the floor in front of her.

And on the floor, slithering and coiling in a writhing mass, was a cluster of rattlesnakes, but they weren't right. Their scales were peeling, flesh hanging from their sides in ragged strips, exposing the pulpy meat beneath. Some had eyes clouded over with death, others were missing patches of skin altogether, their ribs visible through open wounds. Yet they hissed and snapped viciously, their hunger undiminished by their decaying state. Blood and mucus oozed from their fanged mouths, pooling on the floor.

As soon as Fisher stepped into the room, the snakes sensed him. Their heads snapped in unison, dead eyes locking onto fresh prey. With a sickening squelch, they began to slither toward the group, their mutilated bodies dragging themselves across the floor, leaving dark, viscous trails in their wake.

Fisher opened fire and the room immediately exploded into a spray of blood and mucus. The air filled with the acrid stench of gunpowder and burning flesh as the bullets ripped through the snakes. Their bodies convulsed and thrashed, bits of meat and bone flying across the tile. But it wasn't enough.

A handful of the creatures were still moving, their heads twitching, jaws snapping even as their bodies were blown apart. The macabre dance continued until the floor was littered with grotesque, dismembered corpses.

"Jackson, secure the door!" Fisher barked as the rest of the group funneled in. Jackson slammed the door shut, bracing it with a nearby chair. Meanwhile, Guerera guided Ashley to the far side of the room.

Andrea approached the woman huddled on the desk, who was sobbing uncontrollably, her face streaked with tears and blood. Andrea kneeled beside her, keeping her voice calm, gentle. "It's okay. It's over. You're safe, for now. What's your name?"

The young woman sniffed, her entire body trembling in

fear. "J-Jan—Janet. My name's Janet."

"Well, Janet, you're safe now," Andrea said, though even she wasn't sure if those words held any truth.

When William heard her name, he immediately walked over. "Janet? Are you hurt? Are you okay?"

Janet threw herself off the desk and into William's arms. Her thin body shook violently against his chest, her fingers clutching his jacket like he was the last solid thing in the world. "Oh God, William! It was horrible! They came out of nowhere! It all happened so fast!"

William held her for a moment, his jaw clenched, before pulling back. "What happened? Where is everyone else?"

Janet's face twisted in horror as she turned, pointing to the far side of the room. William followed her gaze and felt his stomach lurch.

A severed foot lay in a thick pool of blood, not far from a workstation. The blood was still fresh, glistening under the harsh fluorescent lights. The jagged stump of bone jutted from the ankle, the skin torn and chewed. And it wasn't alone —more pieces of bodies, unrecognizable, were scattered across the floor, among overturned chairs and broken equipment.

Janet's voice broke again, barely a whisper through her sobs. "Dr. Richards... He... he burst in, screaming. They were all over him, biting, tearing him apart. He only made it a few steps before he... before he fell. And then they... Oh God, William, what is happening? What's going on here?"

William had no answer. He looked down at her tear-streaked face, feeling the weight of her despair. He wished he could tell her it would be okay, but the words stuck in his throat. Instead, all he could manage was a hollow whisper. "I wish I knew."

CHAPTER 35

The crash was like a cannon blast, echoing through the house. It ripped Melinda from the shallow haze of sleep she'd drifted into in the recliner. Her heart skipped and her muscles tensed. Kate's scream, high-pitched and filled with terror, came right after. Melinda shot up from the chair, her eyes wide with panic.

"Mom!" Tommy's voice cracked as they bolted out of the living room and down the narrow hallway. She could hear his quick, panicked breaths behind her, almost in sync with her own. They rounded the corner to the bedroom, and that's when she saw it.

Kate was on the floor, scrambling backward, her legs kicking uselessly as she tried to push herself away from the bed. The look in her eyes, wide and glazed with fear, paralyzed Melinda for half a second. Then she saw it—the black, feathered thing on top of the bed. A large blackbird, its wings shredded, twisted limbs jerking in grotesque spasms, squawked and screeched in a way that sounded more like gurgling than anything else. Blood and feathers coated the bedspread like a macabre tapestry. It thrashed, trying to claw its way toward Kate with a single-minded hunger, its body mangled, but still alive—somehow.

The damn thing should've been dead. The glass from the broken window had torn it to pieces when it had burst through, but like all the other horrors today, death didn't seem to mean a damn thing anymore. Its wings were mangled, legs broken and bent at impossible angles, yet it still moved, still fought to get at her daughter.

Without thinking, Melinda snatched up the nearest object, her fingers closing around the cold, smooth base of a table lamp. She swung hard. The lamp made contact with the bird's head with a sickening crack. Blood splattered across the floor as the bird's head crumpled inwards like an overripe melon. But she kept swinging, desperate, frantic. She didn't stop until the thing's twitching body finally lay still, the lamp now slick with gore in her shaking hands.

She dropped the lamp with a metallic clatter and scooped Kate into her arms. "Oh God, baby, are you okay?" She pulled her tight, feeling the trembling in her small body and the soft sobs as Kate buried her face into her mother's shoulder. Melinda stroked her hair, murmuring reassurances, words that felt empty even as she said them. "It's okay...it's okay...you're safe now."

But was she? Melinda's mind raced. Was safety even a possibility anymore?

"Mom!" Tommy's voice cracked. "There's more of them! They're coming this way!"

Melinda whipped around and followed Tommy's trembling finger that pointed through the jagged remains of the window. Her stomach dropped. A dozen, maybe more, of those black-winged nightmares were descending in a chaotic swarm. Their silhouettes blotted out the sky as they swooped down, dark as death, their unholy screeches filling the air.

"Go! Move!" Melinda screamed, shoving Kate toward the

door as the birds crashed into the house. Their bodies slammed into the walls, into the furniture—everywhere at once. She could hear the rest of the glass shattering, followed by hollow thuds as they slammed into the walls.

Melinda tried to yank the bedroom door closed behind her, but her hands slipped on the knob. Panic throbbed in her chest as she struggled, fumbling, while the dark mass of feathers closed in.

They barely made it down the hallway, racing toward the bathroom, before one of the birds grazed past Tommy, its claws slicing through the fabric of his sleeve. He screamed, clutching his arm, but Melinda shoved him forward, forcing him inside the bathroom. She slammed the door shut behind them, and for a second, all they could hear was the pounding of their own hearts. Then came the clawing. The scratching. The birds threw themselves against the door with wild fury, their talons scrabbling at the wood, their beaks pecking, pecking, pecking. The sound filled the small room like a demonic metronome, pushing at the edges of their sanity.

Melinda locked the door with shaking hands, her breath coming in ragged gasps. She pushed Kate and Tommy toward the bathtub, trying to shield them as best she could. They huddled there, pressed tight against the cold porcelain, their small bodies trembling, the terror etched on their faces reflecting her own growing panic.

For a long moment, the only sounds were the relentless scratching, the screeching, and their muffled cries. Then...it stopped. Silence, thick and suffocating, settled around them like a shroud. They all held their breath, too afraid to move. *Was it over?* Melinda dared to think.

A deep, guttural growl then shattered the silence. It reverberated through the thin walls, low and menacing. Melinda's blood ran cold. Whatever was out there...it wasn't one of the birds.

The door shook violently as something enormous slammed into it, the frame splintering under the force. The bathroom mirror rattled on the wall, the ground beneath them seeming to shift as the beast outside rammed again. Melinda's mind screamed at her to do something—but what?

Instinct kicked in. Melinda's eyes scanned the tiny bathroom, desperate for anything she could use to defend her children. Her gaze landed on the towel bar. With a surge of adrenaline, she ripped it from the wall, the metal rod coming free with a groan of protest just as the creature outside rammed into the door once more. This time, the wood cracked and splintered.

The head of the thing that broke through was a twisted nightmare. A mountain lion—or at least it used to be. Half its face was gone, the other side covered in patches of matted fur and dripping black saliva. Its eyes glowed with an unnatural hunger. The door splintered further as it snarled and lunged, its massive jaws snapping just inches from Melinda's face.

Kate screamed, the sound so piercing it sent shock-waves through Melinda's already rattled nerves. With a cry of her own, Melinda thrust the towel bar forward, driving it into the creature's eye. She pushed, hard. The rod pierced through flesh and bone, sinking deep into the brain with a sickening squelch. The mountain lion let out one final wheeze before collapsing, half of its mangled body still wedged through the doorway.

Melinda fell back, trembling. The beast was dead. Finally, truly dead. She stared at its motionless form for what felt like an eternity, waiting for it to twitch, to rise again, like all the others. But it didn't.

She dropped to her knees beside the tub, pulling Kate and Tommy into her arms, holding them tight. Her body was shaking uncontrollably now, and tears stung her eyes. "It's... it's okay," she whispered, her voice barely a breath. "We're okay..."

But the distant howls outside told her the nightmare was far from over.

Melinda pulled away from her kids, her heart still hammering in her chest. Tommy and Kate clung to her for a moment longer before she gently pried their small, trembling hands from her arms. She could see the fear clouding their eyes and she hated herself for turning away from them, even for a second. But she needed to hear William's voice. Maybe his words could give her enough strength to keep going.

Her hands shook as she fumbled for her phone. She prayed he'd pick up, that she wouldn't hear the dreaded ringing that would then lead to the cold, hard voice that would tell her to leave a message and he'd get back to her. In her mind, that could only mean he was gone, swallowed up by this growing chaos.

She breathed a sigh of relief when he answered on the second ring. "Melinda?"

William's voice was a lifeline, pulling her back from the darkness. It was like breathing for the first time in hours. She closed her eyes, gripping the phone tight.

"Is everything alright?" William asked.

She didn't know how to answer, so she lied. "It is now," she whispered.

But William wasn't fooled. He knew her too well. "What's wrong? Are the kids okay?"

She glanced back at Kate and Tommy, huddled together on the floor, their small bodies trembling. "They're fine, William. We just... we just had a little scare, is all. But we're okay now." She swallowed. "I just needed to hear your voice."

On the other end of the line, William's silence stretched out too long, and she knew his mind was racing. She could picture him, pacing, running through every terrible possibility, imagining every horror. She knew him all too well—knew that the helplessness was clawing at him. The distance between them felt like an infinite chasm she'd never cross.

"Don't worry, Hun. We'll get through this." He finally said, trying to sound confident, but there was a crack in his voice, a hesitation that betrayed his words.

"I need you to tell me you're sure, William." Melinda's own voice shook, barely holding together, like a dam ready to burst. Even she could hear the despair leaking through, the fragile thread she was hanging onto unraveling by the second.

She could almost feel William closing his eyes on the other end, struggling to find the right words, the ones she needed so desperately to hear. He drew a long breath, and when he spoke again, his voice was softer. "I'm sure, Melinda. Haven't we always come through the hard times together?"

Memories of their old struggles surfaced—lost jobs, overdue bills, nights spent worrying about how to keep the lights on. But those problems felt so far away now, so small compared to what they were facing. "But this is different," she whispered, her voice cracking. "Before, it was just stupid things. Money, jobs, stuff... Not this." She could barely get the words out. "Not monsters. Not dead things coming back to life."

William was quiet again, and she knew was as terrified as she was, maybe more. "We just have to have hope, Melinda," he said finally, but even as he said it, it sounded hollow. "We have to believe we can get through this."

Melinda's resolve was crumbling fast. She'd used up every

last drop of courage in the fight against the mountain lion—or whatever the hell it had become. She felt herself slipping, and her voice betrayed her desperation. "I'm so scared, William."

"I know," he said, his voice softer now, strained. She could hear his fear too, creeping in, no matter how hard he tried to hide it. "Me, too."

Just then, a deafening boom rocked the house. The walls shuddered and the floor seemed to tilt beneath her feet. Melinda flinched, her breath catching in her throat as dust fell from the ceiling in a fine, gritty rain.

William must have heard it too. "What was that?" His voice was sharp.

Melinda swallowed hard. "I—I don't know," she whimpered.

"Where are you now?" William asked.

"We're...we're locked in the bathroom." Her voice was barely a whisper, the small space around her closing in, making it harder to breathe. It felt like the walls were pressing in, squeezing the air from her lungs.

"The bathroom?" William's confusion was palpable, laced with growing panic. "What are you doing in there?"

"We were attacked," she said, the memory of the mountain lion's rotting face flashing in her mind. She could still smell its rancid breath, still feel the weight of its snapping jaws so close to her face. "We ran in here to get away."

His breath caught. "Attacked? By what?"

"I... I think it was a mountain lion." She paused, the reality of her words sinking in again, colder this time, heavier. "Or at least... it used to be."

William went silent for a long moment, and she knew he was trying to process the impossible. His family was trapped, hunted, and he was miles away. The helplessness was suffocating. When he finally spoke, his voice was low and urgent. "Can you make it to my office?"

Melinda hesitated. Her mind screamed that it was impossible, that they wouldn't make it through the gauntlet of horrors outside. But she couldn't tell him that. She couldn't let him hear the hopelessness in her voice. "I... I think so," she said, though the words tasted like a lie.

"There's a lock-box in the bottom left-hand desk drawer," William said, his words clipped, focused. "The key's under the wolf statue on the bookshelf. Get the box, Melinda. Whatever happens, you have to protect the kids."

Tears welled in her eyes. "I will." She hesitated, swallowing hard, feeling the weight of the words she was about to say. "I love you, William."

"I love you too," he replied, his voice breaking. "More than you'll ever know."

And then the line went dead.

Melinda stared at the phone in her hand, the silence ringing louder than the chaos outside. The tears finally came, and she clutched the phone tight to her chest, sinking to her knees on the cold tile floor. She couldn't shake the feeling that she had just spoken to him for the last time.

***

As William hung up the phone, a wave of regret crashed over him, leaving him hollow. He hadn't told Melinda he loved her enough. How many times had he thought to say it, only to let the moment slip away? He had vowed, once, to never let that happen. But vows were made in the light of hope, not in the face of a crumbling world. And now, with everything falling apart, all he could do was pray he'd get the chance to fix it before the end swallowed them all.

His fingers lingered on the phone, the cool plastic grounding him for a moment longer. But there was no time for self-pity. With a heavy sigh, he rejoined the Marines by the door.

Janet, who was feverishly collaborating with the scientists, looked more ragged than ever, her face pale, eyes bloodshot from the relentless grip of terror she had only recently escaped. Sweat beaded on her brow as they scoured through various notes, screens, anything to find an answer before the thin thread of humanity snapped. The room felt suffocating—hope eroding with every second that ticked by. Everyone knew the truth: they were working on borrowed time, and the debt was coming due.

William scanned the room, his gaze landing on Guerera. She was slouched against the wall in the far corner, just beside an old brown recliner that looked as if it had seen better days. On it, Ashley lay curled up, her breathing shallow, her face smudged with grime, lost in an uneasy sleep.

"What's the story with the little girl?" William asked.

Fisher, his face grim, answered without looking up. "We found her under a car when all hell broke loose. Guerera pulled her out. Just in time."

Fisher's voice tightened, his jaw clenched as memories flooded back. He didn't need to say it—William could see the ghosts in his eyes. "That's when you lost your men?"

Fisher's silence was all the confirmation William needed. He didn't push for more. Some wounds didn't need words. "I'm sorry for your loss. I'm sure they were brave men."

Fisher's gaze shifted to Guerera, who hadn't moved, her eyes focused on the sleeping girl as if watching over her might somehow make everything right. "She feels responsible for the kid now. There's something in her past—

something she's trying to make right." He paused, then added, "If Guerera says the girl's with us, she's with us. No questions."

William nodded, his hand resting briefly on Fisher's shoulder. "You're a good leader, Fisher. Don't ever doubt that."

Before Fisher could respond, a sudden cry rang out from the far side of the room. It was sharp, frantic—the kind of sound that froze the blood in your veins. Fisher snapped to attention, spinning toward Jackson. "Stay here. Guard the door." Without waiting for a reply, Fisher and William rushed toward the source of the commotion, their hands instinctively tightening around their weapons.

Guerera was on her feet in an instant, gun raised, eyes wide and ready for anything.

As Fisher and William neared the workstation area, the tension in the air felt like static electricity—dangerous, explosive. But what they found wasn't an attack; instead, Andrea and Samuel were practically vibrating with excitement, their voices overlapping in a rapid, breathless exchange.

William's heart was still pounding as he reached them. "Have you found something?"

Andrea's face was flushed with a strange blend of fear and exhilaration. "I think so. The organism... it's extraordinary. It behaves like a swarm of locusts—congregating, feeding, multiplying—but it's more than that. It's also displaying behaviors like honeybees, responding to a single, central entity."

William's brow furrowed, his mind struggling to catch up. "Locusts and honeybees? That doesn't sound like anything good."

Samuel chimed in, "The difference is, when we isolated a

few specimens in a shielded environment, they stopped swarming. They just... floated, aimless. It means they're being controlled, like a queen bee commanding her hive."

Fisher's face tightened. "So, what, we take out the queen, and the rest follow?"

Andrea hesitated, her eyes flicking between Fisher and Samuel. "It's not that simple, but yes. If we can destroy the queen, the swarm will lose its coordination. We haven't found a way to kill them all yet, but they're showing some vulnerability to sodium tetra borate."

"Sodium tetra-what now?" William asked, his face a mask of confusion.

Andrea cracked a small, tired smile. "Borax. It's a natural pesticide."

Fisher let out a dry laugh. "So, you're suggesting we head to Lowe's, grab some bug spray, and wipe these things out?"

Samuel shook his head, though there was a spark of humor in his eyes. "Not quite. We need to focus on the queen. If our theory holds, eliminating her will either weaken the rest of the creatures or, if we're lucky, immobilize them."

"But how do we even find this queen?" William asked. "And when we do, how the hell do we get close enough to kill her?"

Before anyone could respond, Guerera cut in, her voice holding a hint of excitement, "When we were attacked earlier, I hit the center of the swarm with the flamethrower. There was this... screech. Then the whole swarm just scattered."

Andrea's eyes lit up. "You must've hit the queen. If she's injured, she might be more vulnerable."

Fisher's expression darkened. "Or she'll be even more guarded. Harder to kill."

William's mouth tightened into a grim line. "So where do we find this swarm, and when we do, how do we take out the queen before she tears us all apart?"

Before anyone could answer, Samuel's phone rang, the sound slicing through the thick tension like a knife. He fumbled for it, checking the screen. It was Sergeant Anderson.

An icy dread settled over the group as Samuel answered the call.

"Sergeant?" Samuel began, but Anderson's voice cut him off, frantic and desperate. "The base is under attack! Please tell me you've figured out a way to kill these fucking things."

"Maybe," Samuel answered quickly. "Do you see a large black mass in the sky nearby? Something that looks like a funnel cloud?"

There was a brief silence on the other end as Anderson scanned the sky. Then, a sharp intake of breath. "I see it. It's coming right at us—looks like a goddamn tornado."

"That's no tornado," Samuel said. "It's an insect swarm."

"Jesus Christ," Anderson muttered.

Samuel forced his voice to remain steady. "We think if you destroy the queen controlling the swarm, we might be able to stop them."

"Might?" Anderson responded in disbelief. "That's all you got? A fucking theory?"

"I'm afraid so."

There was a moment of silence, then Anderson's voice came back, cold and resolved. "What do you need me to do?"

Samuel's words were simple. "Hit that bitch with the biggest fucking gun you've got. And hope to God it's enough."

Anderson didn't hesitate. "That I can do."

The line went dead.

As Samuel lowered his phone, the room was suddenly

plunged into a tense silence. And then, without warning, a thunderous bang erupted from the other side of the door. Everyone froze, holding their breaths, with their hearts pounding in their chest, as they waited for the next nightmare to burst through.

CHAPTER 36

Ashton rushed out to the heli-pad like a child on Christmas morning eager to tear into his gifts. Despite his plan teetering on the edge of collapse, he could barely contain the excitement bubbling within him. After all, he was about to unlock a door to something far greater than the world had ever known. He wasn't just unveiling secrets—he was unleashing a force that would finally prove humanity wasn't alone in this universe. And that power was soon to be his to command.

Flanking him were Frank Vogel and Victoria Kafka, each pushing heavy rolling carts loaded with various metal containers. Unlike Ashton, whose face was covered with feverish glee, they wore the grim expressions of soldiers marching to war. But they were loyal—devoted to a man whose vision of the future had pulled them into his web. They might not share his exhilaration, but their fear of him was enough to keep them close.

As the wind from the helicopter's blades whipped Ashton's coat, the pilot hopped out and met them halfway, shouting over the deafening hum of the rotors. "Your packages are in the back!" He yelled through the noise.

Ashton's eyes narrowed as they settled on the pilot. "Did my associate tell you anything about their contents?" he asked.

The pilot shook his head vigorously. "Nope! Didn't ask, he didn't tell!"

Ashton studied him for a moment longer, weighing the man's fate in his mind. His cold smile flickered for a heartbeat, then vanished. "Good," he said quietly, deciding the pilot would live—for now. Without another word, he moved swiftly toward the helicopter's rear compartment, where the specimens awaited him.

The two large metal trunks were loaded onto the first cart, accompanied by a small, inconspicuous brown satchel. Ashton knew what lay inside: the samples Clause had painstakingly extracted from Samuel. But it was the other cart that held the real prize—beneath the dark, weathered tarp lay a body, now cold and silent, an unwilling participant in Ashton's grand experiment. Silently, they made their way toward the elevator at the edge of the heli-pad.

Ashton's mind raced, replaying the day's events. He had been forced to reveal more than he wanted—opening up to Vogel and Kafka about his hidden laboratory. As much as it grated on him, even a man as brilliant as Ashton needed help from time to time. He'd tested their loyalty in the field months ago; now they were proving themselves useful again, and for that, they had earned his reluctant trust.

The elevator doors slid open with a hollow chime, and the trio descended into the belly of the complex. Vogel and Kafka peeled off, pushing their cart toward the primary lab where they would begin their twisted research. Ashton, however, guided the other cart—his precious cargo—down the narrow hallway leading to the hidden lab. When he reached the inner sanctum, a shiver of pride coursed through him as his eyes settled on the stasis tubes, each holding its own grim trophy.

He stood before them like a twisted god, his eyes gleaming as he looked at his collection—the journalist, the cameraman, the police officers, the construction worker, and now, the soldier. All of them suspended in their final moments, each one representing another piece of his puzzle, another step toward his ascension. But there was still one tube left. One space reserved for someone special. Someone whose capture would complete his masterpiece.

A smirk curled across his lips as he sent a quick message to Clause, inquiring about his current location. Ashton no longer needed Samuel or his team. The specimens had arrived, the experiments could proceed, and the world was at his feet. If Clause arrived before Samuel and his ragtag crew discovered anything, he'd eliminate them without hesitation. But if they had stumbled upon something useful, Ashton would need to play the part of the diplomat—for a while longer, at least.

A short buzz in his pocket signaled Clause's reply. He was close, just minutes away from his destination. Ashton slid the phone back into his coat pocket, his smirk widening. Soon, this would all be over. His triumph, sealed. He turned on his heel and made his way back to the lab where Vogel and Kafka worked feverishly.

The corridors felt darker, yet more alive, as he approached them. Victory was close—so tantalizingly close. If all went according to plan, the world would soon know their names. And he, Ashton Brown, would be remembered as the savior of mankind. Or perhaps something more.

***

The first thing Clause saw when he pulled into the parking

lot was that damned Humvee, standing like a monument to his past failure. His blood surged, a molten rage bubbling up from the pit of his stomach, clawing its way into every fiber of his being. Every instinct screamed at him to storm in and obliterate his former squad members, to make them pay for their betrayal, but he clenched his fists, forcing the fury back down. Not yet. He had a job to do—a higher purpose to fulfill. Revenge could wait.

Stepping out of the car, his jacket caught on the edge of the door, tearing a jagged hole in the fabric. A curse hissed from his lips, but he twisted it into a crooked smile. The rip was perfect—just one more detail to complete the image of a desperate, battered survivor. He ran his fingers through his hair, mussing it up to look a little more unhinged, his face already bruised and bloodied from the earlier accident. The injuries would sell the lie.

He patted his back to ensure the gun was still securely tucked beneath his shirt, the cold metal pressing reassuringly against his spine. Closing the car door softly, almost reverently, he began his approach to the building, stepping over the sprawled body of a woman whose lifeless eyes stared up at the sky, a bullet hole neatly centered in her forehead. Her guts spilled out around her like some grotesque wreath, the stench of decay mingling with the coppery tang of fresh blood. He paused, staring down at her for a moment, almost admiring the brutality. This was the world they lived in now—death and carnage, chaos and survival.

Clause took a deep breath, letting the scene sink in, and continued toward the entrance. When he reached the door, he stopped just short of the frame, careful to peek inside without giving away his position. His eyes scanned the room beyond —a wasteland of dead bodies, blood smeared across the floor and walls like some macabre art installation. A few insects crawled along the surfaces, feeding off the remnants. He narrowed his eyes. The coast was clear, at least for now.

He had been here before, more than once, so he knew the layout. The real challenge was locating Samuel and his pathetic crew. Slowly, cautiously, he slipped inside, his footsteps almost soundless as he moved down the hallway, heart pounding in his ears. As he neared the labs, he stopped, cocking his head, listening. Just beyond one door, he heard a squeal, high-pitched and frantic.

Clause grinned. He pulled a small blade from his pocket, its edge gleaming under the flickering lights, and dragged it down the side of his own cheek. The sting of the cut was sharp, the warmth of the blood dripping down his face like a red river. The pain was nothing, though. It was a tool—part of his disguise.

Satisfied, he wiped his hand across the blood to smear it, giving himself the perfect, desperate, wounded look. His eyes filled with calculated fear, and he raised a fist to the door. Then, with the urgency of a man on the edge of death, Clause pounded against the cold metal, the sound echoing down the hall like the tolling of a funeral bell.

CHAPTER 37

Melinda looked down at her children nestled in her arms, their small bodies trembling with fear. She bit down hard on her lip, fighting back the tears that threatened to spill over. She had to be strong for them, but how? Every fiber of her being was exhausted, drained by the sheer terror of the nightmare they had been living. After her last conversation with William, she couldn't shake the feeling that the end was closing in, suffocating her like a dark shadow. Her mind kept replaying the attack—the demon-cat's twisted, undead body tearing through the house, its bloodthirsty eyes burning into her soul. A shiver passed through her.

Then, as if sensing her inner turmoil, Kate lifted her tear-streaked face, her wide, innocent eyes locking onto her mother's. "It's okay, mommy," she whispered, her voice trembling as she tried to be brave. "I'm scared too."

Something inside Melinda snapped into place. Those soft, pleading eyes—her child's courage despite the fear—ignited a fire deep within her. A surge of fierce determination coursed through her veins, pushing back the suffocating dread. She would not let these monsters take her children. She wouldn't allow them to be devoured by the horrors

259

outside.

"Come on," Melinda said, her voice suddenly steadier than before, though every muscle in her body screamed in exhaustion. She nudged Kate and Tommy away gently and stood, towering above them like a shield. "We have to get out of here."

Kate clung to her brother, trembling. "But... it's safe here."

The fear in her voice broke Melinda's heart, but she crouched down to meet her daughter's eyes, brushing her damp hair away from her face.

"It's not safe anymore, baby," Melinda said softly, though her gaze was firm. "There's something worse out there now. We have to move." She turned to Tommy, her voice low but urgent. "Stay close, and protect your sister. Do you hear me?"

Tommy swallowed hard, nodding without a word. His silence told Melinda everything—he was trying to be brave, but she saw the terror in his eyes. It was the same fear that churned in her gut.

With trembling hands, she turned to the bathroom door, grimacing as she pried the demon-cat's mangled head from where it had wedged into the hole in the door. The lifeless eyes stared back at her, the remnants of its last growl frozen on its blood-stained muzzle. With a sickening squelch, she finally managed to pull the door free, its grotesque form crumpling to the floor.

Stepping carefully over the remains, she peered out into the hallway. It was eerily quiet—no scraping claws, no howling, just an oppressive silence. But she knew better than to trust it. Gripping Kate's hand tight, she pulled her daughter along, with Tommy close behind. They moved in a hurried shuffle, as if the very shadows might lunge at them. The hallway stretched on forever, each footstep feeling like it brought them closer to death.

They were only twenty feet to the study. But it felt like a mile.

Then came the sound—the one Melinda had prayed she wouldn't hear again—a deep, guttural growl that sent ice down her spine. She spun around just in time to see the creature lurch into view: a coyote, its decaying flesh barely clinging to the bones, blood dripping from the gaping hole where its stomach should have been. Its eyes gleamed with unnatural hunger.

"Inside, now!" she shouted, shoving her children into the study and slamming the door just as the undead beast barreled into it. The force of the impact rattled her bones, her arms shaking as she braced herself against the door, holding it with everything she had. The coyote snarled and scratched, its claws gouging deep into the wood, each slam causing the door to shudder.

"Tommy!" she gasped between breaths, "In the bottom left drawer of the desk—there's a metal box. Get it for me. Now!"

Tommy scrambled across the room, his feet stumbling in his panic. He yanked open the drawer and pulled out the small box, rushing it to her trembling hands as she lay with her back to the door, acting as a shield against the terror.

"Now... the key," she panted, "under the wolf statue on the shelf."

Tommy hesitated for just a second, then ran to the bookshelf, stretching on his toes to retrieve the key. His fingers brushed against it, nearly knocking it off, before he finally grabbed it.

Just as he handed it to her, the coyote threw its full weight into the door again, the impact making Melinda cry out. The key slipped from her hand, clattering to the floor. Panic seized her, but she forced herself to stay focused, scooping it up with shaking fingers. She jammed it into the lock and opened the box, revealing the Beretta nestled inside. Her heart raced as she lifted the gun, the cold steel offering a strange comfort in her grip.

"Go, both of you—hide in the corner," she ordered, her voice trembling with both fear and determination. Tommy and Kate rushed to the far side of the room, huddling together behind a pile of boxes.

Melinda took a deep breath, her heart hammering in her chest. The door was weakening. She could feel it bowing under the relentless assault, the coyote's snarls growing louder, more frenzied. It wouldn't be long now. One more hit and the monster would be inside, just like the mountain lion before it. Her only chance was to take it out before it could strike.

Her hand tightened around the gun as she prepared to move, her breath coming in ragged gasps. Then, suddenly, a chilling sound filled the air—a chorus of howls, rising from all directions. They echoed through the walls, reverberating in her skull, and then everything went deathly silent.

***

Anderson stood frozen, his blood turning cold as he watched his men scatter in every direction, their screams drowned out by the deafening screeches of the nightmare descending on them from above. Moments later, an army of unholy animals followed in the birds' wake, each one a nightmare birthed from the darkest pits of Hell. They poured in like a flood—ravenous, mutilated versions of once-familiar creatures.

He had seen hellish battlefields before. He'd stared into the abyss during his countless tours of duty, but this? This was something else. Something far worse. His mind struggled to process the sheer savagery unfolding before his eyes. The sirens wailed through the base, a desperate cry that announced the apocalypse had arrived.

Anderson's hand shook as he hung up his phone. Every fiber of his being screamed that they were out of time, that nothing they could do would stop the onslaught that barreled toward them. As the call connected, his eyes widened in horror. The sky darkened as the mass of birds—black as midnight—swarmed overhead, blotting out the sun. It was like watching death itself take form, swooping down to claim them all.

His gut told him what his mind refused to accept: they wouldn't survive this. The ground trembled as the tide of twisted creatures surged closer. Wolves, coyotes, and mountain lions—all rotted, their flesh hanging loosely from their bones—moved in alongside the birds, eyes glowing with an eerie, unnatural hunger.

Samuel's voice echoed in his brain, telling him to hit the swarm with something big. Anything big. Anderson's eyes darted toward the MTV—a tactical vehicle equipped with the M142 HIMARS missile system. It was their only shot, but it was nearly a hundred yards away, through a war zone filled with death. His heart raced. He had maybe sixty seconds before the swarm was upon them. In his prime, he could've covered that distance in twelve seconds. Now, he wasn't so sure.

He didn't have time to second-guess himself. Taking one last deep breath to steady his nerves, Anderson exploded into motion, his legs pumping furiously as he sprinted toward the vehicle. His muscles burned, his lungs screamed for air, but he kept running, desperation driving him forward.

Halfway there, a flicker of movement caught his eye. He turned his head just in time to see it—a massive gray wolf, its eyes hollow and dead, its flesh decaying as it hurtled toward him with terrifying speed. There was no time to think, only react. Anderson dropped to the ground, rolling forward as the beast lunged. Its momentum carried it over him, claws swiping the air where his neck had been moments before.

In one fluid motion, Anderson came up into a crouch, his hand darting to his sidearm. A sharp crack echoed as he fired a single shot, the bullet finding its mark between the wolf's eyes. The creature collapsed in a heap of blood and fur, twitching once before lying still.

Immediately, Anderson was on his feet again, sprinting the final few yards toward the MTV. His hands were trembling as he clambered into the driver's seat, flipping switches and powering up the missile system. The seconds ticked by, each one feeling like an eternity as the black swarm closed in.

The targeting system flickered to life, but the swarm—erratic and unpredictable—made it nearly impossible to get a lock. Anderson cursed under his breath, his fingers flying over the controls as sweat dripped down his face. The sky was almost entirely black now, the screeches of the birds mixing with the howls and snarls of the undead horde. His vision tunneled, the walls of the vehicle closing in as panic gnawed at the edges of his mind.

Finally, the system beeped. Target acquired.

Anderson slammed his hand down on the launch button. The missile roared to life, streaking into the sky with a high-pitched whine. For a moment, everything was still. Then, the explosion. The blast rocked the entire base, a fiery ball of destruction ripping through the swarm. The ground shook as the shock-wave rippled outward, sending undead creatures flying in all directions.

A piercing chorus of howls and screeches filled the air—a haunting symphony of death. One by one, the beasts crumpled to the ground, lifeless.

Anderson sat in the silence that followed, his heart still pounding in his chest. Slowly, he climbed out of the vehicle, his boots crunching against the dirt as he made his way through the carnage. Animals lay scattered across the ground everywhere he looked, their twisted, rotting bodies surrounded by pools of inky black ooze. Those that had taken direct hits were still, their unnatural life finally snuffed out. Others, less fortunate, whimpered and writhed in agony, their bodies too broken to continue but not dead enough to find peace.

Steeling himself, Anderson raised his gun. One by one, he put the suffering creatures out of their misery.

After the last shot echoed into the air, Anderson holstered his weapon and turned his gaze toward the base. Bodies lay strewn across the ground—both human and beast alike. The stench of death hung heavy in the air. His soldiers... his men... fallen. He walked among them, his eyes burning with grief and fury. They hadn't stood a chance.

CHAPTER 38

Fisher pressed his finger to his lips, signaling for absolute silence. The tension in the air thick enough to cut. Whatever was lurking behind the door needed to lose interest and move on. But fate, in all its cruelty, had other plans.

Andrea, huddled behind the desk, suddenly sneezed.

The noise shattered the fragile stillness, and in an instant, a loud bang reverberated through the door. They froze. Then came the voice they all dreaded—Clause, calm yet dripping with distaste. "I know you're in there," he called, his tone sending a chill down their spines. "You need to let me in. I need your help."

Guerera's eyes narrowed, her fury unmistakable. She locked eyes with Fisher and shook her head vehemently. The M16 in her hands was steady, her knuckles white with restrained anger. She was ready to blow Clause's head off the second they let him in, and Fisher could see it in her gaze: she would take the shot without hesitation.

Another bang rattled the door, more insistent this time. "I'm hurt," Clause's voice pleaded through the thick metal. "Look, I have information that might help us fight this thing. You need to let me in."

Fisher stood motionless, jaw clenched. Samuel drifted over from his place by the far wall, joining Fisher and William a few feet in front of the door. Jackson remained by the entrance, alert and ready. Guerera stayed close to Ashley, her protective instincts kicking into overdrive, while Andrea shrank behind the centrifuge, eyes wide with fear. The entire room shared one thought: Do not let that bastard in.

But Samuel's voice broke the silence, cutting through the tension. "If he has information... maybe we should listen?"

Guerera's face twisted with rage, her voice sharp. "I don't want that prick anywhere near me!"

Fisher held her gaze, his expression firm. "I don't like it either. But if he can help, we might not have a choice. At the very least, we hear him out."

Jackson added in a low tone, "I'll keep my eyes on him the whole time. He won't try anything."

But Guerera wasn't convinced. Her eyes burned with hatred as she stared daggers at Fisher.

Fisher's voice dropped to a low growl. "You need to control that anger, soldier. This isn't about what you want. Emotions get people killed. Stay focused."

The words hung in the air like a loaded gun. Guerera held Fisher's gaze for a few tense moments before finally lowering her eyes, the battle raging inside her quieting, if only for a moment. She knew he was right. Her fury had to take a back seat, if not for the group's sake, then for Ashley's. She had sworn to protect her at all costs, and that meant keeping her head straight, no matter how much she wanted to paint the walls with Clause's blood.

Fisher's voice dropped to a whisper as he addressed the group. "Stay on your guard. Clause is a snake. He'll try anything if it gives him an edge. Don't trust him for a second."

He turned toward Jackson. "Alright. Let him in."

Jackson hesitated for a split second, then moved toward the door, his hand resting on the latch. The room collectively held its breath, the seconds ticking by like an eternity as everyone prepared for the worst.

As the door creaked open, Fisher's hand hovered near his weapon. Guerera's grip tightened on her M16. They all knew that once that door was open, there was no turning back.

***

Ashton stood beside Dr. Kafka, watching anxiously as she carefully lifted the first specimen from the frosted metal container, placing it into the control area. The hiss of escaping cold air lingered in the sterile room, and the tension grew as the cryogenically frozen black bird began to thaw. As time ticked by, each second seemed to stretch out, and the atmosphere became dense with anticipation. Seven agonizing minutes crawled by before the bird reached normal temperature. What greeted them was nothing short of grotesque—a twisted, unnatural sight.

Its wings hung at broken, jagged angles, and its entire left side was crushed inward, a gruesome testament to whatever had ended its life. Yet, despite its shattered form, the creature sprang to violent life. Its head jerked up, and it screeched—an ear-piercing, banshee-like wail that reverberated through the glass walls. Its good claw scratched and scraped feverishly, leaving long, jagged streaks along the surface as it thrashed wildly, desperate to tear into the humans observing it.

Dr. Kafka gasped, frozen for a moment, her eyes wide with terror as the undead bird flailed against the glass. Her mouth hung open, speechless in the face of such an abomination. Ashton, however, was a picture of delighted madness. His eyes glinted with an unholy glee, a wide grin stretched across his face as though he were witnessing the birth of something magnificent. On the opposite side, Dr. Vogel watched impassively, his face a mask devoid of emotion as the nightmare played out.

The bird's flailing grew more frenzied, its broken body moving with an unnatural strength. Ashton, seemingly unbothered by the creature's savage struggle, turned away and placed the stolen sample from Greenburg under the microscope. His hands moved with precision as he studied the writhing organism on the slide. He marveled at the way the cells seemed to pulse, moving in eerie synchronization as if guided by some unseen hand, some dark force beyond comprehension.

Without pulling his eyes from the microscope, Ashton called out, "Vogel, bring me one of the test subjects."

Vogel nodded silently, walking to the far corner of the lab where small cages lined the shelves like ominous tombs. Moments later, he returned, holding a large, white rat in his gloved hands. It squirmed, oblivious to the horror awaiting it.

"Now, place it in the chamber with the specimen," Ashton instructed.

Vogel calmly dropped the rat into the enclosure with the undead bird and took a step back. For a split second, there was nothing. Then the bird struck with blinding speed, its good claw hooking into the rat's soft belly, splitting it wide open in a vicious blur of red. Blood sprayed across the glass, and the bird's beak followed, stabbing repeatedly into the rat's chest. The rat's squeals were short-lived, its white fur turning crimson in a matter of seconds before its twitching body went limp.

Dr. Kafka recoiled in disgust, her voice trembling. "Did we really need to see that?"

Ashton smiled—an unsettling, twisted smile. "Patience, my dear," he murmured, his voice eerily calm.

Kafka turned back toward the glass enclosure, her stomach churning. But what she saw next drained the blood from her face. The rat, its body mangled and soaked in its own blood, twitched. Its limbs jerked unnaturally, and before she could fully process it, the rat sprang back to life. It began clawing at the glass, its once-dead eyes now burning with the same unholy fervor as the bird. Both creatures, the bird and the rat, screeched in unison, their cries a cacophony of madness.

Kafka staggered back. "What the hell?" she gasped, her voice barely above a whisper.

Ashton turned toward her, his eyes gleaming with manic excitement. "It is my theory that Hell is exactly what you're looking at, Doctor. For what else can reanimate the dead?"

His face twisted into something bordering on lunacy, with a wide smile stretching across his face.. A wave of nausea rose in Kafka. She had followed Ashton for so long, driven by his relentless ambition, but now, standing in the presence of such horrors, she could feel the madness creeping into him. This was no longer science. It was something darker, something evil.

Suddenly, the creatures let out a piercing screech, louder than before, their bodies thrashing violently against the glass. Then, just as quickly as it had started, they collapsed, lifeless once more. An oppressive silence filled the room.

Ashton's grin evaporated, replaced by cold fury. His fists clenched, knuckles white with rage. He knew, somehow, that Greenburg was behind this. The timing was too perfect, too deliberate.

"Ashton?" Kafka asked, her voice shaky.

He snapped into action, barking orders with a ferocity that cut through the suffocating air. "Kafka, get these specimens back into cryogenic storage—now! Vogel, back up all the data to the secure server. We need everything intact."

Neither of them questioned him as he stormed out, his mind racing. As he walked, his fingers flew over his phone, sending a single text to Clause: Find out anything you can. Then kill them all.

Ashton's heart pounded in his chest from the seething fury building inside him. This was far from over. Greenburg would pay for this. They all would.

CHAPTER 39

Sweat dripped down Melinda's face, her hands trembling as they clutched the gun tight. Every muscle in her body was coiled with fear, her heartbeat thundering in her ears. She stood there, frozen in place, waiting for the beast on the other side of the door to come crashing through. The fear felt like a noose tightening around her throat, making it hard to swallow, but she forced it down, gulping back the terror that threatened to choke her.

The minutes dragged on, each one a painful eternity. Her ears strained for any sound, any hint of movement that would signal the creature still lurked just outside, ready to tear them apart. The house had grown eerily silent, but that made it worse.

Tommy, who was crouched low in the corner, holding Kate tightly in his arms, shook his head vigorously as he watched his mom slowly approach the door. "No, Mom! Don't go out there! Please!"

His voice was a desperate whisper that nearly broke Melinda's heart, but she needed to be sure the danger had passed.

With a shaky finger pressed to her lips, she motioned for

silence, her gaze locked onto Tommy's wide, pleading eyes. After a long moment, he nodded reluctantly.

Her hand gripped the cold metal of the door handle, and she took a deep breath, glancing at her children huddled in the corner, their small bodies trembling. The sight of them strengthened her resolve, and without another moment's hesitation, she flung the door open, diving into a crouch, her gun raised just like she'd seen in action movies so many times before.

A strangled cry tore from her throat when her eyes landed on the massive, mangled heap of fur lying in the hallway, motionless, its hulking body twisted and broken, lay in a pool of inky black ooze. The liquid oozed from its ears and mouth, a sickly sheen coating the hallway floor, glistening under the dim light.

Further down the hall, she saw them three black birds, their feathers matted and wet with the same black substance. They, too, lay still, their claws curled in death. The scene was grotesque, surreal, like some twisted nightmare brought to life, yet somehow... it was over.

Slowly, she moved toward the living room, every step feeling like she was in a dream. She edged closer to the window, her heart thumping wildly. Pressing her face against the cold glass, she peered outside.

The sight made her gasp.

The ground was littered with corpses. Wolves, coyotes, birds, even rabbits—everywhere she looked, lifeless animals lay scattered like discarded toys, all leaking that same black ooze. Their eyes were open, clouded over, staring blankly into the sky. The apocalypse had torn through them and left only death in its wake.

Her legs gave out beneath her, and she sank to the floor, the weight of everything crashing down on her all at once.

The gun slipped from her fingers as sobs wracked her body. She buried her face in her hands, her chest heaving as she cried uncontrollably.

"Mom! Are you okay?" Tommy cried as he and Kate rushed into the room in a panic. "We heard you crying!" Both of their faces were twisted with fear.

Melinda looked up, her breath still coming in shallow gasps, and saw her children standing there, alive and safe. She reached out and pulled them close, gathering them in her arms.

"It's okay," she whispered, her voice trembling but steady enough. "Everything's fine now. It's finally over."

But even as she spoke the words, a cold shiver ran down her spine. Something deep inside her, some motherly instinct, told her this reprieve was only temporary. This evil, whatever it was, had not left for good.

Yet for now, in this brief, fleeting moment, she allowed herself to believe it was truly over. For her children's sake, she had to.

***

William's gaze was so locked on Clause, that when his phone vibrated in his pocket, it startled him. He clenched his teeth, forcing himself to stay calm, his eyes never leaving the man standing before him. Without breaking eye contact, he reached into his pocket and answered the call.

"Hello?"

Relief flooded through him when he heard Melinda's voice on the other end. "Melinda! Are you okay?"

Her voice was frantic. "William, I think it's over! I think we're safe!"

His brow furrowed. "What do you mean?"

"The animals... they're all dead," she replied, almost breathless. "Something happened. They just collapsed. All of them. It's like they just... stopped."

William was momentarily stunned. Then he pulled the phone away from his ear and looked at Samuel. "Call Sergeant Anderson. Get an update. Now."

Samuel quickly whipped out his phone and dialed the sergeant's number. William's attention snapped back to Melinda.

"That's incredible news," he said, though his voice remained cautious. "Samuel's checking with Anderson now. Just stay in the house, Melinda. We don't know if it's truly over yet."

"Okay," she replied, though the excitement in her voice hadn't faded. They both hung up, but William's mind was already racing, doubt gnawing at him.

Samuel didn't have to wait long for the sergeant to answer. Anderson's gruff voice rang through the phone. "Doctor! I was about to call you. You're not going to believe this. We hit that damned swarm with one of our missiles, just like you said, and the second it exploded, every animal dropped dead. Just... collapsed. Now there's this black, sticky shit everywhere."

Samuel's voice remained calm, but his eyes darkened with suspicion. "Don't touch it, Sergeant. We still don't fully understand what we're dealing with. The organisms may just be dormant for now. They could reanimate if another connection is established—possibly with a new queen."

"You're telling me these fuckers could come back?" Anderson's voice sharpened.

"We don't know," Samuel said gravely. "But we're close to a permanent solution. We're running final tests as we speak."

"Then hurry the fuck up," Anderson growled. "We need to

end this nightmare before it gets any worse." Without another word, the line went dead.

Samuel lowered his phone, his mind calculating the grim possibilities when Clause's voice broke the tense silence.

"So, you've actually found a way to stop all this?" Clause mocked.

"You sound surprised," Samuel replied.

Clause shrugged, the smirk on his face barely concealed. "Given how fast this whole shitshow spiraled out of control —and considering your rather... limited resources—I didn't think you'd have it in you to pull it off."

Andrea's voice cut through the air, sharp and biting. "You've been underestimating us from the beginning, Clause."

Clause raised an eyebrow, his smirk deepening. "Fair enough," he said with a casual shrug, his tone dripping with indifference. "Maybe I did misjudge you. But I won't make that mistake again."

Before anyone could react, his hand darted to his side, and in one swift, calculated motion, he drew his gun. The crack of the gunshot echoed through the room like a thunderclap, deafening and final. The bullet tore through the air, slamming into Andrea's chest with brutal force. Her body jerked back as if hit by a freight train, her eyes wide in shock as she collapsed, her blood pooling beneath her.

CHAPTER 40

William jolted awake, his heart pounding as if he'd just run a marathon. His chest heaved, and his skin felt clammy beneath the damp sheets. Sweat dripped from his forehead, soaking the pillow—a nightly consequence of the nightmares that stalked him relentlessly. They were always the same. Sometimes the monsters were grotesque, the walking corpses that had ripped their world apart. But more often than not, the ghost haunting him wore the face of Clause—the first man William had killed in over a decade.

He glanced down at Melinda, her peaceful face momentarily creasing as if she could sense his unrest even in her sleep. Carefully, he slid out of bed and slipped on his robe. The last thing he wanted was to wake her with the weight of his demons. She had enough of her own to deal with.

The kitchen was quiet, bathed in the dim pre-dawn light. William waited, listening to the soft hum of the coffee machine, staring out the window as the first slivers of sunlight pierced the horizon. The mountains to the east caught the early light, casting long, jagged shadows that stretched across the desert floor like claws reaching out from the dark.

He took a slow sip of his coffee, the warmth doing little to chase away the cold pit in his stomach. His mind drifted back to that day three months ago. A day that had marked him, left a scar deep in his soul.

He knew he shouldn't dwell on it, shouldn't let it consume him—but the past clung to him like a dark shadow, whispering reminders of who he used to be. William had buried that side of himself long ago, the killer, the man who could pull the trigger without hesitation. But Fate had dug it up, resurrecting what he had hoped would stay dead.

It had been instinct that saved them all that day. Clause had been a man capable of absolute carnage. One wrong move, one hesitation, and everyone in that room would've been slaughtered. William had seen it in his eyes—Clause was already planning the massacre when he gunned down the scientists.

The memory hit him like a cold blade. The shots ringing out, blood spraying as the scientists crumpled to the floor. He could still feel the air shift as the bullet flew past him, narrowly missing. His body had moved on its own then, muscle memory from years long buried—rolling to the ground, drawing his gun like an old friend, and firing.

Two bullets. One after the other. Each one finding its mark in Clause's chest.

He could still see the look on Clause's face as he fell to his knees, a mix of disbelief and rage, as though he couldn't fathom that someone had dared to shoot him. He'd tried to lift his gun one last time, but the Marines riddled his body with bullets, ending Clause's life in a fitting display of carnage.

William took another sip of coffee, though it tasted bitter now. The room was silent except for the quiet creak of the floorboard as Melinda entered. She sat across from him, her eyes soft but filled with concern.

"You okay?" she asked. It was the same question she asked every morning.

"Yeah, I'm fine," William replied, though they both knew it was a lie. "Couldn't sleep. Figured I might as well get ready for work."

Melinda looked at him, her brow furrowed. "You can't keep beating yourself up over this. None of it was your fault."

William looked down, his fingers tightening around the coffee mug. "I can't stop thinking about how I could've handled it differently. If I'd acted sooner, maybe people wouldn't have died."

"How could you have known what Clause was capable of?" she asked.

"I knew," William said quietly. "I'd seen men like him before. Everyone warned me about him. I should've kept my eye on him from the start. If I had, maybe a good man wouldn't be dead."

Melinda sighed, knowing she was losing him to the darkness again. He was stuck in a loop, replaying the what-ifs over and over. "But you saved everyone else. And Andrea's alive, recovering because of you."

He nodded but remained silent, his mind still warring with itself. The battle inside him was relentless, boiling down to two crushing fears: Could he live up to the expectations everyone now had of him? And worse—was he becoming the same monster he once was? There had been a time, long ago, when he wore the same haunted look that Clause had carried in his final moments.

Melinda reached across the table, taking his hands in hers. When William looked into her eyes, he saw the unwavering love, the belief that had saved him time and again from slipping into the abyss. She was the reason he hadn't become a monster again, the reason he could still fight to be a man worth saving.

He leaned forward and kissed her forehead gently, silently thanking her for being his anchor. After a quick shower, he dressed, strapping his badge to his belt as he prepared to face another day. As he walked out the door, he silently prayed he had enough strength left to rebuild what had been so brutally torn down.

The End.

BOOK THREE PREVIEW

Savage Apocalypse
Book Three:
The Roar Of The Dead

By Scott Dokey

CHAPTER 1

Silas floated in the silent void, the only sounds were the faint hum of the ship's systems and his own breath echoing in his head. Below, the mysterious planet loomed like a marble drenched in swirling blue and white, its cloud formations twisting in chaotic dances. It was beautiful, even mesmerizing. Yet, there was also something quite unsettling about the possible life teeming just beneath the surface. It was something unknown. His stomach twisted in knots at the thought.

For all the wonders this planet might hold, Silas couldn't shake the gnawing question clawing at the back of his mind: *Will they think I'm a monster?* It was a question born from past experience. In every corner of the universe, one truth had remained constant—fear. Fear of the unknown, fear of the other. Civilizations didn't need a reason to destroy what they didn't understand. And if this planet's inhabitants saw him, saw any of them, as a threat… his mind conjured up an array of scenarios too terrible to dwell on.

Jeron's voice finally broke the silence. "That's a whole lot of blue down there."

Silas blinked, shaking off the thought. He'd been so lost in his own head that he barely registered the others. He glanced at Jeron, then back at the planet. "I'd say about seventy-five percent of it is water."

Ridley's reaction was immediate. Her wide eyes darted to the viewport, fear creeping into them. Silas didn't blame her. Water meant life, and life meant danger. After everything they'd lost, after the world they'd left behind, the very idea of another planet teeming with life sent shivers down his spine. But Ridley's fear was different. There was something more… personal there.

Aldin sensed it too, squeezing Ridley's hand tightly. "It doesn't mean anything," she whispered, her voice gentle but firm. "We don't know what's down there yet. Let's not jump to conclusions."

Ridley nodded, though the terror in her eyes didn't fade. She retreated against the wall of the ship, trying to look brave. Trying to mask the terror she felt.

Mishka's voice cut through the moment. "What's the plan?"

Ahead of them, the meteors that had shared their journey through the cosmos now drifted lazily in the planet's orbit. Their jagged, blackened shapes seemed almost peaceful, suspended in the void. But then, slowly, they began to shift. The planet's gravity was pulling them in.

Silas felt his throat tighten. "That depends on what happens next. If one of the meteors makes it through the atmosphere… we'll need to be ready."

Mishka scoffed, her sharp eyes narrowing. "Why? What do we care? We don't owe them anything."

Silas paused, his heart heavy with the weight of a billion lost souls. "If one of those meteors breaks through, it could trigger a cataclysm. Whatever life is down there, they might not survive."

"So what?" Mishka's voice was cold and distant. "Our world didn't survive. Why should theirs?"

Her words hung in the air, thick and suffocating. She was right. Their entire world was gone, wiped clean by something unimaginable. And here they were, drifting through space like the last remnants of a broken dream. How could they care about anything anymore?

Silas clenched his jaw, feeling the weight of those billion souls relentlessly pressing down on him. His gaze swept over the others, their faces etched with grief and despair. They had all lost everything. Except for Jeron. He was the only one who didn't seem to care, didn't seem touched by the sorrow that draped over each of them like a thick blanket.

Silas exhaled slowly. "We'll monitor the situation. It's not just the meteor I'm worried about." He hesitated, then voiced the fear that had been gnawing at him since they left their world behind. "The organism… it might have survived. And if it gets loose down there…"

Aldin's face went pale. "You think it could survive in space?"

Silas nodded grimly. "It's possible. We don't know enough to be sure."

A heavy silence followed. The possibility of facing another savage apocalypse on a foreign world was suffocating. Aldin lowered her head, her shoulders trembling. *Not again!* her mind screamed. *Not another world lost because of me.* She couldn't bear it, couldn't endure the thought of watching it all happen again—the death, the destruction. She had already carried one apocalypse on her shoulders. She wouldn't survive another.

"Let's just hope none of them get through," Ridley said, her voice barely a whisper.

Silas nodded, though he knew hope wasn't enough.

"Jeron," he said. "Can you see if you can tie into their communications? We need to know what we're dealing with before we even think about going down there."

Jeron was already at work, his fingers flying over the console. "On it. Their systems are pretty archaic. Nothing too complicated." He smirked, though the humor didn't reach his eyes. "Are you looking for anything in particular?"

"No. Just… anything that gives us an idea of what they are. What we're walking into."

A few tense minutes passed before the cabin was filled with the crackle of static. Then, slowly, voices began filtering in—strange and fragmented. Jeron worked quickly, shifting through frequencies until a video feed flickered to life on the main screen.

They all watched in stunned silence.

"They look… like us," Jeron said, his voice barely containing his surprise. He glanced at Silas and smirked. "Well, maybe not you, big guy."

On the screen, uniformed men poured out of a large transport vehicle marked with the letters S.W.A.T. They were dressed for battle, guns drawn, advancing on a crumbling structure. Moments later, gunfire exploded across the screen. Bodies fell, blood spraying in thick red arcs.

Silas's stomach churned.

Jeron quickly switched the feed, pulling up another scene —a competition of some kind. The combatants were once again clad in armor, engaging in brutal hand-to-hand combat over some strangely shaped object. The violence was measurable.

One more time, Jeron changed the frequency. This time, the feed showed two people sitting behind a desk, calmly relaying the world's news. But even then, the images that followed were more of the same—war, conflict, destruction.

Jeron cut the feed, the silence that followed was even heavier than before.

"So much violence," Aldin murmured. "How are we supposed to survive in a world like this?"

"By sticking together," Silas replied, though even he could hear the uncertainty in his voice. "And praying that what we saw wasn't a true reflection of their world."

No one spoke. They didn't have to. The fear was etched on their faces.

"Get some rest," Silas finally said, trying to muster some semblance of calm. "We'll check again later."

"I'll stay on watch," Jeron offered.

Silas hesitated, then nodded. "Wake me if anything changes."

Silas glanced back down at the planet below, the swirling clouds now more ominous than beautiful. He couldn't shake the feeling that whatever awaited them down there was worse than anything they had ever faced.

***

Jeron's eyes glowed in the dim light of the cabin, the eerie blue hue from the screen reflecting off his face. His fingers danced over the controls, but his mind was elsewhere. He glanced around the ship, his head turning just enough to catch the soft rise and fall of the others' chests as they slept. Quiet, rhythmic snores interrupted the stillness, a comforting lullaby for the exhausted. They were oblivious, trusting.

He smiled. *Good.*

He exhaled, returning his gaze to the monitor. Outside, the meteors drifted silently against the backdrop of space, dark shadows against the glittering stars, just as they had for hours now. Slowly, steadily, they moved toward the planet below, their erratic course becoming more deliberate as they felt the invisible pull of gravity drawing them closer. Jeron's heart pounded with growing excitement. His pulse quickened, fingers tightening on the edge of the console as if by sheer force of will he could guide the rocks himself.

The ship's system displayed the data in cold, clinical figures, but Jeron's eyes flicked past the numbers, focusing instead on the spectacle unfolding before him. The meteors gathered speed as they neared the planet's atmosphere, like wild animals converging on prey, hungry and relentless.

Then, just as quickly, flames licked at their jagged surfaces, and one by one, they began to burn up. Fiery streaks lit up the thermosphere, each meteor a brilliant burst of light before disintegrating into nothing. Jeron clenched his jaw, a flicker of frustration creeping in as he watched them die off, consumed by the planet's atmosphere.

But not all of them.

His heart skipped a beat when he saw it. One meteor, larger than the rest, blazing through the firestorm and punching through the barrier, undeterred. The air around it screamed as it tore downward, descending faster and faster toward the surface of the world below. For a brief moment, Jeron's breath caught in his throat. Then, a smile tugged at the corner of his lips—a cold, predatory smile.

It had made it. *Yes!*

His gaze narrowed as the meteor streaked toward its destination, vanishing beyond the horizon and out of view. He didn't need to see it hit. He felt it—deep in his gut—a tremor that reverberated through the quiet of space, through him.

A few seconds later, a dull thud registered on the monitor from the impact. The screen flashed as the planet reacted to the sudden intrusion. Jeron's smile grew wider, more sinister.

It was done.

"It has begun, Uncle," he whispered under his breath.

He leaned back in his chair, eyes lingering on the now-empty void beyond the ship's viewport, the meteors gone, their purpose fulfilled. The others wouldn't know, not yet. They had no idea what had just been unleashed below, what his real mission was. They thought they were survivors, trying to find a new home, clinging to hope after the destruction of their own world. But Jeron knew better.

He had other orders.

The words of his uncle echoed in his mind, the last conversation they had before the mission. *"You know what you have to do, Jeron. You can't fail."*

He turned back to the sleeping crew. Silas, Ridley, Mishka, Aldin—they had no clue. They thought they were all in this together. How wrong they were.

Jeron chuckled softly. He had waited for this moment for so long, the anticipation gnawing at him since they'd first launched. And now, as the pieces fell into place, that gnawing hunger transformed into something darker, something far more dangerous.

He leaned closer to the monitor, zooming in on the surface of the planet below. The meteor had landed in a remote area, but he knew it wouldn't stay contained for long. Soon, the organism—the one they thought they had left behind—would spread. Relentless. Insatiable.

The crew wouldn't suspect him, not until it was too late. And by then, the world below would be nothing but a husk.

CHAPTER 2

As time passed, Silas shifted in his seat, causing Jeron's heart to skip a beat. Without missing a second, he slumped his head to the side and let his eyes flutter shut, feigning the deep, undisturbed sleep of someone lost in exhaustion. He had perfected this act over years of playing both sides, a talent that had always served him well.

Silas's voice broke the silence a moment later. "Anything happen while I was asleep?"

Jeron held his breath, keeping his eyes closed to sell the act to perfection. He didn't stir until he felt Silas vigorously shaking his arm.

Jeron cracked his eyes open with a slow, practiced grogginess. He stretched, exaggerating the motion, his arms wide and yawning, putting on a show as though waking from a restful slumber. "What's going on?" he asked, trying to sound dazed.

"You fell asleep," Silas stated flatly.

"I'm sorry," Jeron replied, feigning embarrassment. "I guess I was exhausted."

"You should've woken me up. Now we have a big problem," Silas said in disappointment.

Jeron kept his face neutral, forcing a mask of mild confusion. "Why? What happened?"

Silas's eyes narrowed as he gestured toward the screen. "The meteor cluster is gone."

A spark of satisfaction flickered deep within Jeron, but he kept his face carefully composed. He leaned closer, peering at the monitor. "Are you sure? They were on the radar earlier. Maybe they pulled away from the planet's orbit and floated on?"

Silas shook his head. "Highly unlikely. It's more probable that they fell from their orbit and descended toward the surface."

Jeron forced himself to breathe slowly, a smile threatening to creep up, but he bit it back. "Let's hope none of them made it through the entry."

Without responding, Silas began typing commands into the instrument panel as Jeron watched him out of the corner of his eye, trying to maintain his nonchalance. Silas muttered to himself, "Maybe I can rewind the radar and satellite feeds enough to see what happened."

A tense minute passed as Silas's commands locked onto the trajectory of the meteors. One by one, the meteors blinked on the screen, their paths traced as they approached the atmosphere. Jeron's heart pounded in his chest, but he kept still, watching eagerly as he relived the event he had witnessed earlier with sinister satisfaction.

Each one vanished, consumed by the atmosphere's wrath, until there was one. The last meteor, undeterred, streaked through the planet's protective shield and plunged toward the surface below.

Silas leaned back, a frown covering his face and concern filling his eyes.

"Well, that's not good," Jeron said, barely able to disguise his real excitement.

Footsteps approached from behind, and Jeron didn't need to turn to know who it was. Mishka's voice cut through the cockpit. "What's not good?"

Jeron flicked his eyes toward her, maintaining his outward calm. "One of the meteors crashed into the planet."

Mishka's brows furrowed. "So?"

"So," Silas said, his voice low and filled with an edge, "now we have to go down there and find out what the damage was."

The others had woken as well, gathering around the console. Aldin and Ridley stood in silence, their faces hard and cold. Aldin's voice then broke the tension. "You mean, to see if the organism was present?"

"Yes," Silas replied.

"I don't like the idea of going down there," Ridley said nervously. "Can't we just try to find another suitable planet to live on? This doesn't feel right."

Silas's voice hardened. "My earlier analysis indicated there aren't any other such worlds in this galaxy. Plus, if we start skipping from galaxy to galaxy, we'll run out of fuel. We don't have the luxury of options, Ridley."

As the weight of the situation pressed down on them, the ship's console emitted a soft beep. A satellite image of the planet's surface flickered onto the screen, displaying the meteor's impact site. A jagged, smoking crater marred the lush landscape below, steam rising from the smoldering earth.

"What's that?" Mishka asked, her eyes widening as she took in the image.

"It's the location where the meteor crashed," Silas said grimly. "Unfortunately, it's on the other side of the planet."

"How long will it take to get there?" Aldin asked, her voice hushed.

"Not long," Silas replied. "But we'll need to find a secluded place near the crash site to land the ship undetected. This isn't going to be a simple scouting mission."

Jeron leaned in, tapping a few keys on the console. "I can help with that. I'll run an algorithm that generates an energy field around the ship—cloak us from their systems. It'll keep us hidden from whatever they've got down there."

Silas glanced at him with a hint of surprise in his eyes. "You've certainly picked up a few tricks since I saw you last."

Jeron shrugged, his smile just a little too forced. "I've always been interested in quantum mechanics and nano-science. Just never had the motivation to pursue it further until recently."

"When did the meteor crash?" Aldin asked, her voice trembling under the weight of the question.

Silas's response came without hesitation. "A little over a cycle ago. We'll need to move quickly to assess the situation, figure out if the organism survived entry, and if it did—how much damage it's capable of doing."

An eerie silence fell over the group. The organism, the thing that had wiped out their home, was now possibly on another world, wreaking the same devastation that had led to their planet's destruction.

Mishka's face hardened. "What are we waiting for?"

Silas didn't answer right away. His eyes lingered on the screen, watching the image of the smoking crater as if it might suddenly spring to life. "You three," he finally said, addressing Aldin, Ridley, and Mishka, "go check out the storage containers. See what kind of gear we have. We need to be prepared for anything."

Jeron leaned back in his chair, watching them shuffle out of the cockpit. His mind, however, was already far away—

focused on the surface below. His heart raced as a sinister smile crept up his lips, hidden from view.

If the organism had survived, there would be no stopping it.

***

As the women sifted through the cargo hold, their hands running over the cold metal of containers stacked tightly against one another, Ridley's mind was elsewhere. She was silent for a moment longer, but a gnawing suspicion was clawing at her insides, a feeling she couldn't shake. Her eyes darted to Mishka, then to Aldin, before she finally whispered, "I don't trust Jeron."

Mishka paused mid-search, her fingers grazing over the sleek surface of a medical kit, and looked up. "What do you mean?" she asked curiously.

Ridley's lips pursed into a thin line. "You didn't see him back on Terran, before we escaped from the lab. He was... off. Creepy, even. And the way he smirks when he mentions his uncle..." Her voice dropped lower. "It tells me he's hiding something. I think his uncle was Jensen."

The name hit Aldin like a gut punch. Her breath caught in her throat, her lips trembling. Jensen—the man who had ruined everything, whose shadow still hung over them like a curse even after his death.

"That's a stretch," Mishka replied, though her voice was tinged with uncertainty. "His uncle could've been anyone."

Ridley's eyes hardened. "Think about it," she pressed. "It makes perfect sense. Jensen was a control freak. He would've had someone on the inside at the ancillary lab, someone to keep him informed of any developments, someone to warn him of threats to his work. Jeron was there, wasn't he? And now, he's here—right when we're at our most vulnerable."

Aldin closed her eyes, trying to steady her nerves. The idea sent chills down her spine, but she wasn't ready to accept it. "Okay, say Jensen was his uncle," she said, her voice shaky. "What do we do?"

Ridley's hand slid to the grip of her blaster, her fingers tightening around it. "For now, we keep a close eye on him," she said, her voice cold and resolute. "And if he does anything radical... I'll take care of him."

Mishka snorted, rolling her eyes. "That's a little dramatic, don't you think?"

"Jensen fooled us before," Ridley hissed. "I'm not going to let his crazy nephew fool us, too. Not again."

Mishka shook her head, a smirk tugging at her lips. "You're being paranoid." But there was a flicker of doubt in her eyes, a shadow of unease that hadn't been there before.

She moved to the next container, prying it open with a groan of metal. Her breath caught as her eyes widened in delight. She reached inside and slowly pulled out a sleek, black blaster rifle, cradling it like a lover long lost to the void. Her fingers traced its contours, her smile stretching wide, full of a dark satisfaction.

"Now that's more like it," she said excitedly.

Aldin and Ridley exchanged a glance as they watched Mishka's strange reverence for the weapon. Mishka laid the rifle gently at her feet before diving back into the container, pulling out more gear, her grin growing with every item.

Ridley, still tense, crouched beside her and helped dig through the contents. In no time, they had a small cache of weapons laid out before them—blaster rifles, tactical gear, and sleek, dark uniforms that looked too ominous to be standard issue.

Aldin glanced nervously at the door. "We should hurry."

Before they could check the last few containers, Silas's voice rang through the ship's intercom, crackling with static. "We're above the descension point. It might get a little rocky for a few seconds before we hit the lower atmosphere, then it'll smooth out."

The women exchanged tense glances, bracing themselves as the ship shifted, groaning as it began its rapid descent. The metallic walls vibrated, a low hum growing into a violent shudder. The ship lurched, rocking side to side as it plunged downward, the sensation like being caught in a vicious storm. The instruments around them blinked erratically, the ship's engines groaning in protest as turbulence took hold.

Ridley gripped the edge of a crate, her knuckles white. "I hate this," she muttered under her breath, but no one was listening.

The ship jolted violently, the hull screeching as if it were being ripped apart. Then, without warning, they slammed into something hard—too hard. The impact sent a bone-rattling shockwave through the ship, and suddenly everything was spinning.

Ridley's heart leaped into her throat. The ship spiraled out of control, alarms blaring, lights flashing like a strobe of impending doom. Equipment flew across the hold, slamming into walls, scattering the weapons they had just carefully laid out. A cargo container broke free, slamming into the bulkhead with a deafening crash.

"We hit something!" Mishka shouted, her voice barely audible over the screaming alarms.

Ridley's pulse thundered in her ears, her mind racing. They were spinning, hurtling down toward the planet in an uncontrollable spiral. And through it all, a sickening realization settled deep in her gut: Jeron was still up front with Silas, trying to control the ship. What if he had sabotaged them somehow?

Her suspicions suddenly felt terrifyingly real as the ship continued to tumble, each jolt more violent than the last.

CHAPTER 3

The force from the crash hurled the three women across the metal floor, their bodies colliding with the walls of the ship as if they were playthings caught in a storm. The ship groaned in protest, and for a moment, everything felt still—too still. Then, with a few tense breaths, Silas wrestled control of the ship, his hands steady despite the chaos, guiding it into a hidden spot nestled at the base of a rugged mountain range. The ship shuddered one last time as it settled, the metallic whine fading into the silence of the alien terrain.

Jeron rushed to check the spectrum inhibitor, his fingers flying over the controls. Relief washed over his face as the device blinked, still functional. Their location remained cloaked. For now. "What the hell was that, Silas?" he groaned.

Silas shook his head. "No clue. Nothing showed up on the scanner."

Silas turned to Jeron, "Get the communication system back up and see what you can find out. Focus on local frequencies in lower bandwidths. See if you can pick up anything about an alien presence. And if you do, hopefully, it's not about us."

"What are you going to do?" Jeron asked as he watched Silas get up from his seat.

"I need a drink," Silas replied.

He joined the women at the rear of the cargo ship as they were about to resume inspecting the remaining storage containers. Only two large containers and a small row of lockers remained unopened.

Silas immediately went to the row of lockers and began to open each one. They were each filled with personal items, apparently the property of those lost souls who were originally scheduled to depart on this ship. Finally, the fourth locker revealed what he had been searching for: a bottle of Kandrake venom.

He closed his eyes and said a silent prayer for all those that had been recently lost before downing a shot. Immediately, he felt the fire circling through his veins, hoping it would take the pain and heartache away. Although it helped to ease the tension, he knew nothing would ever erase the loss from his mind. He sighed and took another shot before placing the bottle in the pocket of his robe.

"Hey guys, I found something," Jeron suddenly called out.

The rest of the group shuffled to the front of the cabin and watched as a video feed materialized onto the screen. It appeared to be a broadcast concerning recent events, with the letters, KESQ in large letters at the bottom. A woman dressed in business attire was addressing her invisible audience through an audio device she held in her hand: "Authorities have confirmed that the violent animal threat is now over, though experts remain unsure about the cause of the virus that ravaged the Valley's wildlife. In total, nearly three hundred and fifty people have been confirmed dead, including Captain Gerald Henderson of the La Quinta Police Department, along with a significant number of his officers.

Our thoughts and prayers go out to the victims' families."

The feed switched to another topic and Jeron promptly switched it off, leaving everyone speechless.

Finally, Mishka said, "Well, I guess that answers the question about whether the organism found its way here."

"I'm surprised they were able to stop it," Jeron said, "given how primitive their society seems."

"Maybe that's exactly why they were able to beat it?" Silas offered. "For all of our advances in science and technology, the organism itself was raw and savage, and it took something just like it to defeat it."

"And we're supposed to live here?" Aldin said.

"It might not be all that bad?" Ridley said with little conviction in her voice.

"I still want to check out the crash site just to make sure the threat is indeed over," Silas said.

"How far is it from here?" Mishka asked.

"Our incident a few minutes ago—"

"You mean our near-death experience?" Ridley interjected.

Silas raised an eyebrow and continued, "However you'd like to call it, the episode took us away from the site a little bit."

"Just how far?" Aldin asked.

"Not a lot, but we'll need to be extra cautious to avoid unnecessary interaction with local inhabitants. We should also wait until it's dark, just in case."

"Well, I'm excited!" Mishka said sarcastically. "Who else is excited?"

She looked around at each one, in turn, failing to get the response she had hoped for. Then she noticed that someone was missing. "Um, where's Jeron?"

Before anyone could respond, Jeron snuck up behind them, emerging from the rear of the ship with a big smile on his face, "Hey, guys! Come see what I found."

"What are you wearing?" Mishka asked with a cold stare after she recovered from being startled.

Jeron twirled around in front of the group, showing off a long, black robe similar to the one Silas wore. "I found this in one of the lockers in the back." He walked over and stood next to Silas, "We're practically twins now, big guy. What do you think?"

Silas eyed Jeron and merely grunted.

Mishka snickered, "You're not anything like Silas."

Jeron scowled at her for a second before saying, "Anyway, this isn't what I wanted to show you. Come on. I think you'll be pleased."

As the group followed him toward the back, Ridley grabbed Aldin's hand and squeezed it gently once more, nodding toward the quick flash of a blaster rifle that peeked out from inside Jeron's robe when he turned to walk toward the rear of the cargo ship.

Ridley made a mental note of the weapons cache that was now scattered all over the floor of the ship. *I wonder what else he has hidden up his sleeve?*

Jeron brought them to the very back of the ship directly in line with the rear compartment hatch, and pressed a button on the side of the large storage container there that spanned nearly the whole width of the ship. He proudly held his arms out wide as the walls of the container disappeared into the floor to reveal a trio of gyro-cycles flanking a small personal transport.

Ridley squealed as she rushed over to the nearest cycle, while Silas approached the transport like it was a long-lost friend he was reuniting with after a lifetime apart.

"These should help get us where we need to go," Jeron said with a smile.

"But won't they be noticeable if someone spots us?" Aldin asked.

"I can attach a spectrum modifier to each one and link it to a personal transceiver," he suggested. "That'll effectively make us invisible to those outside the immediate area while allowing us to maintain communication between each other."

"Before we can go anywhere, we need to make sure the air outside is safe for us to breathe," Aldin said.

Silas replied, "I ran atmospheric diagnostics as we were descending and everything checks out. Aside from the higher levels of greenhouse gases than we're used to, the air is very similar to what Terran's was."

Aldin cringed inside at the last part of that statement. *I don't think I'll ever be able to quiet these demons*, she thought bitterly.

Ridley asked, "How long before we're ready to go?"

"Are you that eager to jump into the unknown?" Mishka said.

Ridley replied, "No, but the sooner we get out there and check out the site, the sooner we can get back here where we know it's safe."

Mishka replied, "You do realize that we won't be able to stay in this ship forever? Eventually, we're going to have to venture outside and try to fit in with whatever kind of hole we've found ourselves in."

"Maybe so, but we don't have to rush right into it."

Jeron interrupted them, "I'll get everything ready as fast as I can so we can get out there and back quickly. Then everyone will be happy."

Jeron left both of them pouting for a moment and then returned a few minutes later carrying a bunch of electronic components in his arms.

"That was quick," Ridley stated.

"I helped load the cargo onto this ship," Jeron explained. "Luckily, I still remembered where most of it was."

He handed a thin silver neck strap to each one and promptly placed one around his neck. "These will help us stay in contact with each other. Once you press the button on the back, they'll sync with your biometrics. They'll also enhance your vision so we can see where we're going, as well as allow us to see the modified vehicles, since someone here suggested we venture out at night." He turned to Silas with an accusatory look in his eyes.

Silas stood there silent.

Each one placed their device around their necks and pressed the button, the strap glowed a soft blue for a brief second before it changed color to blend seamlessly into their skin, making it basically invisible.

Jeron then went to the nearest gyro-cycle and placed a small round disk on the side of it. After tapping on the disk, a swirl of energy spun around the cycle. A second later, it was gone. Jeron stepped into the energy field and sat on the seat of the cycle, disappearing as well.

He reappeared a moment later, after he had tapped the disk once more to deactivate the spectrum modifier. "What do you think? Pretty cool, huh?"

Ridley stood there with her arms crossed and a flat expression on her face. "I guess it'll work," she said.

"I'll send the location coordinates to each of the vehicles," Silas said. Then he looked around at everyone, "Are we ready to do this?"

A nervous murmur rippled through the group. Only Jeron seemed excited about the prospect of venturing outside into this strange new world—a world they would now have to call home.

A few minutes later, the rear hatch of the ship opened up

and Silas led them out in his new transport. Jeron and Mishka followed him in their gyro-cycles, while Aldin sat behind Ridley on the third cycle, holding tightly onto her waist.

They sat there for a long moment, taking in the landscape. Even at night, the sweltering heat reminded them of the Sandscapes on Terran, although the terrain here was far less barren. It was also teeming with wildlife. Off in the distance, a flock of avians circled overhead; a pack of canines roamed about the base of the mountain nearby hunting for food; the chirps and squeals of insects reverberated throughout the valley.

"Everyone, stay close and go slow," Silas said. "We can't afford to draw attention."

Before they even got started on their clandestine journey a loud howl rose through the air nearby.

CHAPTER 4

Ashton hadn't heard from Clause in hours, and that gnawing sense of unease had evolved into something far worse. Something had gone terribly wrong. He could feel it. As the minutes ticked by, Ashton's agitation grew. He stared at his phone again, his finger hovering over the call button. If Clause was in trouble, he needed to know.

He hit dial, the phone ringing once, twice, three times.

Finally, the call connected.

"It's about time you answered the damn phone!" Ashton barked.

But it wasn't Clause who answered.

William's voice was low and menacing, "Ashton Brown, I presume? I'm sorry to inform you that your boy Clause is dead. And we're coming for you next."

A chill ran through Ashton, coiling itself around his spine. His mouth went dry as he gripped the phone tighter. "Who is this?"

"I'm the man who put a couple of holes in his chest before the Marines finished him off," William growled.

Ashton's heart thundered in his chest. *Clause... dead?*

He immediately ended the call, his mind spinning in rapid

calculation. He knew what was coming. They wouldn't be far behind. He had no time to waste!

He bolted from the office, his heart racing. When he reached the lab, his voice was sharp and urgent. "Drop everything. Follow me. Now."

Kafka and Vogel looked up in confusion. Kafka raised a skeptical eyebrow, while Vogel nervously exchanged glances with her, unsure whether to follow. But there was something in Ashton's eyes—something dark and full of panic—that spurred them to their feet.

They followed him down the sterile corridor, their footsteps echoing ominously in the dim light. At the far end of the hallway, Ashton stopped outside a plain, unremarkable wall sconce. The two scientists exchanged uneasy glances again. "What's going on?" Kafka asked.

Ashton didn't reply, instead reaching for a hidden switch embedded in the fixture. With a soft *click*, the wall opposite them hissed and groaned, sliding open to reveal a secret door they had never seen before.

"What the hell is this?" Vogel muttered, his voice barely a whisper.

Ashton stepped through the opening without answering, and the two followed reluctantly, the air growing colder, heavier. The lights flickered on as they entered a long hallway. The smell hit them first—a faint, metallic odor, like blood or something far worse.

Ashton turned to face them, his grin unnerving. "This is where we can work. Without oversight. Without interference. Here, we are free to explore... the limits."

Kafka and Vogel watched with dawning horror as the hallway opened into a large chamber, where glass containment tubes lined the large room, stretching from floor to ceiling. Suspended inside each tube were bodies floating in some viscous, yellowish liquid, their faces distorted in agonizing screams and their limbs bent at grotesque angles.

Instantly, they realized that the secret lab was a tomb of nightmares.

"What is this place?" Kafka asked, her voice trembling.

"It's our future," Ashton replied coldly. "And now, it's our only chance."

Vogel's stomach churned. The truth settled over him like a shroud. He and Kafka had become expendable the moment they entered this place. If they didn't cooperate, they would end up like the grotesque things floating in the tanks—suspended in some half-death, secrets locked inside their corpses forever.

"We need to move fast!" Ashton said urgently. "Get everything from the other lab. Samples, equipment—everything. Move it here before the authorities come sniffing around."

There was no argument, no resistance. They worked feverishly, the fear of what might happen if they didn't cooperate propelling them onward, through the grueling task of transporting every aspect of Ashton's unholy work.

By the time they finished, hours had passed, and their nerves were frayed. The scientists slumped to the floor, exhausted. Their fear had taken on a new shape—a raw, primal terror that pulsed beneath the surface.

Kafka's voice was hoarse when she finally spoke. "What now?"

Ashton handed them each a small key. Although tiny in size, it was heavy with the weight of the secrets it unlocked.

"You'll come and go as I need you," Ashton said flatly. "No one knows you've seen this place. No one can. If anyone asks, I was here one minute, gone the next. Sick. Vanished. Understood?"

Both nodded, though the dread was plain in their eyes. The keys felt more like shackles than privileges, but they had no choice. They were in too deep now. Too far to turn back.

As they sat in silence, Vogel's hand trembled as he turned the key over and over in his palm. His eyes wandered to the containment tubes again, the bodies swaying slightly as though something unseen moved within the liquid. He blinked, his breath catching in his throat. Was it his imagination, or had the eyes of one of the suspended figures just opened?

And then, just as quickly, they were closed again.

He felt something cold crawl up his spine. He wanted to say something, to tell Kafka, but the words wouldn't come. All he could do was stare in frozen horror, wondering if whatever was in those tubes was waiting for the right moment to wake.

Ashton's voice broke through the thick tension in the room, his expression unreadable. "Guard your keys with your lives," he said, his voice low, almost a growl. "Because if anyone else finds out about this place... you'll end up just like them."

He nodded toward the tubes, where something—*someone*—shifted ever so slightly.

Scott Dokey is a creative force whose storytelling spans across writing, filmmaking, and visual art, delivering haunting, immersive experiences. Growing up in the shadow of Notre Dame's Golden Dome, Scott discovered early on the magic of turning a blank page into a captivating work of art. This love for creation only grew, leading him to explore writing and filmmaking, with a special focus on horror and the supernatural. His novels, including the Savage Apocalypse series, and the acclaimed *Hellish* series (*Tortured Souls, The Chosen, Unholy Religion,* and *Vizibir*), have cemented his place as a master of dark, psychological terror, where human fears are confronted with unrelenting force.

Scott's career isn't just about writing; he's an award-winning screenwriter who has produced and directed several short films, along with a no-budget feature that showcases his resourcefulness and vision. His dedication to the indie film scene is highlighted by his previous role as president of Mid-America Filmmakers, where he helped foster new talent and bold ideas. As with his novels, his films create unsettling atmospheres where the supernatural meets real-world anxieties.

Now living in Southern California with his wife, Jennifer, and their daughter, Kaylee, Scott enjoys the extreme contrasts of desert life—the blistering 120° summers balanced by the bliss of an 85° winter. His life and work continue to push the boundaries of what horror can achieve across multiple mediums. For more about Scott's creative journey, you can visit his website at www.scottdokey.com.

www.ingramcontent.com/pod-product-compliance
Lightning Source LLC
Chambersburg PA
CBHW032015310726
48972CB00002B/409